The Castaway

SHIPWRECK KEY BOOK ONE

STEPHANIE TAYLOR

Ruby

"Ruby, we've got this. I promise you. Leeza's team has assured me a number of times that she won't ask you *any* of the questions on the list. Everyone is in agreement that she'll stick to what we discussed, and that the whole interview will be soft and easy."

The backstage hubbub on America's most popular morning show is distracting, but Ruby wants to make sure she knows what she's getting into. She folds her arms across her chest and watches as a man in overalls wheels a giant light smoothly across the concrete floor of the studio. There's a tame comedian onstage just beyond the tangerine-colored curtain, making easy jokes and warming up the crowd; the audience is laughing appreciatively.

"You're sure Leeza is on board with this?" Ruby is standing behind the curtain, waiting to go out and appear publicly for the first time since her husband's untimely death. Kate, who has been Ruby's assistant only for the past month, is glancing at her phone. Ruby is a bundle of nerves, but this is definitely not her first rodeo.

"I'm positive." Kate taps at her phone as she talks, pauses, looks at Ruby, and glances back down at the screen. "We made it crystal clear that you would not be answering any questions about Jack, about the accident, or about—"

"I want to stick to talking about the future," Ruby says, holding up one hand so that Kate won't say anything else. "I think looking forward is going to be my main goal from now on, and I am definitely *not* interested in digging through my past in front of every stay-at-home mom and retired grandmother in America."

A makeup artist wearing a tool belt full of fluffy makeup and hair brushes is orbiting around Ruby, assessing her as she pulls a palette of powder from one of her pockets. She silently approaches with a brush in one hand and pauses, waiting for an opportunity to powder Ruby's forehead and nose one more time.

Ruby knows the drill here; she turns her face to the makeup artist, but keeps her ears on Kate.

"Definitely, definitely," Kate assures her. "This has all been prearranged, so you just go out there and kill it, alright?"

Ruby feels the slightest buzz of unease inside of her as she listens to the floor directors and camera people murmuring and talking around her. Maybe it's that she isn't the current First Lady and therefore feels irrelevant to a young assistant with a whole career ahead of her, but Ruby is getting the distinct impression that Kate is already imagining herself working for someone far more important than a washed-up widow rather than focusing entirely on the task at hand.

The show's coordinator approaches Ruby with a clipboard held in her hand, which is bedecked with a floral tattoo and several silver rings, and a headset covering one of her ears. Ruby smoothes her emerald green skirt and the white silk blouse that's covered in polka dots in the same shade of green. The shirt is sleeveless and was chosen intentionally to show off Ruby's famously toned arms, and the tulip cut of the skirt does the same thing for her legs, revealing calves shaped by miles and miles of running--both before and after her husband's death.

"Ready, Mrs. Hudson?" the coordinator asks, giving Ruby a smile. She covers her mouthpiece with one hand and looks Ruby up and down. "You look fabulous," she whispers, then turns her attention to whatever is going on in her ear. She nods at Ruby and then points to the curtain. "Andddd," she says to Ruby, holding up a finger. "Go!"

Ruby takes a deep breath and walks through the long, heavy curtain that hangs from ceiling to floor, taking each step carefully so that she doesn't slip or trip in her high heels. She puts a practiced smile on her face as she waves both hands at the audience, trying to infuse every step and every motion with as much excitement as she can muster.

"Today on our show, we are beyond thrilled to welcome a woman you all know well. She's smart, funny, accomplished, and most of all *resilient*. Please help me give a warm welcome to our former First Lady, Ruby Hudson!" Leeza says with a shout, standing up on the set and clapping along with the audience. Her eyes are dancing as she holds out her hands for Ruby to join her.

The audience breaks into wild applause as the woman who lived in the White House for four years walks across the studio, smiling as she approaches Leeza, the tanned, toned, Botoxed host of the morning talk show.

The expectant energy of the audience hits Ruby with full force and she nearly hesitates; this is her first step back into the limelight since losing her husband. This is the first time the public has seen her emerge from behind the curtain--both literally and figuratively--to present herself as Jack Hudson's widow. As a woman wronged. As a person whose future is still unwritten. And the only thing she wants to talk about at all is what life has in store for her now.

Ruby is terrified and she tries not to blink or look like a deer in headlights as the cameras follow her across the studio and up onto the platform where Leeza is waiting.

Leeza takes both of Ruby's hands in hers, grinning from ear-to-ear like a starstruck super fan. But her smile falters as they sit on their respective black chairs, facing one another at an angle so that they're both turned slightly towards the audience.

"I'm so nervous," Leeza admits, straightening her skirt and then patting her glossy brown hair. "And I don't even know what to call you--Madame First Lady? Mrs. Hudson?"

"Oh, Leeza," Ruby says, reaching over and touching Leeza's wrist lightly to set her at ease. Her fingertips are so cold that she's surprised when the host doesn't visibly recoil. "Please, call me Ruby. That's the only thing I want to be called from now on. If I'm going to be me on my own terms, then that's my very first term: I'm just Ruby."

Leeza laughs, her excited smile returning to her pretty face. "Whew!"

she says, brushing a hand past her forehead like she's broken a sweat. "Okay. Got that taken care of!"

The lights overhead are bright and hot, and Ruby's eyes skim the crowd seated in the stadium-style seats, with each row raised just slightly higher than the one in front of it. Most of the audience is made up of middle-aged mom-types with a few grandmothers sprinkled in for good measure; this is the usual demographic for *Good Day With Leeza*. It is also the main demographic for every public appearance that Ruby makes, and most of her fan mail comes from women just like these ones--women who see her as open, kind, and relatable.

"So, Ruby," Leeza says now, turning to the audience theatrically and making an "I can't believe I'm doing this!" face so that they know what a surreal moment she's having. "Tell us what you've been up to in the past year, and what the future has in store for our favorite First Lady."

Ruby folds her hands in her lap and looks right at Leeza, her gaze direct and firm. "Well, as you all know, I've been through some things." She says this and then pauses ever so briefly; just long enough for the crowd to acknowledge the events of the past year, but not so long that Leeza feels obligated to say anything or to offer her condolences. That would throw off the momentum of the show, and because Ruby knows herself so well, she knows that it might also bring tears to her own eyes. She wants to avoid that at all costs, because this show is meant to be her comeback, not a setback.

Ruby waits for Leeza to ask the first straightforward, leading question. The things she'd agreed to discuss were all laid out for everyone on the show beforehand: Ruby is happy to discuss her daughters, her plans for the future, and anything about her own upbringing or her mother, who she looks up to and admires. She is willing to discuss—in broad terms—living in the White House, decorating it for the holidays, and what her favorite perks of living there were (never having to grocery shop or cook are at the top of her list, and she knows these things will garner laughter from the audience, because most of them will be able to relate).

But as Ruby looks straight into Leeza's eyes, she sees a shift, and it's one she recognizes well, because she's dealt with journalists and done interviews for so many years now that she could do them in her sleep.

The new look in Leeza's eyes is one of hunger. She sees her chance, and she's going to take it.

"Ruby," Leeza says slowly, and Ruby can feel her stomach turn. "A year out of the spotlight is quite a long time. We've missed you."

"I've missed all of you," Ruby says firmly, turning just her upper body in the chair so that she's gazing out at the audience in the studio, as well as at the audience beyond the cameras.

"It's understandable why you might have wanted to take some time away, given the circumstances."

Ruby steels herself; she needs to handle this with kid gloves so as not to lose control of the interview. "Yes, losing my husband was a huge blow to my entire family," she says, folding her hands in her lap and shooting Leeza a warning look.

"Right," Leeza says, leaning forward slightly. "But on top of losing your husband in a tragic accident, you also found out along with the rest of the world that the President had a mistress, not to mention a child you'd never known about. How did that feel during a period that was supposed to be one of mourning? Were you angry?"

Ruby can feel the fury building inside of her and she wants to stand up and walk off the set. Actually, the first thing she wants to do is to push Leeza and her smug smile off of her chair, and *then* she wants to walk off the set. But she won't, because she's been groomed to be a First Lady, and she'll be one until the end, whether she's living in the White House or not.

"Well, Leeza," Ruby says, the ice in her voice apparent to anyone with ears. "It felt like my heart had been stepped on and crushed into a million pieces. I didn't know how to protect my children, and I didn't know how to feel about any of it." She pauses, eyes blazing as she watches Leeza's face. "But I'll tell you what: nearly every person who has ever lived has gone through something heart-wrenching and private that they don't want to discuss."

Leeza is nodding intently and squinting her eyes so that her face is set in the mask of a seasoned journalist. She looks like she thinks she's Barbara Walters, but Ruby knows that Leeza isn't even in the neighborhood of Barbara's league in skill, technique, or humility.

Ruby leans forward in her chair so that she and Leeza appear to be going head to head, which—truth be told—they are. Ruby knows how to handle things with class and dignity, but Leeza has punched some buttons inside of her that she didn't even know were there. "You know, Leeza, it's kind of like when someone in the public eye finds out that their husband has spent nearly a million dollars acting as—wait, what's that called when a man pays for much younger women to 'keep him company' or send him questionable photos?" Ruby turns to look at the audience and sees that every single woman in the studio is hanging on her words and doesn't appear to be breathing for fear that she might miss whatever comes next. Ruby looks back at Leeza as she snaps her fingers. "That's right, a *sugar daddy*."

Leeza opens and closes her mouth like the words have died on her tongue. She's gone from looking hungry and ready to pounce to looking like a deflated balloon in a Donna Karan wrap dress.

"Anyhow," Ruby goes on breezily, her reddened cheeks the only thing betraying her outward calm, "life can get extremely complicated, and now I'm doing my best to figure out how I want it to look going forward. It's time for me to start the next chapter of my life. So to *that* end," Ruby says, her eyes grazing the front row of the audience. "I'm going to follow a lifelong passion of mine and open a bookstore."

Leeza blinks a few times and then tilts her head to the right like she's checking to see if she has water in her ear; it's clear that she hasn't fully accepted that Ruby Hudson just completely owned her on camera, and the stunned look on her face gives away the fact that she's still reeling from being reminded of her own personal PR disaster right there *on her own show.*

"That is amazing," Leeza says, tossing her hair as she crosses one leg over the other. Her eyes are glassy and her tone rings false, but she won't deviate from the script again. "And where exactly can we shop for books and look forward to having our purchases rung up by former First Lady Ruby Hudson? Will there be multiple locations?"

Ruby smiles in a way that says she's holding back; they have now returned to the predetermined plan, and so long as Leeza stays the course, so will Ruby. "I'm still scouting around for a location—as in singular. I have a vision for my store," she says, "and I'll know the spot when I see it. But there will only be one, and it will be my pride and joy."

Leeza looks out at the crowd; everyone is listening intently. "Can you give us any hint at all? North? South? East? West?"

Ruby laughs coyly. "All I can say is that I'll never be shoveling snow in winter, and I'll end every day with a clap of thunder as the sun sets."

A tiny frown pierces Leeza's smooth forehead and she turns to look directly into the camera. "Hmmm, warm winters and thunder...put your thinking cap on, guys! The first viewer to email me the correct guess wins a five hundred dollar gift card to Ruby Hudson's mysterious new bookstore, and it's on me!" Her jovial tone and even smile have returned, but Ruby knows from sitting this close to the host and watching her body language that Leeza is going to lock herself in her dressing room after they're done and send angry texts to every underling on her show's staff just to take out what she's feeling right now on someone beneath her.

"It's feeling southern to me," Leeza says, putting her chin in her manicured hand as she looks at Ruby steadily, hoping for more. "I know there are lots of thunderstorms in Florida."

"You might be right," Ruby says. "But ending my day with a 'clap of thunder' is simply another way to say that I'll be ending it with a strong drink, which is *definitely* on the itinerary in my new life."

"I hear that," Leeza says, giving Ruby a faux-playful wink to show the audience that they're on the same team again. "And we can't wait to find out what the future holds for you, Ruby Hudson. Thank you for stopping by to visit with us, and best of luck with your new bookstore!"

The crowd claps and hoots at this, and the cameraman signals a countdown till the next station break. When the red light flickers off and the woman in the headset from backstage gives them the all clear, Ruby turns to Leeza and leans in closer.

"Nickel's worth of free advice, Leeza," Ruby says quietly so that no one else can hear her. "In the future, be a girl's girl, not a python in lipstick."

Ruby stretches her legs and stands up, waving at the crowd with both hands once again as she walks back toward the orange velvet curtains and to the car waiting for her right outside the studio.

Athena

Athena is the eldest of Ruby's two daughters, and for most of her life, her parents had joked that she was the lone adult in the family. When Ruby wanted to skip dinner and raid the fridge in the White House for ice cream and cookies, or when Harlow, Athena's younger sister, went out at night as a teenager and got herself splashed all over the tabloids for one misdeed or another, Athena was always the one to calmly impart reason. She even knew how to talk her father—the President of the United States of America—down off the ledge with her patient, wise counsel. Most people would call Athena an "old soul," but Athena just thinks of herself as someone with common sense.

"Mom," she would say as a child, "Harlow and I need to eat better meals than just ice cream and cookies. You know that!" Or, "Harlow, you can't just go out and get your bellybutton pierced at a street fair. You know that's going to be photographed and show up online. How will that look for Dad?" She was so much like a mini-adult that Ruby used to joke about her joining Jack's team of advisors when she was still in elementary school.

As for Jack, he was rarely carefree and childish, but on occasion, he might lose his cool over something small, and Athena would soothe him with her words like no one else could. "Daddy," she might say. "Do you think you can afford to throw a tantrum when you're talking to the president of Mexico? No, you cannot." Far from angering him, her words would be like balm to his troubled soul. No matter if he was in the midst of a political impasse or if he was simply tired and rundown, Jack would crack a smile and look at his daughter with total adoration.

Athena has been the anchor of the family for twenty-three years.

Harlow Hudson is another story entirely. Harlow is everything that Athena is not: she is whimsical, spontaneous, wild, and untamed. That bellybutton-piercing-at-a-Brooklyn-street-fair scenario is anything but hypothetical; it happened, it was recorded and photographed for posterity, and when some random guy walked by and bent forward to kiss the bare belly of one of the First Daughters, every camera phone in the vicinity caught the moment and shared it widely. Then just a fifteen-year-old girl, Harlow had been more entertained than apologetic about the brouhaha caused by the Bellygate scandal, as Ruby called it, giving Jack one more reason to lose his temper, and Athena one more opportunity to swoop in and calm her father down.

Now, on her lunch break from her job as librarian of electronic resources at the Library of Congress, Athena takes a seat at a table by the window of a sandwich shop in Washington D.C. and pulls out her phone to text her sister.

She's ordered a cup of tomato basil soup and a grilled cheese sandwich. When the harried looking waitress sweeps past and sets her tray down, Athena looks up at her with a grateful smile before returning to her phone.

Athena: I assume you're aware that Mom has gone viral today.

Harlow: Of course! Ruby went so hard. It was epic. She's trending on Twitter, and I've already seen like seven different stitches of it on TikTok.

Athena: Do you think she overdid it? I'm just worried about her image.

Harlow: Um, no? Listen, if Leeza is going to come at her, then Mom needs to clap back, which she did.

Athena: Yeah...I guess so.

Harlow: No, there's no "I guess so" about it. Mom is at that age where women start to not care. She can do and say whatever she wants, and wear crazy things because she's old. Old people are supposed to be colorful.

Athena: She isn't even 50, Harlow!

Harlow: Whatever. Leeza deserved it. You know, people who live in glass houses and all that...plus Leeza once dated my boyfriend and I hate her for it.

Athena: Ryan Gosling is not your boyfriend. And I don't think they really dated—that was just a photo of them together like fifteen years ago.

Harlow: STOP WITH THIS HATEFUL TALK IMMEDIATE-LY!!! I will not be forced to relive that trauma again.

Athena: Girl. Pull it together. Refocus. We're talking about MOM.

Harlow: Okay, okay. I'm back on track. So, she put Leeza in her place, and she mentioned her future plans to sell books. What's the big deal?

Athena: She told the world that she's opening a bookstore someplace where it never snows in the winter.

Harlow: Uh oh. Pirate Island is about to become the most popular place in the universe.

Athena: It's called Shipwreck Key.

Harlow: Pirate Island...Shipwreck Key. Same difference. Hey, maybe I should move down there and get into real estate? Or would that be like insider trading?

Athena: I'm not sure...

Harlow: Okay, gotta run. And keep tabs on Mom while you're down on the pirate island, will you? We can't have her doing anything crazy while no one is watching.

Athena: No one keeps tabs on Ruby Hudson. You know that.

Harlow: Bet.

Athena laughs at her sister as she holds her phone in one hand, looking out at the busy sidewalk. It's late winter and painfully chilly in D.C., and people are wearing trench coats with their collars turned up to fend off the rainy afternoon. There are puddles of water in the street and umbrellas dotting the sidewalk.

Athena is headed down to Shipwreck Key with Ruby in a few days to stay with her in the new house that her mother has just purchased, and she's looking forward to being on the beach and to seeing where her mom is going to be living. It's a whole different direction that her mother's life is taking, and Athena is totally supportive of it; she *wants* Ruby to have a fresh start and to live her life the way she wants to live it. It's just going to be hard to let her go, and to finally accept that their lives will no longer overlap in Washington. With her father gone for a full year now, her sister living in New York, and her mom moving to Florida, Athena isn't even sure what's left for her in D.C., but it's where her job is, so she needs to make it work. At least for now.

With one quick emoji sent in Harlow's direction, Athena sets her phone down and picks up her spoon. She has an hour with the book she's reading before she has to go back and finish that day's project at the library.

Ruby walks through the lower level of her new house. She's right on the ocean, and the salty air is already seeping into the pores of her soul, filling her with a sense of well-being that she hasn't known in ages. She opens windows and stops to breathe, closing her eyes, and exhaling at each window before she moves on to open the next one. Since Jack's death, it's been something she's had to do with intention—just pause, let everything go, and breathe.

This house was her first purchase when everything came raining down on her head a year earlier. She'd visited Shipwreck Key once with Jack—for their fifteenth wedding anniversary—and she'd sworn that time as they walked around eating ice cream cones and watching boats come and go that she'd own a house on Shipwreck Key someday. And now she does.

The house itself is a stunner: two stories, right on the water, and with a white railing winding around the home's wraparound porch. The weathered-looking shingles give the house an upscale Nantucket vibe, but it's the inside that truly sold the place to Ruby.

Polished hardwood runs throughout the entire downstairs area, with a spectacular living space right at the center that boasts thirty foot ceilings. Couches, chairs, enormous rugs, and lamps in shades of cream,

sand, khaki, and brushed denim fill the huge area, and hanging chandeliers, glass coffee tables, and huge windows that reach the ceiling flank a
wood-burning fireplace that's been painted white and has a beautiful
painting of a stormy sea hanging above it. The house was obviously
decorated by a professional, and when Ruby toured it—her Secret
Service agents stationed outside on the wraparound porch like sentries
—she'd asked if she could purchase it exactly as it was.

In her experience, money can buy anything, and she wanted this
house. So she got it.

"Mom?" Athena calls out, her bare feet padding against the wood
floors.

Ruby's older daughter has come with her to the island while she gets
settled in, and having Athena there to bounce ideas off of has been
invaluable. Of the two girls, Athena is her wise, patient, listener, while
Harlow is everything spectacular that Ruby always wished she herself
could be: charmingly unorganized, unfiltered in a way that makes her
seem brave, and fearless when it comes to life choices. Since Jack died,
Harlow has gotten engaged and broken it off because "the vibe wasn't
right," she's gone skydiving, and she's moved from D.C. to Manhattan
to take a job at a marketing firm that even Ruby has to admit she probably got mostly because of her last name.

But Athena has played things closer to the vest. She's stuck close to
her mother, staying in an apartment in Washington that's just a ten
minute walk from Ruby's condo, and she hasn't even considered leaving
her job or striking out in a new city. As the coverage from the Leeza
interview has rolled on and on, spawning memes, jokes, and plenty of
debate, it's been Harlow sending the funny stuff to Ruby with all of the
"you go, girl" energy attached to it, but it's been Athena who talks to
her seriously about how Ruby really felt in that moment on the set, with
her boundaries being ignored in favor of the potential for Leeza to get a
salacious, career-making interview.

"Mom?" Athena says again, walking into the kitchen where Ruby is
standing with her hands on the cold marble counter of the island,
looking out the giant window that faces the beach.

"What, honey?"

"There's not really much to do here since you bought the place totally furnished." Athena leans a hip against the counter and props one bare foot on top of the other. She is long and lanky, and her hair naturally falls in the kind of waves that come from unbraiding your hair after sleeping with it in plaits. "Do you want to go to that main street in town and see what's going on?"

"Seadog Lane," Ruby says helpfully.

"Huh?"

"The main street is called Seadog Lane. We could take a run up there and order a couple of grogs while we people watch. What do you think?"

"*Grog*, Mom? Seadog Lane? Will we be talking like pirates for long, or do you think this will wear off soon?"

Ruby laughs and pulls her pale blonde hair back with one hand, securing an elastic around it to hold it in a low ponytail. "I think the newness will wear off, but trust me when I tell you that the pirate theme is *deeply* ingrained in this place."

"Someone needs to tell these people that a little bit goes a long way," Athena says, rolling her eyes. "It's charming though."

Ruby walks over to the window and stares out at the ocean, keeping her back to her daughter. The late February sun outside is slanted at an angle that sends its rays directly into Ruby's bright kitchen. She stands there, letting it warm her skin while she watches the blue water beyond the sand.

"How are you doing, Bean?" Ruby asks, using her daughter's nickname. Her whole life, she's been some version of Athena Beana, Theen Bean, or just Bean. "Are you okay?" Ruby can almost feel her daughter go still behind her, and for a long minute, Athena says nothing.

"Are we talking about Dad?" she finally says.

It's Ruby's turn to be still and pause before going on. "We are."

Athena walks across the kitchen and stands next to her mother so that they're shoulder-to-shoulder, looking out at the sea.

"I'm still pissed," she says. "I'm angry at him, and at everyone who knew what was going on. They left us—they left you—in the dark. No one should have to feel like they were married to a stranger."

Ruby considers this. "I don't think I feel that way, Bean. I knew your father better than anyone else did." Athena turns her head and stares at her mother's profile. She says nothing. "I don't think even *she* knew him like I did. In fact, I know she didn't. She couldn't have."

Athena looks back at the water and they watch the waves roll in and out several times before either one of them speaks again.

"So, about that grog," Ruby says, using a shoulder to nudge her daughter, who stands five-foot-ten and is a full three inches taller than Ruby is. "I could go for a walk and a drink."

A soft smile spreads across Athena's face as they make eye contact. "A walk and a drink?" she says, her smile cracking into a full grin. "Aye aye, matey. Let's do it."

* * *

Seadog Lane is like a movie set. Its pirate-themed perfection is reminiscent of something straight out of Walt Disney World, and Ruby fully expects to see a pirate with a peg leg and a hoop earring come stumbling out of a storefront. Everywhere she looks there are nods to pirates and nautical life.

"This is actually insane," Athena says, following Ruby through an old wooden door with an iron ring for a handle. They walk into a dark bar called The Frog's Grog. There are flickering lanterns on every table, and from the ceiling hang yellowed lights that cast a warm glow on the dark wood that makes up nearly every surface of the bar: counter, floors, tables, chairs, beams and posts.

A man wearing a vest and a jaunty pirate's cap walks over to their table with a pronounced hobble.

"Is that for real, or do you think he's in character?" Athena whispers, smiling widely at him when he reaches the table.

"Two grogs, please," Ruby says, folding her hands together and smiling up at him.

The man stares down at her with an amused look. "Aye, miss," he says, "mind if I see some ID?"

Athena pulls out her wallet dutifully and starts to fish out her drivers license, but the bartender is looking at Ruby with a twinkle in his eye.

"It's you I'm going to need to double-check, miss," he says to Ruby as his gray mustache twitches with mirth.

It takes a second—it usually does—but then Ruby gets his joke and decides to play along. She pulls her purse onto her lap and unzips it. People pretending not to know who she is might be the most popular gag that strangers play on her, but she always goes with it because Ruby wasn't raised to be famous. She wasn't brought up in a world where being well-known was her reality, and a tiny part of her still feels like, well, maybe there *is* someone in America who truly has no clue that she was married to their former president.

"Only kidding, Mrs. Hudson," the man says, holding up a hand before she goes to the lengths of taking out her identification. It's clear that while he wanted to have some fun with her, the idea of actually examining her license and seeing 1600 Pennsylvania Avenue listed as her last address might actually be taking it a step too far. "Welcome to Ship-wreck Key," he says, pulling a white rag from where he's looped it over the apron around his waist. He twists the rag in his hands as he talks. "We're thrilled to have you here along with..." He turns to Athena and frowns. "Your sister?"

Athena laughs politely; this isn't the first time a man old enough to be her grandfather has flirted and teased her mother in her presence. It's always cringey and weird, but she figures it must be flattering to her mom, so she lets it slide.

"Thank you," Ruby says, nodding slightly. "Please, call me Ruby. And this is my daughter, Athena."

"Bev Byer," he says, reaching up to twist one end of his mustache between two fingers. "I've lived on this luscious and beautiful island my whole life, and I like to think I'm sort of her caretaker. Unofficially."

"Like a lighthouse caretaker?" Athena asks, putting her wallet away when she realizes that Bev isn't actually going to look at her ID.

"Of sorts," he says. "I know the whole history of the island, and I know everyone who lives here. I never seek out gossip, but somehow it always finds me."

"Seems about right for a bartender," Ruby says knowingly.

"True enough. And I think I just have that kind of face, you know?" His eyes are the gray-blue of a stormy sea, and his hair is as silvery and untamed as his mustache. He's obviously somewhere in the ballpark of seventy, but his arms are strong, and he's tall and lean. "Now, two grogs for our newest residents," Bev says, patting their table. "Coming right up."

He turns and walks back to the bar, leaving Ruby and Athena to resume their whispering.

"Is everyone on this island going to be in costume?" Athena wonders.

"Not everyone. The last time I was here, I saw lots of people just going about their business in street clothes. But I have to admit, there are quite a few who run businesses that rely heavily on the pirate thing. It's definitely a tourist attraction."

Ruby glances around the bar, half expecting to see a few wenches in tight corsets as they deliver foamy mugs of beer to thirsty sailors, but Bev Byer seems to be running the place pretty much singlehandedly. Over in one corner is her Secret Service agent, Banks, and in another is Athena's agent, Corbin. The two men look far more serious than anyone else in the bar, and their eyes constantly scan the room, clocking the patrons, and watching the door.

It had been a real point of contention for Ruby and her daughters when they left the White House: keep their Secret Service agents, or refuse them? President Obama had signed the Former Presidents Protection Act, which provides lifetime Secret Security to all former presidents, their wives, and their children, and while both Ruby and the girls had battled the urge to refuse protection and just get on with their lives as private citizens, they'd been encouraged by several sources to consider maintaining it indefinitely. Sometimes it still feels weird to Ruby to have another human being shadowing her everywhere she goes, but she knows it's for the best.

"Okay, let's talk about the bookstore." Athena waits politely while Bev delivers their grog (which turns out to be rum, lime juice, and sugar), and then looks at her mom again. "I know you've got the location and that you're showing it to me tomorrow, but what about a name? Are you going to staff it with locals? Does Banks have to sit outside the bookstore all day, every day in the hot sun, having a heatstroke to protect the Great Ruby Hudson, bookseller extraordinaire?"

Ruby reaches across the table and pinches her daughter's arm playfully. "No!" she says. "I'm not going to make Banks stand out there in a black suit every day. In fact, once I get things set up the way I want them and the initial curiosity dies down, I figure I'll be just another local around here. No one will give me a second glance."

"*Mom*." Athena lowers her chin and gives her mother a disbelieving look. "Come on."

"What?" Ruby asks innocently, sipping her drink. "I was a regular gal once, and I can be again. In fact, I *will* be again. It'll just take some time."

Athena shakes her head; Ruby is anything but a "regular gal." She still has the high cheekbones, almond shaped eyes, and the pretty face that makes her approachable and attractive at the same time. Before marrying Jack and devoting her life to being at his side through all his political endeavors, Ruby had been a reasonably busy commercial actress who paid her way through UCLA by hawking chewing gum, jeans, and dish soap in a variety of national commercials. In fact, when she first met Jack, he'd commented almost immediately on how much he liked seeing a pretty girl on his television screen frolicking on the beach in a pair of worn-in Levi's. It had tickled Ruby that a man who was already a senator would have seen and remembered her in a commercial, and that charming admission had won him a date with her when he asked for one.

"I'm not holding my breath on you being a regular gal, Mom, but I do want this to be a good choice for you, coming here."

Ruby's eyes shine over the rim of her glass as she takes another sip. "Thanks, Bean. I appreciate that."

In order to keep herself from crying, Ruby pulls a map from her purse and spreads it on the pockmarked and scarred wooden table. The flickering lantern between them throws off just enough light for Ruby to read the map as she flattens it with both hands.

"So," she says, "we're starting at one end of Seadog Lane. After this, I say we hit the Bodacious Booty Salon for manicures—"

"Stop," Athena says, choking on a sip of grog. "You're making that up! Like pirate's booty?"

"I am not making it up," Ruby says haughtily. "And after that, we need to run into Jolly Roger Rags and pick up some pirate gear for your sister. A t-shirt, or maybe a bandana."

"Some pantaloons," Athena adds, warming to the idea. "And maybe we can convince her that she has to show up here dressed like that, or they won't let her on the island."

Ruby lifts an eyebrow. "Do you really think Harlow needs an excuse to put on pantaloons and a bandana?"

"You're so right." They giggle together for a second, thinking of how game Harlow is for pretty much anything. "But Mom? I do have one question."

"Shoot." Ruby knocks back her drink and feels it warming her from within. A relaxed feeling of goodwill washes over her.

"Was there actually a shipwreck here, or is it all a marketing ploy?"

"Aye, lass," Bev says, sneaking up behind Athena and answering her question before Ruby can even open her mouth. "The *Flor de Azucar* wrecked in a storm just off our shores in 1513. Every man on board died, and they say that the only survivor was a woman who was a stowaway on the ship. Mistress of one of the sailors—everyone refers to her as Flora. She made her way to dry land and lived out her life here on Shipwreck Key."

A creaking sound like a wooden boat listing from side to side on a rollicking sea comes from overhead, and Ruby glances up, wondering if it's being piped in via sound system to add to the ambience. It wouldn't surprise her.

"What does *Flor de Azucar* mean?" Athena asks, clearly reeled in by this little bit of local folklore.

"It means 'sugar flower,'" the bartender says. "And rumor has it that the island is haunted by the ghosts of the men who died on that vessel. If you stay here more than a day or two, you might see one sitting on a bench on Seadog Lane, sipping a pint of beer. And Flora is rumored to walk the shores of the island at night, watching the ocean for signs of her lost lover."

Ruby scoffs; she doesn't believe in ghosts or in hauntings. Or rather, she doesn't *want* to believe that a man who crashes and burns spectacularly has the ability to come back and haunt the living, tormenting their souls for all time while he tries to work out the penance for his own sins in some last-ditch bid to get to heaven.

But just to be on the safe side, she crosses her fingers under the table and shoots Banks a look across the bar. As always, he is impenetrable, which soothes and calms her more than she can measure.

Ruby

In her dream, Jack is alive. He's at the helm of a small boat, and Ruby sits next to him, trying to make out his words over the rush of the wind. He's intentionally chosen this location to tell her the real reason for his betrayal, and Ruby strains to hear him.

"I need you to understand, Rubes," he shouts. The sharp rush of air blows his lightly graying hair around. His eyes are shielded by dark sunglasses. "I need you to know why I did it."

Her voice is choked in her throat, though she has a million things she wants to ask, like *Why? Are you sorry? Did you ever think of me? What kind of an asshole secretly carries on with a whole other family for more than a decade and then just dies and leaves everyone in the lurch?*

"I just—" Jack says, but he's cut off by a loud noise. Ruby waits for him to say more, only to have the same loud, insistent sound drown out his words over and over. She begins to reach for him frantically, trying to get him to speak again, but instead of her hands landing on her husband's arm, she jerks awake with her heart hammering in her chest. She's clutching a pillow tightly and sweating through her t-shirt.

Ruby sits up in bed. The banging sound that's woken her is an open window shutter, unlatched and blowing in the wind that's coming through her bedroom window. The clock on the beside table says one forty-two, and Ruby slides out from between the sheets, putting her feet on the floor.

It's far from the first time that she's had this dream, and it leaves her awake and disturbed every single time. There is no good reason why Jack should have betrayed her and their girls after she'd devoted her life to him. She'd been more than just a wife and a helpmeet for her husband; Ruby was a true partner. Whatever he needed to think or talk through, she was there. If he needed a plethora of ideas laid out before him for his consideration—like a customer who wanted to see a variety of carpet and wallpaper options for a remodel—then Ruby did that. She was quick on her feet, nimble when it came to sussing out the intricacies of foreign policies, and secretive to a fault about whatever Jack told her. She'd given up her own private ambitions of somehow using her English degree in order to raise their daughters and to help smooth Jack's way to the White House, and she'd done it all without a single bit of regret, because Jack Hudson had made a damn fine president, and probably would have done so for another four years if tragedy hadn't intervened.

Ruby passes Athena's closed bedroom door on her way downstairs to the kitchen, but she stops on the landing, looking down from the second floor at the gigantic, open living space. Even in the dark it's a grand house. The empty fireplace waits for a stormy winter afternoon or a festive holiday, and the room is ready to be filled with family, friends, and laughter. She walks down there, turning on one single lamp next to a couch so that she'll have just the faintest glow of warm light around her as she makes her way to the kitchen.

Banks is living in the guest house that's detached from the main house, but it's still close enough for him to reach her in under a minute. Living with a Secret Service presence isn't always easy; it took Ruby some time to get used to sharing her personal space with people who barely speak to her, but over time, Banks has loosened up enough that Ruby feels comfortable in his presence. She found out that he's been married and divorced once, and that he grew up in Philly and played basketball at Notre Dame. Banks has an extremely dry sense of humor and can spot a threat from what seems like a mile away. One time he realized that a sketchy looking man was walking along the periphery of a Target store, and Banks had intercepted him just before the man could approach Ruby. Sure enough, this guy had a razor blade tucked into the bottom of his sleeve, and some sort of weird notion that the opposing political party needed him to hurt Ruby in order to regain its footing in the White House. The whole thing had terrified Ruby and reminded her how much she needs extra sets of eyes—professional eyes—to watch what's going on around her.

The stainless steel refrigerator opens up to reveal a riot of colors: grapes in red and green; chunks of cut cantaloupe in a clear container; shiny red cans of Coke Zero; a variety of wedges of expensive cheese; washed butter lettuce, spinach, and kale; and perfectly aligned containers of Ruby's favorite Icelandic yogurt. She reaches in and pulls out a bowl of homemade macaroni and cheese that's leftover from dinner, and pops it into the microwave to warm up so that she can eat it at the kitchen island in the semi-darkness.

With the microwave whirring behind her, Ruby's cell phone lights up where she left it on the counter. It's an incoming call from Banks.

"Ma'am?" he says as soon as she answers. He sounds relatively calm. "Everything alright?"

"Yes, of course. Everything is fine," Ruby says, puzzled. How did Banks even know she was up at two o'clock in the morning?

"There are sensors in each downstairs room of your house that are set to kick on at midnight," he says, answering her unasked question. "My Spidey senses told me it wasn't anything urgent, but I'm up and on my front porch anyway. Want me to come over?"

"Ah," Ruby says, reaching up to open the microwave door just as it dings. "No, no—I'm fine. I was just restless and wanted a snack. Would you like something?"

"No, but thank you. I just wanted to confirm that things were fine. I'll sleep a few more hours. Please let me know immediately if you need me."

"Goodnight, Banks."

"Goodnight, ma'am," he says, ending the call.

Ruby sets the phone down and reaches for the pepper grinder, twisting it over the bowl of macaroni and then digging in with a heavy fork. It's delicious warmed up, and she sits in the kitchen as she eats and looks out at the way the moonlight reflects off the ocean. She hasn't once yet been sorry that she bought a house with a view of the powdery white sand and the sea just beyond, and absolutely no part of her misses D.C. Not even a tiny bit.

For Ruby, this is truly heaven. All these years, paradise was just an island waiting for her off the coast of Florida, and all she had to do was get on a boat in Destin, and then head ten miles out into the ocean to get to Shipwreck Key. Because the house was already perfectly decorated, other than ordering a golf cart to get around the island (the preferred mode of transportation on Shipwreck) and sending trunks of clothes, books, mementos, photos, her computer, and her collection of vinyl albums down from Washington D.C., Ruby has essentially just shown up and started living her new life. It's been easier than she ever hoped it might be.

She forks another bite of macaroni into her mouth and chews, thinking of her recurring dream about Jack on the boat. Most times when she has the dream, Jack is about to tell her something and she can feel fear bubbling up in her chest as she waits for him to speak, wishing he wouldn't say a word. But this time she'd been waiting to hear it, full of anticipation and a need for closure.

Of course, in her waking life, she knows what "it" is: it's Etienne. Her name might be masculine, but everything else about her is ultra-feminine. Chic. French. She is wealthy, Oxford-educated, and moves in the upper echelon of French society. Several Google searches had schooled Ruby on Etienne Boucher, and the things she'd found out had given her far too many sleepless nights.

It isn't fair, she thinks. *Jack got to live the life he already had and also the life he wanted to have, and nobody stopped him. Nobody told me I was helping him live a double life. Everyone had* his *back, and nobody had* my *back.*

A light goes on in the kitchen and Ruby startles. She turns to see Athena there, blinking and looking half-asleep in a pair of pink shorts and a matching tank top. Her feet are bare, and without her contacts in, she's put on her adorably thick glasses so that she can see.

"Mom? You okay?"

Ruby stands and takes her bowl to the sink, filling it with soapy water. She'll leave it for morning, because doing dishes in the middle of the night defeats the purpose of sneaking an illicit snack like microwave-heated mac and cheese.

"Of course, Bean. I'm good. I was just feeling peckish. Should we go back to bed?"

Athena nods as she yawns, wrapping her arms around her own narrow ribcage. Ruby walks over to her daughter and rubs her back. They turn out the light and go back to bed.

* * *

By the time Athena leaves the island three days later, she's satisfied that her mother is firmly grounded, has chosen a good location for the bookstore, and is at home in her new beachfront house, and Ruby is honestly excited to be on her own. She's got a list of things she needs to tackle, and she's ready to roll up her sleeves and get to work.

"How do you feel about this color palette, Mrs. Hudson?" Miranda, the decorator Ruby has hired for the bookstore, is standing there in an ivory colored shirt dress, holding a book full of paint samples in her hands.

"Please--Ruby is fine. I insist," Ruby says, blowing a stray lock of hair out of her eyes as she approaches Miranda. The decorator has the book open to a page with five possible paint colors, each a mere variation on the one before it. Ruby reaches out to take the heavy tome. "May I?"

Once Miranda hands it over, Ruby walks to the window that looks out onto Seadog Lane. She holds up the samples, letting the natural light hit them.

"Well," she says, squinting and trying to imagine what color will go where. "I think this shade of pink needs to be outside, for sure." Ruby walks to the front door, which is currently propped open to let in the pleasant breeze. The calendar has just flipped over to March, and spring is everywhere. She steps out onto the sidewalk in her olive green cargo pants and white Converse sneakers. A white cable-knit fisherman's sweater has slipped off of one shoulder, revealing the strap of a white tank top.

From across the street, a small group of people stop and stare, which

Ruby completely ignores. She's used to people gawking at her and knowing who she is, and she's even used to the idea that they're gossiping about her personal life—or at least about what they think they know. Since her appearance on Leeza's show, Ruby has encountered a lot more people who want to take selfies with her, and several who want to high-five her for calling Leeza out on her own show, which Ruby always tries to downplay. Because who cares about tabloid-worthy gossip like Ruby Hudson and Leeza exchanging words? Ruby isn't the First Lady anymore, and she never will be again. She smiles at them and carries on.

"Where are you thinking for the pink?" Miranda asks, stepping out the door and standing next to her on the sidewalk.

Ruby waves a hand over the storefront, pointing at the trim around the windows. "I want the main color to be that gray we picked out, and the pink to be for the front door and the trim around the windows. I think that'll really pop."

"I think it will too," Miranda agrees. She looks up and down Seadog Lane at the other businesses. "Especially since every other building is totally tame and neutral."

Ruby turns to her with a grin. "That's exactly what I want. I'm thinking of a cottage vibe, and obviously my interior style is kind of a shabby chic beach look, which you know from the million things I've added to our Pinterest board."

Miranda smiles at this and nods. "You do have a strong sense of what you want, and we will definitely make it happen."

The women go back inside and look at a few more paint samples together. They settle on varying shades of white with prominent gray and blue undertones that will look understated in the different rooms of the bookstore. The walls should be muted enough that anything Ruby wants to display will stand out against them.

After she and Miranda finish choosing upholstery for the couches and chairs that will be scattered throughout the store, Ruby walks through the rooms. She eyes the tall, custom-built white wooden bookshelves fitted with ladders that slide along the length of the shelves so she can access the overstock that she'll store up high. The walls have built-in shelving that will be filled with curios, some with spotlights aimed at the objects that will sit there.

This was part of Ruby's plan all along: to incorporate her whole life from the beginning to this point, and to use some of the things that were swathed in bubble wrap, boxed, stored, and essentially forgotten. And there are so many things she doesn't want to forget! On every trip she took as First Lady, Ruby had both given and received gifts. Some of the things are treasured and cherished items that she wants to take out and display here in the store. Gifts like the mother of pearl nativity scene from the King of Jordan, the silver humidor from the Soviet Premier, and the silver Aztec calendar she got in Mexico, will all be preserved in glass cases and displayed on the shelves. Other items will be displayed on the walls, like artwork received from the governments and leaders of various countries, and a circular platter with bands of elephants, bulls, lions, horses, and lotus petals that Ruby received from the Prime Minister of Sri Lanka.

From her former life—the life she lived before she met Jack—she wants to display the things that brought her the most joy and that she's had to keep tucked away in storage for decades. There is the lovely lamp she bought in Santa Barbara one summer that was handmade by a local glassblower. It throws off sparks of light and color whenever she turns it on, and Ruby wants it at the front counter of the bookstore. There is also a collection of flower pots made by local artisans in the places she visited all throughout California during her college years. She'd intentionally stopped at roadside stands and poked around thrift shops and art galleries, hoping to find hand-thrown pots. Her flower pot collection is a gorgeous hodgepodge of smooth and jagged mosaic tiles, painted terra cotta, and ceramic, and she can see them already, standing on the high windowsills that line the upper row of squat, rectangular windows near the ceiling.

Ruby walks around the shop in her Converse, stopping here and there to admire her little kingdom. She stands on a staircase that leads to a tiny upper office area, and she stops in the back room of the bookstore, where she can look straight through the shop to the front desk. Finally, she stands at a side table next to the huge window at the front of the store, looking around and daydreaming about what the future holds for her new shop. It's all hers, really and truly hers. She is the sole proprietor of a shop that will sell romance novels, cookbooks, biographies, gardening manuals, and every kind of book in between. She is the mistress of this place—the brains behind the whole operation. And the very thought of it thrills her. To be her own boss, to make her own rules...it's been so long, and the novelty of it almost overwhelms her for a moment.

She answers to no one. Not anymore.

When it's complete, Ruby wants her store to be light and bright, and to be a reflection of a life that has taken her from the west coast to the east coast and around the world. It should be a testimonial to a life lived as a wife, a mother, an English major, a book-lover, and a First Lady.

Ruby glances down at the stainless steel tank watch given to her by the president of the Czech Republic on her last official visit to the country as First Lady, and she lays a hand gently over its face. She'd unearthed the watch along with all her other artifacts, happy that she'd had the foresight to pack the things she'd wanted to hang onto for senti- mental and aesthetic purposes—rules about gifts valued at over four hundred dollars not leaving the White House be damned.

After all, who was going to stop a grieving woman from taking a few mementos and keepsakes? Who amongst the White House staff would step in and ask Ruby to put a halt to her packing, particularly when most of them had been privy and played a part in the deception that led to Jack's untimely death? As it turned out, none of them had the guts to confront her, and she'd wrapped up all of her keepsakes and packed them alongside the girls' baby books, her winter coats, and the blanket her grandmother had made for her when she was a child, taking it all with her when she left the White House.

But enough of that, Ruby thinks, walking behind the front counter of her bookstore and opening the top drawer to reveal the letterhead and business cards she'd had made for the shop. She pulls out a card and holds it up, admiring the embossed palm tree with a Jolly Roger flag flapping from its trunk. Across the top of the card is the name of her store: *Marooned With a Book*. And beneath that, her name: *Ruby Hudson, Proprietress*. It's the first time in so long—so long that she can't even remember how long—that she's owned something for herself. Something that is truly, honestly, with no strings attached, *hers*.

Ruby glances around to make sure she's alone and does a little happy dance right there at the front counter of Marooned With a Book.

The thought that she's completely reimagined her whole future suddenly fills her with such awe and wonder that her heart begins to race. She's on an island where she knows almost no one, and she's starting a business of her own that she'll be running as a one-woman show. Ruby's whole future is a mystery, but that feeling is okay, she thinks, because up until now, every minute of every day has been planned for her by someone else; every outfit selected, everything she will need to say carefully laid out and vetted for meaning and intent.

But now...*there are no rules.*

Now, the rules are hers to make.

A chill runs up Ruby's arms as she looks again at her business card and thinks of all that her little shop could become: Marooned With a Book is like a baby she's about to give birth to, its potential still unknown.

With a feeling of satisfaction, Ruby locks up her shop and heads to her golf cart, with Banks following close behind.

Athena

February in Florida is always preferable to February up north. No question. Coming back to D.C. has left Athena questioning all of her life choices up until this point. All except for one, that is: Diego, a man she has recently decided is the one that she's spent all twenty-three years of her life waiting for.

Diego Santana is the Romeo to her Juliet. He is the Clyde to her Bonnie. The John Lennon to her Yoko. Okay, none of those are fabulous examples, but essentially he is the other piece of the puzzle that completes her, and she desperately wants him to feel the same way. She knows deep in her soul that he's the man for her without ever even going on a date with Diego. Instead, she watches him every day as he enters the Library of Congress, his dark and wavy hair combed carefully into place, his suit usually navy and cut just so. He is a Lead Contract Specialist, and while Athena isn't one hundred percent sure what he actually does, she knows that he is the most beautiful and soulful man she's ever seen.

The truth about Athena that she likes to keep to herself (because *judgment*, duh) is that she's a virgin. A twenty-three-year-old woman with no experience to speak of. In college she'd been kissed by exactly two boys and one girl (that last one had been confusing and sort of an accident, because she hadn't realized that a lacrosse player named Shar wasn't just inviting her out for Thai food and a movie, but she doesn't really count that kiss because she pulled away so quickly). So discounting women, two boring guys had kissed her and found her not interesting enough to push for more.

Athena sighs and clicks from one computer screen to another. She's mid-project and has a deadline, but she can't keep her mind from conjuring images of Diego. Outside it's spitting cold sleet against the window of her third floor office, but inside her mind, she and Diego are walking along the beach of Shipwreck Key together, holding hands. She likes to do this when work gets boring, to daydream and turn an image over in her brain like a shiny penny. She makes a movie with a full soundtrack, a plot, and a resolution, and enjoys it over and over and over until—

"Athena?"

She nearly jumps out of her skin, then turns in her chair to face the door. Against all odds, it's Diego. Six-foot tall, smooth-skinned, eyes the color of fizzy root beer, *Diego Santana*. Diego, who, until now, has *never* shown up in the doorway of her office.

"Quick question," he says, looking serious and glancing down at a folder in his hands. "I have several pdf documents that I need to have compiled into one database. It pertains to this particular Supreme Court case," he says, taking a step into her office with his long legs and thrusting the folder in her direction. "And if you don't mind, I'd really like to be able to send out the link to the appropriate parties by this afternoon. Do you think you could set that up?"

Athena flips through the papers in the folder. Her heart is thumping so hard and so loud that his voice actually gets quieter in her ears. She can feel her face redden, and for some reason, she keeps her eyes trained on the paper in a sort of *if I can't see you, then you can't see me* game. As if this will somehow make it so that Diego can't see her cheeks flamed up and turning a violent shade of red. As if somehow it will mask the sweat that's instantly forming in the shallow valley of her cleavage under her black Anne Klein sweater.

Athena glances up at Diego. She just has to accept that she looks like an idiot with her red face and sweaty chest and move on with it.

"Yes, Diego," she says, trying out his name on her tongue. It's delicious, so she does it again after clearing her throat. "Diego, I can do this for you." Athena glances at the watch on her wrist. "If you give me until two-thirty, I can have it done."

A slow, pleased smile spreads across the most handsome face Athena has ever seen in person. He steps back and pats her doorframe with one perfect hand. Fingers: long and tapered. Nails: short and perfectly filed. Wrists: strong and square. Athena's eyes linger on his hand longer than they should, and another wave of heat washes over her as she imagines his hands on her.

"Thanks a lot," Diego says, watching her face. "I owe you a cup of coffee, Athena." He walks away and leaves her staring dumbly at the spot where he was just standing.

"Oh god," Athena whispers to herself, using the folder in her hand to fan herself. She pulls her sweater away from her body and unsuccessfully tries to push some cool air down the front of her body. Walking around all afternoon with a sweat-dampened bra is not the move. She wonders if Diego could smell the pheromones seeping from her every pore.

Athena tosses the file folder onto her desk and quickly picks up her phone. In an instant, she realizes that she has no girlfriend to call so that she can dissect this interaction between her and Diego. No confidante, no college bestie, no coworker/friend who knows her secrets. Instead, Athena quickly finds her mom in her phone.

"Hi, sweetheart." Ruby's smooth voice fills her ear and her heart rate instantly slows. "What's going on?"

"Hey, Mom." Athena smiles. "Not too much. I was just thinking about how beautiful it must be on Shipwreck Key right now." Her eyes cut to her window and she watches again as the gray sky pours cold, frozen droplets of rain all over the city. "It's horrible here."

Ruby laughs. "Yeah, it's pretty fabulous here. Seventy-nine and sunny. I'm wearing sunglasses and drinking coffee on the front step of the bookstore while the painters do their thing inside. But tell me about you."

Athena sits back in her chair and folds one arm across her stomach, using her other hand to hold the desk phone to her ear. "I'm just working on a couple of projects here—nothing exciting." She decides to keep her interaction with Delectable Diego to herself just a little longer, though telling her mom that she has a crush on a coworker isn't totally out of the question. She just isn't quite ready for advice or input. "I miss you."

"I miss you too, Bean. You know you can come back down for a visit anytime, right?"

"I know," Athena says. The prickling sweat that had covered her body the second Diego entered her airspace has cooled and left behind a chill. "I know, Mom."

"Okay, then let me tell you all about the bookstore," Ruby says, launching into a series of stories and little details about her progress at Marooned With a Book.

Athena smiles and laughs in all the right places, missing her mom a little bit less as they talk and talk. She'll get started on Diego's Supreme Court project soon enough, but right now what she needs is less rain, less emotional upheaval, less gray sky.

What she *really* needs is a dose of her mother's sunshine.

Ruby

~~~~~~

How do you distill a woman's entire life down to one single moment? How do you sift through it all: marriage, motherhood, success—and come up with a clip of the moment that perfectly encapsulates who she is?

For Ruby, it's not Jack's inauguration. It isn't her on the set of her first big commercial, shaking with nerves as someone touches up her hair and makeup. And it isn't even the birth of her beloved children. It's the opening night of Marooned With a Book that happens at the beginning of April, and all that it represents. For Ruby, this night is a culmination of her dreams, her plans, and her hard work. It is also the crossroads of the life she's had so far, and the one she's embarking upon. Excitement flutters around inside of her like fireflies caught in a glass jar as she stands in the middle of the bookshop, which still smells of fresh paint masked by the rich, sweet scent of cardamom and vetiver candles that burn around the store.

"Mom," Harlow says, appearing at her elbow and looping her arm through her mother's. "You did it." Ruby's younger daughter looks proud, and maybe even a little surprised at her mother's competence. Ruby smiles at her indulgently.

"Yes, Lolo, I did it."

Ruby always calls her daughters by their nicknames: Lolo and Bean. Bean and Lolo. To her, her babies are the perfect girl-women; the human embodiments of every joy and amazement she can possibly imagine. Harlow leans into her now, putting her head on Ruby's shoulder for a moment.

Unhooking their arms, Ruby snakes an arm around the shoulders of her youngest child and pulls her closer. As always, she fights the urge to run her fingers through Harlow's wild hair to tame it, or to hand her a tissue and discreetly tell her to blot her overly bright lipstick. At this point, Ruby knows exactly who Harlow is, and she loves her for her stubbornness and fierce independence.

And Harlow is a force to be reckoned with. Her short skirts, late nights, and penchant for swearing at paparazzi were all things that Ruby and Jack used to argue over. In Harlow, Jack saw a liability: a president's daughter who went to nightclubs, shopped at Goodwill for fun, and once got caught smoking weed with the son of a White House groundskeeper just off the property and within view of the early morning delivery trucks (unforgivable, in Jack's eyes), but Ruby saw her as a spark plug. How many times had she defended Harlow to her husband, reminding him that while he had signed on for his job and she had supported his run for the Oval Office, the girls had done nothing but be born into the family? They couldn't be expected to slip from the womb and into adulthood with no mishaps, no awkward mistakes, no friction. Jack had always looked exhausted during these arguments and had referred to Harlow as "a pound of whipped cream that you have to scoop into a teacup with your hands." There were times when Ruby had to agree that it was an apt description, but she was always supportive of her younger daughter's independent streak.

Watching Harlow now as she moves through the crowd that's growing inside of the bookstore, Ruby feels nothing but pride. Harlow helped her think up some of the key marketing strategies that she's now prepared to implement, and while Athena is the organized and prag-matic one, Harlow has a keen eye for design and for visually appealing details. In fact, it was her choice to hang a different chandelier in every room of the bookstore, from an ornate brass light fixture with strings of cut glass beads draped over it, to a chipped, antique white metal chandelier whose arms are shaped into flowers that boast petals of pink, and green glass leaves. When the lights are turned on, it adds a flair of femininity to the Romance Room, as Ruby thinks of the very back room, which offers visitors two wing chairs upholstered in different floral patterns to sit in while they browse their books.

"Well," Ruby's own mother says, walking with with completely erect posture as she moves from the front of the store into the center room. "Looks like you've done it, doll." There is a massive, round wooden table laden with various book displays beneath a heavy chandelier covered in seashells and sea glass in the middle of the room, and Patty Dallarosa stops next to the table to admire her nearly fifty-year-old daughter as she basks in the glow of her bookstore success.

Patty is seventy-eight, and to this day she is still one of the most regal women Ruby has ever encountered, heads of state and formidable female politicians included. When Ruby was a young girl, her mother had once told her to "never leave your bedroom if you aren't going to be dressed enough to answer the front door." She abhors people who schlump around in sweatpants and pajamas, and Ruby can honestly say that she's only ever seen her mother in a nightgown a handful of times in her life. When Ruby was young, Patty was always up before the sun, dressed, sipping coffee, and being more productive than any other human she's ever known.

"Thanks, Mom," Ruby says quietly, stepping closer to her mother. "I'm so glad you're here."

"Wouldn't have missed it," Patty says, her eyes glittering with pride.

When Ruben Dallarosa died of a heart attack at the age of forty, he'd left Patty a widow, and his namesake and only child, Ruby, a fatherless eleven-year-old. Patty had used her resources and her dormant law degree and had become, in her forties, a lawyer with a reputation for being fierce and tireless. It was through her constant encouragement and pursuit of perfection that Ruby had excelled in her own ways, and had ultimately become the kind of woman that one of the country's most popular senators—and the future President—had fallen hard for.

"This is quite an island," Patty says, reaching out to pluck a glass of champagne from a silver tray as a waiter in a pristine white shirt and starched black pants passes by. "Bit heavy on the pirate kitsch, but it's cute nonetheless. You think you'll be happy here?" Patty's words are sharp and fast, and Ruby feels like her mother has slipped into lawyer-mode, which she frequently does.

"I actually really like it," Ruby says, watching as people filter in off the street, looking around with curiosity and more than a little awe at the fact that they've been invited to a cocktail party/bookstore opening thrown by Ruby Hudson. "I think the people are wonderful, and the whole pirate thing is very tongue-in-cheek. Trust me, it'll grow on you."

Patty sips her champagne, her heavy gold rings and stack of tasteful gold bangles and chain bracelets catching the light of the chandeliers. She lifts a groomed eyebrow as a trio of women Ruby's age pass, their hair blown out and their grays covered. They're dressed in beach-chic dresses and sandals and carrying expensive purses. It's clear that Patty has instantly clocked them as ladies who lunch, but Ruby already knows the women, who have dropped in to introduce themselves as she's worked on the bookstore, brought her coffee, and offered to show her around, and they are each far more than meets the eye.

"I'm so glad you all could make it," Ruby says, walking over to the women and extending both hands so that she can reach out and touch each of them in a warm, friendly way. "I'd love for you to meet my mother, Patricia Dallarosa."

Patty smiles, holding the stem of her champagne flute as she looks at them all expectantly.

"Mom, I'd like you to meet Shelly Winetraub, who runs the most successful real estate company in Okaloosa County." Patty offers a hand. The faintest flicker of amusement passes over her face as she hears the words *Okaloosa County*. As a native Californian who loves big cities and all that they have to offer, Patty eschews anything that smacks of small-town, backwoods charm. "And this is Marigold Pim, the former—"

"Model," Patty interrupts. "Of course. I recognized you right away," Patty says, shaking Marigold's hand as the model turns up a thousand-watt smile and her spine immediately straightens. "Lovely to meet you."

"And last but not least, this is Heather Charleton-Bicks, who—"

Heather thrusts out a hand and takes over. "Who has been married to every rich old man under the sun," she says with a honeyed Southern accent.

Patty can't help herself: she laughs out loud. "Well, I do admire a woman who can distill her own highlights down to a single sentence. It's much harder than you think." She lifts her champagne in a toast to the three women she's just met and then takes a sip.

"If you had to distill *your* highlights down to a single sentence," Heather says to Ruby's mother with a challenge in her voice, "what would it be?"

Patty's eyes twinkle; she loves a sharp cookie, and Heather is clearly far more than she appears to be. She squints for a moment as if thinking.

"A woman who was once a shark of a lawyer, and who likes her men young and her cars old." Patty casts a glance at her daughter, knowing that Ruby will approve. Even when she was living in the White House, Ruby had supported her mother's unwillingness to mince words. Ruby likes to think that Harlow has inherited some of her sass and sauciness from her grandmother, and that from Patty, Athena has gotten her work ethic and sense of self.

Heather nearly chokes on her own champagne. "Oh, Patty—may I call you Patty?"

Mrs. Dallarosa nods her assent. "You may."

"Patty, I think we're going to get along like a house on fire." Heather reaches out and takes Patty's sun-spotted hand in hers. Patty's nails are perfectly manicured a sedate but glossy shade of coral, and she lets Heather lead her away with nothing but a glimpse over her shoulder at Ruby and the other women. "Now, Patty. The first question I have for you is which of the naughty books in the romance section you'd recommend to a lonely divorcee who loves to read in bed..."

Ruby watches her mother walk along next to tall, toned Heather, whose long legs are bare beneath a clingy jersey knit dress, and whose jewelry rivals anything Patty has ever owned, in terms of carats or clarity.

Marigold sighs as they all chuckle to themselves. "Incorrigible," she says, shaking her head.

"Heather, or my mom?" Ruby asks, turning her attention back to Shelly and Marigold.

"I'm going to say both," Shelly pipes up, turning her hand over to inspect her own manicure. Patty has always had that effect on other women: she intimidates and excites them, but everything about her silently urges them to rise to the occasion—whatever that occasion may be. Ruby has watched it happen her entire life.

"I'm sure you're not wrong," Ruby says with a smile as she sees several new groups of people wandering in through the front door. "I'm sorry, ladies. If you'll excuse me, I see some new guests and I'd love to welcome them in."

"Oh, of course. And everything turned out amazingly well in the store," Marigold says, reaching over and putting a hand on Ruby's arm lightly before she and Shelly wander off to browse the shop.

As Ruby winds her way through the guests, nodding, smiling and welcoming each of them personally as she passes, she takes stock of the room, a habit she's had for years. Her daughters are talking to three men in golf attire who appear to be in their fifties, and who are no doubt pumping them for information about their late father. Ruby suppresses a wave of annoyance, though this is nothing new. People can't help but ask questions about Jack, always hoping for tidbits of unknown gossip or stories they can share during cocktail parties or business lunches. But her girls have always been good about knowing what's fit for public consumption and what isn't.

Along the back wall stands Banks, who has ditched his sunglasses but not his earpiece, which tethers him tonight to the girls' Secret Service agents—Corbin, who is there with Athena, and Watkins, there as Harlow's guard. Just to aggravate her father, Harlow had once threatened to date Eldrick Watkins, who'd played tight end for Ohio State before enlisting in the Marines and eventually being recruited into the Secret Service. Of course the mere idea of Harlow acting up—yet again —had aggravated Jack to no end, but Ruby had soothed him, swearing up and down that Harlow was only doing it to get his goat. As Ruby's eyes flick over her daughter and Watkins now she isn't one hundred percent sure that Harlow hasn't harbored some sort of naughty intentions for the poor man, but Watkins is tough, strong, and silent, and surely he would never bend or break to the whims of a young woman when it would put his job on the line.

Probably.

Maybe.

Ruby pushes the thought from her mind as her eyes graze Watkins, who is stationed at the front door, and Corbin, a short, stocky, ginger-haired bodybuilder who has taken the spot in the center room. They are attempting to be as unobtrusive as possible, but Ruby finds that it's more difficult for them to blend in here on Shipwreck Key than it was in D.C. After all, people expect Secret Service agents to trail and track the First Family in Washington, but no one knows quite what to do with men who look like tanks with serious faces and boring fashion sense on an island that's been cultivated almost entirely for fun and relaxation.

Ruby spots her mom and Heather talking and laughing amongst the shelves of romance novels in the back room, and as she passes by two women and two men who are clearly in the throes of early retirement from the kind of white collar jobs that afford vacation homes on tropical islands, she overhears their heated whispers.

"Everyone knows he was assassinated. No question," says a tall man whose right hand is tucked casually into the pocket of creased trousers that break cleanly across a pair of polished loafers.

"But when they found his body," says a woman wearing a tangle of pearl necklaces and a giant ruby ring, "it left even more unanswered questions."

"That's where you're mistaken," says the other woman, looking as though she is about to solve a great mystery. "The questions weren't unanswerable, but the answers were not passed on to *us*, the general public. Trust me—people on the inside know *exactly* what happened."

Ruby can tell by the tone and by the content of the conversation that it's about Jack. Rather than slink away from it, she knows she needs to press forward. In order to truly begin living her life amongst civilians, Ruby is going to need to buck up and accept that there will be conversation about her, about Jack, and about how he died...maybe for the rest of her life.

"Are you kidding?" says the man who hasn't yet spoken. "This is one of the great presidential mysteries in history, and—"

"Welcome to the bookstore," Ruby interrupts, stepping up to the group and forcing herself to hold a firm, unwavering smile. "I'm so glad to have you here on opening night. Ruby Hudson," she says, offering a hand to the woman closest to her, then shaking hands with each person as they sheepishly introduce themselves. No one acknowledges what they all know—that Ruby walked up and overhead them indiscreetly discussing her husband's death.

"So happy to have you here on Shipwreck Key," says the woman with the pile of pearls. She twists her fingers through them nervously as she speaks. "My husband and I are here for six months of the year," she says, nodding at the man in the polished loafers. "We're both voracious readers," she adds, "so I'm sure you'll see us in here far more often than you'd like."

"Oh, that can't be true," Ruby says, shaking her head. "After all, how will I keep the doors open if you all aren't in here buying up my Elin Hilderbrands and John Grishams?"

Those particular authors are a random guess based on their ages and appearances, but Pile of Pearls laughs and cocks her head to one side as she lets go of her necklaces.

"You got me there," Pearls says. "I do love my beach books!"

"And I'm not above a good Grisham to read by the pool," Loafers says, lifting a graying eyebrow. "In fact, can you point me there now?"

Ruby gives them all a quick overview of where each genre is shelved in the store, then excuses herself with a smile and moves on.

By the end of the evening, the two young women she's hired to work in the shop have rung up an impressive two thousand dollars in sales (Ruby really only expected to have people in to see the shop and to meet her and her daughters out of curiosity), and she's handed out over a hundred business cards. There have been requests to bring authors in for book signings, questions about where Carl Sagan, Jack's beloved Golden Retriever, was (sadly, he'd died of cancer not long after his master's death), and several people had wondered whether Ruby might have any famous visitors dropping in to the shop in the near future. Not too surprisingly, there were also a few comments about her February appearance on Leeza's show, and one woman asked if it had felt good to bring such a sanctimonious bitch to her knees on live television. Ruby had blinked at this in surprise and was surprised at the words that came out of her own mouth: "Yeah, actually it felt great!"

All in all, it's been a successful opening night, and Ruby feels satisfied that Marooned With a Book has been met by the locals with open arms.

After Athena and Harlow have taken their grandmother back to the house in Ruby's golf cart, accompanied by Corbin and Watkins, Banks is left behind to keep an eye on the shop and on Ruby, and things are finally quiet. Ruby kicks off her sandals and walks through the store barefoot, watching as the catering crew cleans up and packs everything away efficiently.

Ruby is wearing a gingham dress with an oversized white collar, the skirt of which is pleated at the waist, giving it a 1950s feel. It brushes against tables and bookshelves as she walks through, straightening piles and picking up discarded cocktail napkins and champagne flutes. The shop isn't a mess, by any means, but it still makes Ruby shake her head as she wonders what kind of people set trash next to brand new books and then just walk away.

"Ma'am?" The woman from the catering crew is standing near the front counter, her black apron rolled up in her hands as she waits for Ruby to walk through the shop. Ruby is still in her bare feet and holding a stack of paper plates and napkins. She tosses them all in the trash and brushes her hands together.

"All done?" Ruby asks with a smile. "You guys were incredible. I think the salmon puffs and bruschetta were a huge hit."

"Thank you, ma'am. We were thrilled that you chose us for the job."

Ruby takes the bill from the woman and skims it. The fact that she's had to bring the catering crew over from the mainland adds to the cost of hosting the event, but it's worth it.

"Can I pay this online?" Ruby asks, glancing up from the bill as she sets it on the counter next to the register.

"Oh, of course," the woman says, nodding her head slightly in what almost looks like a bow.

Ruby is used to this kind of deference, though she's never grown comfortable with it. She watches the woman, wondering when and if it will ever end. Will there be a day when people stop calling her "ma'am" and acting like they're in the presence of royalty? She certainly hopes so. For a girl who grew up on a beach in the 80s—even with a mother who never wore jeans and who served lunch with mineral water in wine goblets—Ruby has never truly felt at ease with a household staff or with strangers who get visibly excited while speaking to her.

"Have a safe trip back to Destin," Ruby says, waving at the catering crew as they pack their crates and boxes out the front door and down to the dock to meet the boat that's waiting there for them. She steps out onto the front step of her shop, putting her hands into the pockets of her gingham dress as she watches them go. "I'll definitely book you guys again the next time I have an event!"

She knows it's unnecessary to stand out there shoeless, waving at the team of tired caterers, and for a moment Ruby feels a wave of loneliness. It's been a long time since she had a core group of friends in her life, people who have nothing to do with politics and nothing to do with the White House, and she longs for that. More than anything, she wants a group of ladies with whom she can talk about music and books, ladies she can drink wine with while they laugh about the indignities of being middle-aged women. It's a void in her life that she feels more frequently now that she's a widow and not in the public eye, and it's something that she hopes to remedy as she embarks upon Act Two of her life.

As the caterers disappear from view, Ruby folds her arms across her chest and leans against the frame of the open door. Seadog Lane is paved and lined on both sides by sidewalks. Along the edge of the sidewalks nearest the street, weathered wooden posts with rusted iron rings affixed to them sit at regular intervals, and long lengths of heavy rope run from post to post. Above each business on Seadog Lane hangs a wooden anchor with the building's street number burned onto the thick stock with a branding iron, and spaced out at twenty foot intervals are heavy black lanterns on light posts that look like they've been salvaged from a sunken pirate ship.

An image of women of all ages and walks of life sitting inside her cozy bookstore on a warm night pops into Ruby's head and she rubs her hands up and down her bare arms. They could meet there once a month —maybe twice? Weekly?—for a book club. For a chance to talk, to laugh, to connect. Ruby pushes away from the doorframe and turns back to look into her well-lit bookstore. It could use a good vacuuming after the foot traffic of the evening, and she wants to dust all the surfaces and reorganize the books and displays, but overall, the shabby chic decor and the neutral paint on the walls are inviting. The throw rugs and the mismatched prints of the comfy chairs and lampshades throughout the store give it a soft, whimsical feel, and the items she's chosen to display from her time as First Lady are positioned around the shop, housed in the nooks and crannies that she had carved out just for that purpose. She'd seen people stopping to look at them all evening, and it pleases her to know that she's salvaged these gifts from languishing in storage somewhere.

As Ruby turns off lamps, closes the white wood shutter blinds throughout the shop, sets the alarm, and locks the front door behind her, she gives a satisfied look up at the wooden sign that hangs over her store.

Marooned With a Book, she thinks, putting her keys into her purse and stepping around the rope that divides the sidewalk from the street.

She climbs onto the front seat of the golf cart that Banks is driving, and thinks about her theoretical book club all the way home.

Harlow

Of course Harlow hadn't enjoyed making her dad angry with her—not really. Admittedly, there was *some* level of amusement to getting under his skin, but don't most daughters feel that way? At least a tiny bit?

Some of the things that Harlow had done as a child and as a teenager had truly just been because she wanted to do them. She'd *wanted* to shave her head that time in middle school, and she'd *wanted* to eat all the cotton candy at Coney Island before going on the Tilt-a-Whirl the summer before her sophomore year. Now, had she wanted to throw up all over a very sweet grandmother the minute she stepped off the ride? No. And was it part of the plan for a photographer to be there, following her and her best friend Maya? Definitely not. That same photographer had gotten photos of Harlow washing the cotton candy down with vodka, and naturally the whole thing had enraged her father and gotten her grounded for the rest of the summer.

At heart, Harlow truly believed that no woman wanted to be as good as she was expected to be (okay, maybe her mom and her sister really enjoyed it on some level, but most normal women wouldn't), and she'd spent the majority of her life on a mission to wreak havoc—but just enough that she was still considered lovable. Just enough that she could have fun and not forgo the freedoms that every other kid in the universe seemed to have.

When she was sixteen, Harlow's dad arranged a formal sit-down dinner for his daughters to hostess, and much to their surprise, the guests of honor were Chelsea Clinton, Jenna and Barbara Bush, and Sasha and Malia Obama. They'd tried hard not to be wide-eyed as the other First Daughters strolled into what had once been their home, greeting Ruby and Jack politely, handing their coats to the butler, and sitting down at the dining room table for what turned out to be a pre-arranged program of events.

Harlow had gritted her teeth once she realized that her dad had arranged the entire dinner so that these women who'd gone before her could share their words of wisdom. They shared funny stories about growing up in the White House, but also advice about how to behave in a way that wouldn't cost their fathers any votes or give them any gray hairs. At the end of the night Harlow had admitted to herself that it had been fun and interesting, but to her parents she said nothing, just rolled her eyes and retreated to her own bedroom with a huff.

Still, the advice had stuck in her brain, worming its way into her cranium and setting up camp there. After that dinner, every time she considered going home with some guy she met in a nightclub, or anytime she unhooked her bikini top on Miami Beach, secretly hoping there might be some paparazzi there to capture it, she paused. She remembered how proper Chelsea Clinton was as a First Daughter, or how sweet and well-mannered the Obama girls were.

She's back home in New York now after her trip to Shipwreck Key to attend the opening of her mother's bookstore, and Harlow is thrilled to be back in the city. Her job is easy enough, and she gets to be creative and social, which she loves. The marketing firm she works for is filled with young people who come and go as they please, getting their work done with no regards to "working hours," and the owner is totally comfortable with people making their own schedules, coming to work wearing tie-dyed pastel sweatsuits, fanny packs, and ironic eyeglasses that look like something a wood shop teacher might have worn in the 80s.

Harlow prefers a more upscale look for herself: tight black pants (denim, heavy cotton, or sometimes strategically ripped at the knee or thigh for a tougher look), a cropped black leather jacket, and expensive t-shirts that hug her toned upper body. She gets her dark hair blown out every week, and she keeps her gel manicure fresh, choosing bright colors or a classic nude nail. Her shoe collection largely revolves around black motorcycle boots, black Doc Martens, or shiny black Manolos with dangerously spiky heels. She knows as well as anyone that her name is what got her in the door at the firm and not just her marketing degree from NYU, but now that she's here, she wants to enjoy it. Harlow takes her work seriously, and frankly, she thinks she's damn good at it.

"Drinks at Hive tonight," Dart says, poking her head into the office and winking at Harlow. Dart is a gorgeous lesbian with a short, black haircut that reminds Harlow of James Dean. She wears cuffed jeans with highly polished black penny loafers everyday, but she turns the menswear look on its head by going with tight bodysuits over push-up bras on top. The combination of masculine and feminine looks is alluring, and every time their little gang of coworkers hits a bar or goes out for dinner, Dart sees more action—from both genders—than the rest of them combined.

"I'm in," Harlow says, sucking on a lollipop that she removes from her mouth so that she can talk. "I just have to finish what I'm working on here and then I'll be ready."

"No rush, sugar tits," Dart says, blowing Harlow a kiss. "I'll text you when we're heading out."

She vanishes again, leaving Harlow to keep working on the images she's going to present to a client the next day.

That right there is another thing that Harlow loves about living away from D.C., and away from her old life as a resident of the White House: she's made friends who seem to not care at all that she's the daughter of a former president. She can't imagine anyone in Washington ever feeling comfortable enough around her to call her "sugar tits," and if she worked some boring job like her sister, Harlow would be stuck in a stuffy building all day with other snoozy, sedate people who just like to talk about books.

At six o'clock, Harlow heads to Hive with Dart and the others: Julia, a marketing intern with her septum pierced; Mika, an extremely good-looking guy in his thirties who has loudly declared himself asexual, which meant that almost immediately, every woman wanted to be the one to conquer him; and Ulysses, a former gymnast for the US Olympic team who is so short, stout, and muscular that he's almost wider than he is tall. Ulysses has skin that is so black and shiny that he looks burnished, and someone recognizes him every single time they go out, buying him a drink and wanting to take photos with him. To be fair, they do it to Harlow as well, but the level of excitement that Ulysses generates is on a whole other level.

The evening is fun—it always is—but there's a low-energy vibe coursing just beneath the surface. Dart flirts half-heartedly with a young couple who both seem interested in her, but her eyes keep flickering toward the door; Mika dances unselfconsciously to 90s music even when no one joins him; Julia keeps excusing herself to use the bathroom, which Harlow figures could either be a UTI or a coke habit, and Ulysses looks just a little tired and detached every time someone comes up to talk to him, high-five him, or ask for a photo.

As for Harlow, she sits at the bar with her Lemon Drop martini, trying to meditate with her eyes open as the vodka works its magic.

Nobody would say that they're having the *most* fun they've ever had, but it beats a jab with a dull stick, and the music is decent. Harlow is actually contemplating knocking back her drink and joining Mika on the dance floor when a feeling of unease sweeps over her. She glances at the door of the club and sees Eldrick, her Secret Service agent, rushing at someone.

Harlow sets her drink down and the alcohol splashes over the sugared rim of the martini glass and onto her wrist. Later, this will feel sticky and she will scrub it with soap and a washcloth in a daze, feeling like a different person than the one she is at this exact moment.

But Eldrick is moving like he's on a mission. Harlow watches, mouth open, as someone barrels through the door and dodges Eldrick. Before the two connect, the interloper brandishes a gun and starts firing. Harlow is only aware of what's happening because of the way each shot creates a blinding flash of yellow in the dimness of the bar and fills the air with a temporarily deafening explosion. Harlow's first instinct is to cover her ears and slide off the stool, pressing her body against the wooden bar, though this isn't exactly a hiding spot.

Several more shots ring out as people scatter, screaming. The feeling of unease in the bar has morphed into one of panic and terror, and Harlow fights the urge to squeeze her eyes shut. She has to know where this guy is so that she can move if she needs to, but getting up and bolting right now will do nothing but draw attention to her.

Everything is happening at warp speed, but to Harlow, it all feels endless. Could this guy move *any* slower? She keeps her ears covered against the blast, tracking the number of gunshots (eight, nine, ten), as she thinks of her father. If someone had asked her beforehand what she might be thinking about during a random act of violence, her father wouldn't have necessarily made the list. Her mother, definitely. The way her potential future is vanishing before her eyes like Michael J. Fox's arm in the photograph in *Back to the Future*, yes. But her father and the way he must have worried about getting trapped in a situation just like this one, with a crazed gunman on the loose, no. To Harlow, her dad's job was just that: a job like any other dad might have had, only one that came with a house and some staff. She didn't ask questions about what he did all day, and she never wondered about his safety, but here in this bar, she's thinking about the risk he took as president just waking up every single day and going to work.

Someone ducks under the lip of the bar next to Harlow and she glances over to see that it's Ulysses. He's saying something to her, but she can't hear him. His lips are moving, but all she can hear is the ringing in her ears from the gunshots and the music that's still playing loudly throughout the bar.

Without waiting for her to understand, Ulysses grabs Harlow by the wrist and drags her up, pushing her ahead of him so that he's essentially covering her from behind. He guides her with a firm push to her lower back, and somehow Harlow understands that he wants her to get behind the bar, so she does. She ducks and curls herself into the smallest ball that she possibly can, covering her ears again and this time closing her eyes. Everything suddenly feels smoky and she's frightened. Harlow is positive that she actually stepped over a blood-covered person on her way from the front of the bar to her new spot behind it, and she pushes the image from her head as she hides, inexplicably whispering the Pledge of Allegiance to herself over and over as she waits for it all to end.

Ruby

It's the annoying uncertainties—or even the things you *are* certain about, but don't particularly like—that Patty has always told Ruby are the "annoying creases of life." Kind of like a brand new shirt taken out of a package that still has the folds in it, they're the parts you just want to shake out and smooth over. They're the uncomfortable seams in the toes of your socks; the place you folded the paper and then realized too late that it wouldn't fit into an envelope that way; the spot where the wallpaper doesn't quite line up.

Getting a phone call from a police officer in Manhattan telling her that she needed to get up there as soon as possible to be with her younger daughter is more than an annoying crease; this is the stuff that real, horrifying, unfiltered life is made of. Once Ruby had pulled enough information from the police officer to know that Harlow was alive and safe, she'd calmed down. Ursula, her virtual assistant, had booked her a flight and made her arrangements to get from Shipwreck Key to Destin, and Vanessa and Tilly, her employees at the bookstore, had agreed to run the shop in her absence.

Her hand shakes now, rattling the ice cubes in her plastic cup as she sips a vodka and orange juice in First Class and hides behind her sunglasses. This isn't the time to have people asking her questions about

Jack, her appearance on Leeza's show, the bookstore, or anything else, really. All she wants to do is sit quietly and let the pilots fly her to Harlow.

Ruby drains her mixed drink and sets the empty cup on the folding tray table in front of her, looking out the window at the earth far below. She needs to think about something other than Harlow because imagining her baby in a bar where there is gunfire makes her feel like she's having a panic attack, and she *cannot* have a panic attack while trapped in a flying metal tube with two hundred strangers. She racks her brains for another topic--any topic--that will distract her from the horrors of what she's already seen on the news.

Jack. She'll think about Jack and let her anger and emotions about him take over in the interim here as she's winging her way to Harlow. That should keep her distracted.

Jack's affair with Etienne is another one of Ruby's annoying creases. She can shift it around, mentally take an iron to it to smooth it out, and close her eyes to try and ignore it, but it's still there. A crease in their marriage. A mar on the perfect wallpaper that was their life together.

And why had he done it? Why does any man do it? When he's married to a woman who is everything a life partner should be, why does he stray? There was no question in anybody's mind that Ruby was the ideal First Lady, even when talk of them landing in the White House was still just hushed discussion behind closed doors. They powers that be had done their due diligence, searching through her history, turning over every rock, trying to find something that might cause a scandal and drag down Jack's bid for the presidency.

But they'd found nothing. No illicit drug use beyond a little pot in the 80s, and who hadn't gone to the sand dunes with friends and smoked a little weed while listening to Duran Duran on a boombox? No domestic violence with ex-boyfriends. No secret babies put up for adoption. Truly nothing. In fact, Ruby had been willing to spill all of her own tea: she'd lost her virginity to a guy named Ted at the age of seventeen. There was no real story there; he was her first boyfriend, and her first real love. It had ended when they both went to college. During her college years, she'd had a few lovers, none noteworthy in any way. She did not experiment with girls in college, though many of her friends had and she'd just smiled and carried on. Not for her, but not a problem if it was for others.

As for the rest of it, Ruby had been hyper-vigilant about taking her birth control pills. She'd eschewed smoking cigarettes but didn't mind a little beer or marijuana at a party in her teens and early twenties. And thanks to the fact that this all happened before the advent of cell phones, there were no photos or videos, and none of her high school or college friends cared enough about their shared youthful indiscretions to share them with anyone in the press. The guys Ruby had dated up until she met Jack were all bland and cut from the same cloth: college athletes with good families and high GPAs, they'd gone on to careers in medicine, finance, and business. None had sparked any particular passion in her, and when she'd parted with them, it had been amicable and without incident.

Until Jack. He was anything but bland. The night they met was at a political fundraiser in Los Angeles held by a friend of Ruby's who owned an art gallery. Jack was a young senator from California with a record for being socially liberal and fiscally conservative. And he cut an impressive figure both on screen and in person, with his wavy, dark blonde hair cut into a perfectly casual swoop that he pushed back from his high, tanned forehead. Jack's eyes were the clearest, most bottomless eyes Ruby had ever seen. When he walked up to her and asked if she wanted a glass of champagne, she'd instantly gone into a daze.

"Do *I* want a glass?" she'd asked, holding a silver tray in one hand. The friend who owned the gallery had hired Ruby and several other twenty-something friends who needed the cash to act as servers for the event. Ruby stood there before him in a short, black skirt and a sleeveless white dress shirt with a black bowtie. On her feet were pointy black oxford shoes with shiny silver buckles, and her hair was scraped back from her forehead with a black velvet headband. This was the late 90s, and though her skin was clear and luminous and youthful, Ruby felt exhausted. She was already tired of living the life of a starving young woman. She was over fighting L.A. traffic as she scampered from commercial audition to commercial audition, and even with her English degree in hand from UCLA, she knew that the best money she could hope to make was if she landed another national commercial. Worst case scenario, she'd get acting out of her system, get certified to teach, and end up in some high school in the suburbs, teaching English to a bunch of fifteen-year-olds, though the very thought sent waves of panic through her.

In short, she would have killed to set down the tray and have a glass of champagne with the handsome senator.

As if he could read her mind, Jack took the tray out of her hands and handed it to the next waiter who walked by, but he never took his eyes off of Ruby. She was stunned.

"Hey," Jack said, suddenly turning to the waiter who was retreating with Ruby's tray of champagne flutes. "We'll need two of those."

The waiter—a guy named Rob who Ruby had encountered at several commercial auditions—shook his head as he watched Ruby take her first sip of champagne.

"Let's go out to the balcony," Jack said, putting one hand on the small of her back and leading the way.

Outside, the early evening was swallowing the hot afternoon sun, and three stories below them the traffic crawled along the maze of roads and streets, glass and metal glinting as people went to and fro. But all Jack and Ruby had to do was sip bubbles and stare at one another as they leaned on a railing and watched the world below.

Jack broke the silence first. "You know. We'd have beautiful children," he said confidently.

Ruby nearly choked on her champagne. "Excuse me?" The California sun had left her arms and legs with a warm tan, and she smoothed one hand over her forehead, touching the velvet headband self-consciously. Had she heard him correctly?

"Our kids. They would be stunning." Jack tipped back his champagne and the bubbles sparkled in the light of the golden hour. "I remember you from that Levi's commercial," he said, letting his eyes skim her bare arms. "That black-and-white one, shot on the beach. Very Herb Ritts."

Ruby blinked; she was surprised that a senator knew anything at all about a famous fashion photographer known for his work in black-and-white.

"I wanted to buy stock in Levi's after watching that commercial." He laughed at his own joke.

Ruby looked down at the toes of her oxfords and then back up at him, feeling light years younger than she was. For all the life experience she'd had up to that point, she was still nothing but a naive, fresh-faced innocent next to a suave politician like Jack—at least in her own mind.

"Then you should have," she said, bucking up her own courage with a swig of champagne. "And here's an insider tip for you: I have a Chapstick commercial coming out next month, so you might want to grab stock in that one while it's low." Ruby reached for his empty champagne glass. "I should really get back to work," she said. "I could get fired just for being out here with you."

"Don't," Jack said, reaching for her arm as she walked away. "Please stay." Ruby paused, looking back at him. "How old are you?"

Ruby groaned inwardly. Of course it had come to this. But she wouldn't lie, and she wouldn't even pretend. "Twenty-five. You?"

"Thirty-six," Jack said, lifting his chin defiantly. "That's a true May-December romance right there."

"Who says there's any romance between us?"

"It's my prediction that there will be."

They stood there, eyeing one another, each waiting for the other to back down first. He had nerve. Ruby had to give him that.

"Let's leave," he said. "I have a car waiting. We'll go wherever you want to go. The beach. A restaurant." He glanced down at her outfit, which made her look like a cast member who'd escaped the set of *Beverly Hills 90210.* "Or bowling. You pick."

Ruby weighed this carefully: walk out and upset the friend who'd hired her for this gig, or stay and possibly lose a date with the most interesting man she'd ever met?

She set their empty champagne flutes on an outdoor table and stared at Jack. "Let's go."

From there, things had snowballed. The flame between them burned hotly—throughout the entire marriage, if Ruby is being honest with herself—and there's no one she's ever admired more than she did Jack. He looked at her adoringly, and was over the moon with the birth of each of their girls. Ruby had needed no real work to be brought up to speed in terms of how to behave like a politician's wife, and she'd set aside her own aspirations fairly easily, tucking her English degree away in a box and throwing herself headfirst into motherhood and marriage. As First Lady she'd focused and honed a platform that supported reading initiatives for children, and Ruby had been able to travel with her girls to elementary schools all around the country, donating books and sharing the joy of reading with young children and their parents. It had all been incredibly rewarding, and she'd been good at it. Good at talking to the parents she met, at connecting with the school administrators and teachers, and, frankly, she'd been beloved by the press.

Which leads her back to the same question that still runs through her mind on so many sleepless nights: what went wrong? Had their sex life grown cold, she might have understood better why Jack needed to look elsewhere for affection. But that wasn't the case. As far as Ruby knows, she was always his closest confidante, and if she ever felt even the slightest twinge of wonderment about where her own life had veered off track and so fully merged with Jack's, then she never let on about it to him. After all, he was busy running the country, and she was busy doing exactly what she'd signed on to do.

But Etienne was still a fact. She *is* still a fact. She'd shown up at Jack's memorial—she'd stayed quiet and at least attempted to shroud herself in discretion, but not enough that Ruby hadn't known instantly who she was—and since then, Ruby's lawyer has heard from Etienne's lawyer, but Ruby has rebuffed all of Etienne's attempts at making contact. It's messy and it's heartbreaking, and it's nothing that Ruby wants in her new life.

When her plane lands in New York, she's off the aircraft first, whisked away by a concierge sent to meet her. Banks is with her (he'd been seated right behind her in First Class because he preferred it that way), and they rush through JFK, find their car, and make it to Harlow's apartment in record time.

The first thing Ruby does when she sees her daughter is break down. She drops her purse, her small carry-on bag, her sunglasses. Arms are wrapped tightly around one another as both women sob openly, the fear and the anger and the relief taking over and leaving them both a crying mess.

"Mom," Harlow says, burying her face in the crook of Ruby's neck. "I was so scared."

"Baby, I know." Ruby pulls Harlow into the apartment and leads her to the couch where they sit, thighs and shoulders touching one another. It's as if now that they're finally together, they can't stand to be apart.

Harlow puts her hands to her face and lets her chin drop so that it's almost touching her chest. "But, Mom...my friend Ulysses."

Ruby puts her arm around Harlow and her daughter collapses, her head falling into her mother's lap while she cries.

"He was a very brave man," Ruby says. "I called his parents and gave them my sympathies. And I told them that we all know about his bravery. The last thing he did was get you behind the bar, and because of him, you're still here. It's cold comfort to a parent, but there is something to knowing that your child saved someone else before they died."

The room stills. Banks and Eldrick are stationed right outside the door of the apartment, and the women have been left alone. The afternoon sun streams sideways through the window into Harlow's small living room, falling on Ruby and Harlow at an angle.

Ruby's eyes scan the room. There are potted plants on windowsills, hand-knotted throw rugs on the floor, a framed poster from a concert in Central Park on the wall, and a giant bean bag stationed on the floor in front of an oversized television. But over the arms of the couch, a chair near the kitchen, and on the table, there are piles of clothing. Discarded jackets, last minute wardrobe changes, and things that need to be dry cleaned or otherwise attended to. It's so Harlow that Ruby almost laughs over the solid knot of tears in her throat.

"Mom," Harlow says, picking at a loose thread on her couch. "I can't sleep. I'm scared. Every time I close my eyes I see gunfire. I can see Ulysses' face. I think of Dad dying. I'm afraid I'll never be okay again."

Ruby takes Harlow's hand in hers. "You will be okay," she promises. "The human heart has an amazing capacity to heal itself. And your brain knows how to sort through trauma and to take away the sharpness. Over time, it becomes more like a butter knife than a sword."

Tears fall down Harlow's smooth cheeks and she nods, staring at a spot on the wall in the distance.

"This might be crazy and it might be too soon, but what would you think about coming to Shipwreck Key for a while?" Ruby asks gently.

The first thing she'd wanted to do when she got the call from the police was to bring her daughter to her, to keep her safe, to never let her out of her sight again. But that's unreasonable—Harlow is an adult—and Ruby needs to present it as an option, and not as though she thinks that Harlow can't function on her own in New York City. Because she certainly can; she's made from tough stuff, and Ruby believes wholeheartedly that both of her daughters can move mountains.

Harlow nods slowly, considering this. She sniffles. "I need to go to therapy," she says, as if this is an answer to her mom's question. "Not just because of what happened at the bar, but because of a lot of things." She's quiet for a long minute. "I thought a lot about Dad as I was hiding behind the bar, and I realized that I need to figure some things out. I always accepted him being President at face value, but there's a lot more to it, you know?"

Ruby can't hold back a hard little laugh. "Oh, I know. Believe me, I know."

Harlow looks at her mother in surprise; it's probably never occurred to her how Jack's life and death have changed or derailed Ruby's life, which is common for kids. Don't they all pretty much assume their parents are totally functioning, self-reliant, and able to see the forest for the trees at all times?

"You too?" Harlow asks, looking oddly hopeful.

Ruby understands that her own lack of clarity, her own true emotions of anger, confusion, and uncertainty, will certainly be comforting for her daughter to hear about. Finding out that your mother—who successfully managed being the backseat driver to the most powerful man in the free world—doesn't always have her it together either has to be a relief.

"Me too," Ruby confirms with a sad smile. "And I've considered going to a therapist for a number of reasons, but..." She looks at Harlow sheepishly. "But can I really do that?"

Harlow blinks at her. "Yeah, Mom, you really can do that. A therapist is bound to secrecy—they have to keep whatever you tell them to themselves. So don't worry that you can't go just because you're famous."

Ruby laughs heartily. "Oh, honey. I don't think of myself as famous. Not at all. I think of myself as someone who knows a lot of important secrets. Someone who knows things that she maybe shouldn't share... with anyone."

With a hard shake of her head, Harlow disagrees. "No way. You have as much right to access mental health support as anyone."

Ruby reaches out to take Harlow's hand in hers; she appreciates that her daughter, who has just been through a life-changing trauma of her own, wants to make her feel better about seeking help. But Ruby is firmly planted in Generation X, a group of humans who pride themselves on being self-sufficient, tough, and not in need of anyone's help. She'd seen and heard plenty of jokes during the pandemic about how Gen X was the only generation fully prepared to withstand the boredom of quarantine. How, as a group, they were almost wholly self-sufficient, having come of age without much parental guidance (after all, most people's parents were busy working, divorcing, and generally just doing their own thing while kids let themselves into the house after school, dug up a wildly unhealthy snack, and sat in front of MTV until they were sent to bed without bedtime stories or any other sort of fluff or frippery).

"I hear you, Lolo, but I'm not sure if I'm the kind of person who lets my guard down easily enough to talk to a therapist." That's Ruby's most succinct way of brushing the suggestion aside for the moment, but she hangs onto Harlow's hand. "I want to help you right now, though. I want you on your feet and feeling solid again."

A tear slips down Harlow's cheek and she swipes it away with the hand that her mom isn't holding onto.

"Would you consider coming down to Shipwreck Key with me for a bit?" Ruby asks, hoping that Harlow might consider it. "I know it's a tiny island, but I think it would be good for you. It might help you to decompress. And if there's no one actually on Shipwreck Key for you to talk to, I bet we could find someone in Destin."

"Therapists do Zoom sessions now, Mom," Harlow says patiently, patting her mom's hand with pitying like she's an out-of-touch invalid.

"So does that mean you'll come down with me and stay for a while? We can pay your rent here and I'm sure your boss will give you a leave of absence—"

"Yes," Harlow says, nodding and smiling for the first time since Ruby arrived. "Yes, I want to go home with you, Mom. I don't want to be here right now. I'll talk to my boss, but a lot of my work can be done remotely anyway, so I don't think it will be a problem."

Ruby nearly shudders with relief; leaving Harlow in New York after the shooting is the very last thing her mom heart wants to do, so the thought of holding her youngest child close and taking her back to Florida for a little R&R makes Ruby insanely happy.

"How soon can we leave?" Ruby asks. She's already thinking about booking plane tickets, setting Harlow up in the bedroom she'd stayed in when she was down for the bookstore's opening, and cooking her dinners that they can eat together out on the porch, watching the water and breathing in the soothing ocean air.

"Let me call my boss and pack a few things. Want to leave tomorrow?"

"Yes, let's get a good night of sleep, and then we'll head out on the first flight," Ruby says, opening her arms and hugging Harlow as she falls into them.

"Mom?" Harlow asks, her voice muffled by Ruby's hug. "I know it sounds babyish, but can you sleep in my bed with me tonight? I don't want to be alone."

The pain her daughter's voice brings tears to Ruby's eyes and she holds her tighter, pressing her lips to Harlow's head and inhaling the intoxicating scent of her own child.

"Yes, baby girl. I'll be right there next to you. Don't you worry about a thing."

Athena

Athena is almost entirely sidetracked by news of the bar shooting. She feels a cold chill running the length of her body the second she hears that Harlow was involved, and she literally cannot get warm again until she gets to New York and sees with her own eyes that Harlow is okay.

Her trip to Manhattan is quick—she gets there late at night after Ruby has arrived—and she sleeps on the couch, happy to have her mom curled up with Harlow. Eldrick and Banks take turns standing guard with Athena's agent, Corbin, and there isn't a single second when someone isn't on hand to watch over the three women. But when Harlow and Ruby leave the apartment the next day to board a flight to Florida, Athena has no choice but to get back on the train bound for D.C. and carry on. After all, she has a job to go back to, and her mom is going to take amazing care of her sister on Shipwreck Key.

All eyes are on Athena as she walks through the Library of Congress. People know what's going on in her private life whether she wants them to or not, and the fact that her family is still front and center in the twenty-four hour news cycle means that every update on the bar, the shooter, the victims, and the fallout is everywhere.

At her desk, Athena makes the mistake of logging in to a couple of her favorite news sources just to see what else is going on in the world, and the headlines scream at her:

WAS GUNMAN TARGETING HARLOW HUDSON?

CONNECTION BETWEEN SHOOTER AND FORMER FIRST DAUGHTER?

GUNMAN TAKES HIS OWN LIFE AFTER KILLING EIGHT, INCLUDING FORMER OLYMPIAN; FORMER FIRST DAUGHTER SURVIVES

Athena feels a headache coming on and reaches for her coffee, nearly knocking it over as someone raps on the open door behind her. She jumps and spins in her chair.

"Diego!" she says, feeling torn between surprise, excitement, and the mix of emotions she's still feeling about her sister. "Hi."

"Welcome back," he says, leaning against the door frame with one suit-jacketed shoulder. He slides his phone into his pocket and watches her seriously. "I'm so sorry to hear about the situation with your sister, and I won't ask if she's okay because I'm sure you get that question a million times a day, and we can all see on the news that she's fine."

Athena is using a paper napkin to mop up the little bit of coffee that sloshed from her mug when Diego knocked.

"She's getting there," Athena says diplomatically, remembering how her dad told her to always say things that had a positive spin, but that revealed nothing.

"Good, good," Diego says, running a hand through his dark, shiny hair. "What I really wanted to ask is, how are *you*?"

Athena pauses her coffee mopping, holding the wet napkin in her hand. "I'm fine," she says, forgetting for a second to say something more upbeat. She reconfigures her answer. "Actually, I'm processing the whole situation and trying to figure out how to help my family from a distance. My sister went home with my mom for a while, so they're together, and I'm here in D.C."

Diego makes a face. "I've been away from family. No fun." He puts his hands into his pockets casually. "Hey, would you want to go out—maybe have dinner? I know you've got a lot on your mind, and making dinner alone is probably the last thing you want to do."

He's assuming she's single. Athena feels a wash of shame to know that a gorgeous man in her age range has looked at her and immediately clocked her as a sad singleton. Diego sees her and knows that she's a boring librarian who goes home alone at night to hand wash her cardigans and hang them in her small bathroom, to order takeout from the various restaurants in her neighborhood, and to watch documentaries in her fuzzy single girl pajamas while she folds laundry on her coffee table.

"Yes," she says without thinking. "Dinner would be amazing. I would really appreciate the company." The words are out of her mouth before she knows what she's saying or doing. Dinner with Diego. Of course she's going to have dinner with Diego. It was always going to happen, because when you watch a man hungrily for months on end, he notices. And if he's interested, he rises to the occasion and asks you out. Which is exactly what is happening right now.

Diego looks pleased. He smiles widely and stands up tall. "Perfect. How about if I swing by here to get you at closing time?" He pulls his phone from his pocket and checks the time. "Also known as seven hours and forty-three minutes from now."

Athena laughs and pats her curly hair nervously. "I'll be ready," she says, already plotting how quickly she can make it back to her apartment during her lunch break to grab cuter shoes, a bag of makeup to touch up her face at the end of the day, and some perfume to spritz on and cover up the wilted, stagnant smell of the library that seems to cling to her every day.

Diego gives her a nod and a smile and goes on his way, and Athena picks up her phone to set one of those countdown timers. She titles it *Dinner with Diego* and smiles as she sees that they're now at seven hours and forty minutes even. Seven hours and forty minutes until she gets to sit across from Diego, sip a glass of wine, and get to know him better.

Athena spends a good part of the morning Googling Diego and browsing his social media accounts. His Twitter reveals that he's fairly liberal (but not too); his Facebook account doesn't have much but a handful of friends who appear to be family (because people their age aren't too excited about the platform, but most given in grudgingly and sign up for an account); and his Instagram is public and is entirely comprised of pictures of him running marathons, waxing poetic about trees after the rain (with accompanying photos), and a handful of pictures of his dog, Chester. He hasn't posted on there in almost two years, but surely the pandemic killed a lot of people's desire when it comes to sharing photos of daily life.

With every photo and every blurb she finds online about Diego (apparently he was a chess champion in high school in Trenton, and his family owns a food truck that's extremely popular there—this tidbit is accompanied by a picture of a young, fresh-faced Diego that makes Athena nearly squeal with joy), she gets more excited.

When she finally closes out all of her search tabs and opens her email, she glances at her timed countdown to *Dinner with Diego*: only five hours and twenty-six minutes to go.

* * *

Athena is still at her computer at five-thirty, waiting impatiently for Diego to stop by and pick her up, but trying to look like she got so busy working on something that she lost track of time. She'd run home at lunch and changed her underwear from white cotton to black satin (hey, a girl should at least *feel* like she has the potential to be a vixen, even if deep down she has no clue whether a vixen would choose black satin or opt for no panties at all), and while there, she'd grabbed her deodorant, the small bottle of Lancôme that she dabs behind her ears and in the hollow of her neck each morning, and a collection of makeup and brushes so that she could reconstruct her morning face.

"Hey," Diego says, breezing in and looking as fresh as he had that morning. Athena is sure that he didn't run home at lunch, and instead just looks and smells this heavenly all the time. "Ready?"

She locks her computer and stands up, grabbing her purse but leaving her makeup bag locked in the drawer. She'll just slip in tomorrow morning and put on her makeup and deodorant before anyone sees her.

Athena turns off the office light and follows Diego. Her stomach is a shaken bottle of soda, and she's having a hard time finding words, so she starts with, "So, how was your day?" as they step into the elevator and Diego punches the button for the bottom floor.

"I was counting down the hours until we got to hang out," Diego says with a nervous laugh, stepping back so that they're shoulder to shoulder in the elevator.

Athena can feel sweat forming on the back of her neck. "Me too," she admits, turning to look up at him. "So where do you want to go?"

"How do you feel about Mexican food?"

"Love it," she says with relief, glad that they aren't going to play the "What do you want? No, what do *you* want?" game.

"Awesome. I picked a place close by that my family loves. Are you into spicy food?"

They walk down the rainy street together, both a little shy as the conversation bounces back and forth between them. Mercifully, the sky has stopped pouring buckets, and now they're just dodging puddles and waiting for the walk signals under a gray sky.

"I'm good with spicy food," Athena says, tucking her hair behind one ear as she looks up at him playfully. "Or is that supposed to be a joke because I'm a white girl?"

Diego laughs, throwing back his head and showing a set of perfect teeth. "Nah, I just thought it was polite to ask before I take you somewhere and order a salsa so spicy that it burns your esophagus. But now that you mention it, I hadn't even noticed that you were white."

Athena bumps him playfully with her elbow and suddenly her nerves fade away. She's walking next to Diego Santana. They're about to have dinner together. He's teasing her. Athena hates to even admit it to herself, but for a second, it's like nothing horrible has ever happened-- her dad is still alive, he never cheated on her mom with some weird and mysterious French lady, and Harlow was never caught in a shooting in New York--the only thing that matters is the happy feeling she has *right now* as Diego reaches down and slips her hand into his while they cross a busy street together.

The restaurant, El Paraguas, is a cozy place tucked in between a bookstore and a dry cleaner. As soon as they walk in, Athena is charmed by the open umbrellas that hang from the ceiling. A hostess seats them under a yellow umbrella covered in pink polka dots.

"*Paraguas* is Spanish for umbrella," Diego says with a smile, watching as she looks around at all of the different colors and patterns.

"But that's just in case you didn't know. I'm not trying to be a mansplainer." He takes the menu offered by the hostess with a nod of thanks.

"I never took you for a mansplainer." Athena skims the margaritas on the front page of the menu and decides on a frozen strawberry one, brain freeze be damned. "Are you fluent in Spanish?"

"I grew up speaking only Spanish at home. When I got to kindergarten, I had my work cut out for me, but kids adapt, you know?"

Athena nods as the waitress stops at their table. They order drinks and Diego asks if she minds him ordering for both of them. She assures him that she's fine with anything, so he orders mole and tacos al pastor for them, and a boy in a black apron and a white shirt sweeps by and delivers a basket of warm tortilla chips and fresh pico de gallo to eat with their margaritas.

Dinner goes well, and the conversation is easy. The margaritas don't hurt things, as Athena is always better when she's relaxed, and by the end of the meal (two margaritas for her, and three for Diego), they're both laughing and talking like old friends. Diego helps her on with her coat after he pays the bill, and she loops her arm through his without even asking, leaning on him just slightly as they weave through the wooden tables beneath what must be fifty colorful umbrellas.

Athena isn't even sure how they end up at his place, but they do. She isn't impaired enough not to remember Diego's hand sliding up her inner thigh in the back of the Uber, and she certainly remembers the way he turned to her and kissed her full on the mouth, his tongue salty and sweet after the tortilla chips and margaritas. The Uber driver was polite enough to keep driving without so much as a glance at them in the rearview mirror, and when he dropped them off, all he said was, "Y'all have a good night now."

When Athena finally parts the fog of lust that's taken over her entire being, she realizes that Diego is unzipping the back of her flowered dress and sliding it off her shoulders as they stand in his bedroom.

Do I want this? she thinks as his lips cover her neck, her collarbone, her earlobes. *Of course I want this. I'm twenty-three years old. If not now, when?* Her arms come free of the dress and it slides over her torso, leaving her standing there in just a black lace bra.

"You're so beautiful, Athena," Diego says, unbuttoning his own shirt hurriedly. She sobers up entirely as he takes it off, revealing a smooth, toned upper body. She'd expected chest hair, but instead he's got muscular pecs and biceps honed through hours at the gym, and waxed by a professional. His body looks less like the tangled forest she's been expecting, and more like a desert of windblown hills of brown sand. He's breathtaking.

"You are," she whispers back, letting her fingertips touch his tight abs. "You're beautiful."

In seconds, he has her dress unzipped an inch more and it slides over her hips, falling into a puddle at her feet. Now she's just in her black bra and the black satin panties she'd chosen earlier, secretly hoping but not *quite* thinking that this might happen. Diego takes off his own pants, and stands before her in just a pair of black boxer briefs. His legs match his upper body: smooth, muscular, waxed. He looks like an Olympic swimmer, and Athena's brain can't help but think up ridiculous things, like: *Thank god my first time wasn't with some guy from my high school with pimples all over his back. And I wonder if Harlow's first time was with a guy this hot?*

But Diego gently pushing her onto the bed clears her mind of anything but the feel of his body on hers, and she gives in to the sensations, the wonder, and the momentary pain of the act, which is completely eclipsed by a sense of peace once it's over and they're lying next to one another.

Diego is quiet and breathing rhythmically like he might fall asleep.

* * *

Athena floats into work the next day like she's on a hoverboard that lifts her off the ground. She wears a beatific smile, because she now knows what love is. Or at least lovemaking. Diego had opened his eyes and they'd done it all again, and at one point, he'd looked startled and even a little fearful as the realization that it was Athena's first time had settled over him.

"It's fine," she'd promised him, tucking his dark hair behind one ear as she smiled up at him. "I'm glad it was you."

But the palpable feeling of nervousness hadn't left him, and while he hadn't exactly rushed Athena out of his apartment, he had gotten her dressed and called her an Uber, kissing her at the door and letting her walk downstairs alone.

Athena had barely slept—not that there were a ton of hours left in the night anyway—and when she'd gotten up and showered, it was with the knowledge that soon she'd be seeing Diego at work. She doesn't even care that she's left her makeup bag in the drawer of her desk, and she drifts towards Diego's office barefaced, her curly hair pulled up in a bun to leave her neck visible, which will hopefully remind him of how much he'd loved kissing that same neck the night before.

But Diego's office is empty and the light is still off. The middle-aged secretary who sits at the desk right outside the cluster of four offices that includes Diego's glances at her curiously. Athena thinks her name is Ellen, but she's new enough that she isn't sure, so she settles for a simple, "Good morning."

"Good morning," maybe-Ellen says. "Can I help you, hon?"

"Is Diego coming in late today?" Athena asks, hooking a thumb at his empty office. It's Friday, and she can't remember a day that she didn't see him around the library at least once.

The secretary frowns and lifts her fingers from the keyboard. "No, hon, he's not coming in at all. And he'll be out all next week."

Athena's heart pounds; she knows instinctively that she's on a collision course with disaster. Diego hadn't said a word about being gone from work, and all she can imagine is that something horribly tragic has happened. The parents he'd spoken of so lovingly over dinner have been in a terrible accident; he woke up feeling ill and needed to be rushed to the hospital for an emergency appendectomy; someone has stolen his identity and he's working with the FBI to break up a massive ring of forgers and thieves.

But it's worse. So much worse.

"Why?" Athena croaks. Her face feels hot. She knows she looks like exactly what she is: a woman about to be scorned.

The secretary takes a beat before answering. "His wedding, hon. He's supposed to fly out today for Bali to get married on the beach."

Athena's knees buckle and she reaches out for the nearest surface to hold her steady, grabbing for a tall filing cabinet against the wall.

She can hear the woman asking her if she's alright, but rather than answering, Athena gathers herself and flees, rushing down the hallways and ignoring the greetings of her coworkers. Finally, she gets to her office, closes the door, and sits on the floor with her back against the heavy wooden door.

She stays that way for almost two hours, eyes unblinking, heart broken.

When she can finally rouse herself to get up off the ground and crawl to her desk, she picks up the phone and calls her mother.

Ruby

The store has been open for a while now, and Ruby knows all of the other shop owners on Seadog Lane. She knows when the tide is out so that she can walk the beach by her house, picking up shells or drinking coffee while she watches the waves and breathes deeply. She has come to understand that Shipwreck Key is, quite literally, an island unto itself, and that the way things function here is entirely different from the way they function anywhere else. For instance, if she goes to The Frog's Grog for a drink of any sort, she's telling Bev Byer that she's happy to sit and talk about pirate tales and island folklore (which, to be honest, she usually is). If she drops into the Bodacious Booty Salon for a manicure or a pedicure, then she becomes both privy to the gossip of Shipwreck Key, and potentially a part of it, as everyone will want to know whether the former First Lady chose Red Riot for her toes again, or whether she's a good tipper.

But more than that, things have settled into a routine with just a few hiccups. Harlow coming down to the island has been, in some senses, easier than she might have imagined, because the young woman was so shaken by the shooting that she'd allowed her mother to set her up in a guest room with a view of the ocean, and since then, she's been content to wander the house with a blanket hanging from her shoulders like a cape, watching television while Ruby goes to Marooned with a Book, or sitting on the sand and staring at the water while Eldrick stands close by, watching over her in silence.

Their routine has become an easy one, with Ruby going back and forth from the bookstore and being home to cook dinner most nights, but she hasn't yet convinced Harlow to get dressed and join her for dinner or a drink on Seadog Lane or anything.

Things got a tiny bit more complicated when Athena called her mother from the floor of her office, stunned and crying. Ruby hadn't fully understood between the sobs what was going on, but she got enough of the story to know that her first baby needed to be with her mother. She'd arranged for Athena's trip to Shipwreck Key, Athena took a leave of absence from work, and now Ruby has both of her girls living with her under one roof for the first time since Athena left for college five years earlier.

Even though the circumstances that brought them all together are not good ones, Ruby gets a secret thrill each morning as she walks quietly past the closed bedroom doors, knowing that her girls are tucked safely into their beds. It hasn't all been sunshine and roses, and Athena hasn't opened up to them entirely yet about what happened with the man at work, but the three women are happy to all be living in one place again. They function well as a unit, and they all know that they're safe when they're together.

Ruby feels at peace. She feels needed again in the way that mothers do when their kids come home. Her heart feels whole.

Which is why it's so unsettling when she receives a phone call from Helen Pullman, Jack's former Chief of Staff.

"Ruby," Helen says warmly. "It's so good to hear your voice. You stunning beauty, what are you doing?"

Ruby is, in fact, standing on Seadog Lane with a paper to-go cup of coffee in one hand and the keys to Marooned With a Book in the other.

"Hi, Helen," she says, sticking the key into the lock and twisting it as she wedges the phone between her ear and shoulder. "I'm just opening up my shop here. How are you?"

"Listen, honey, I've been better. I'm not going to yank your chain here: I need to see you. Can I come down to your island?"

Ruby gives a throaty laugh as she punches the code into the alarm system and sets her coffee and keys on the front counter. "Technically the island isn't mine, Helen, and I would love to see you. I truly would." She puts the phone on speaker and sets it on the counter, looking around at the shop in the morning light. It could use a few plants here and there, but still, there's nothing Ruby loves more than unlocking the door and staring at a day ahead with all its unwritten potential.

"Fabulous. I'll be there tomorrow," Helen says, sounding thrilled that it's settled.

"Oh," Ruby says, tilting her head to one side as she puts both hands on the counter. "Tomorrow? I was thinking you and Kent might be planning a weekend down here or something." She loves Helen and her husband Kent; both are in their late sixties and both are lifelong politicos. The best part about having dinner with Helen and Kent is the fact that they're complete opposites when it comes to their politics; they agree on nothing, but they do it so cheerfully and with such gusto, and they always lean over and kiss one another full on the lips after every debate, no matter how messy it gets.

"No, no, honey—no Kent this time. Just me. I can stay at the local hotel or wherever. I don't care about that. I just need a few hours of your time."

"Nonsense," Ruby says, turning on the computer at the front counter and adjusting the air conditioning so that it's cool enough in the shop. "You'll stay with me. I have plenty of room."

"Thank you, Ruby. Just one night—I need to get back here as soon as possible, but this is face-to-face business."

Ruby is instantly on edge. "Is this about...her?" she asks softly, breathing in and out as she stares at the counter in front of her.

"Maybe," Helen allows. "It's important. I'll be there at eleven o'clock tomorrow morning."

"I'll meet you at the dock." Ruby is grim-faced. This feels like it's definitely going to be bad news.

"Okay, honey," Helen says, then pauses before saying goodbye. "Have a good day, and don't worry too much. We'll talk tomorrow."

But Ruby does worry. All day long. She worries about the new crease that Helen is about to put into her life. She worries about how she'll handle whatever twist is coming her way, and whether or not it will be one more thing to upset her girls and send shockwaves through their lives when they're both currently in a semi-fragile state. Every single thing that happens needs to be vetted, dealt with, and shared accordingly, and this is exactly the kind of drama that Ruby wants to leave behind. She wants to shed that skin and leave it all back in D.C. In her old life. In the past.

She sighs and scratches her forehead, then puts her phone and keys into the drawer behind the front counter. Vanessa and Tilly are both scheduled to cover the bookstore tomorrow so that she can pick up Helen and spend the day listening to whatever she needs to tell her.

Ruby is already lost in thought as she straightens the store and turns on the appropriate lights in each room. She chooses a jazz station on Spotify and connects it to the speakers so that music is playing, then runs through her list of orders that she's going to place in the next few days. A handful of people walk past the front of the shop—a woman with a giant, loping Dalmatian on a leash; a dad with a little boy perched on his shoulders; two elderly women with their arms looped together—but no one comes in for nearly an hour.

And then, like a hurricane blowing the door off its hinges, Marigold Pim bursts in, holding a piece of paper in her hand. Ruby nearly jumps out of her skin, but she can see Banks sitting in his golf cart out front, looking alert but relaxed as he drinks a cup of coffee. It's clear that Marigold does not raise any alarm with him, so Ruby turns her attention to the tall, lithe woman in front of her. It's nearly as surreal for Ruby to see a supermodel in the flesh as it is for Marigold to see a former First Lady.

"Hey," Marigold says breathlessly. She's dressed in a pair of biking shorts and a tank top. Anyone with eyes can see that she is in the best shape of her life, despite that fact that she's solidly into her fifties. The whole world knows her not just as a model, but most recently, as an extremely vocal advocate of aging gracefully, and a staunch proponent of women not being written off or ignored the minute they pass forty.

"I saw this hanging up at The Frog's Grog." Marigold holds up a wrinkled page that Ruby recognizes as the flyer she made and hung around the island advertising her potential book club. "We need this," Marigold says, nodding firmly and definitively. "We need this, and I want to help."

Ruby

Helen's boat pulls up the next morning at 10:58. Ruby is standing at the dock with her blonde hair tucked under a hot pink Martha's Vineyard baseball cap, wearing a pair of black leggings and a white t-shirt that whips in the wind coming off of the water. Between Vanessa and Tilly, the bookstore is covered all day, and Ruby has already planned out the dinner she'll serve Helen on the porch of her house that looks out on the water.

From the fish stand on Seadog Lane, she's purchased four lobsters, and with them she'll serve her famous sriracha potato salad, homemade buttered biscuits, sweet corn and tomato salad, and an apple crumble with a bottle (or two) of a California Chardonnay. Ruby has fixed up the third guest room and covered the queen-sized bed in clean, cool sheets, but she resisted the temptation to pick out a 1000-piece puzzle to work on while they talk, because this visit is not a social one, and even though it might be nice to have something to do with her hands while they talk, she wants to be fully present.

Ruby reaches up to hold her hat in place while the boat docks. Helen stands up, reaching out to take the hand of another woman, someone much younger and more petite than Helen is. Ruby squints and tries to make out a face.

It's…no, it can't be…

"Sunday?" Ruby shouts, cupping her hands to the sides of her mouth. "Oh my God! Sun!"

Sunday's head whips around so that her shoulder-length, light brown curls bounce in the breeze. "RUBY!" she screeches, jumping up and down and clapping her hands like a cheerleader.

Ruby's heart leaps. Sunday Bond is the former Second Lady, married to Jack's Vice President, Peter Bond, and she's one of Ruby's absolute favorite people in the world.

Ruby rushes to the edge of the dock and helps Helen up the steps and onto dry land, which is no easy feat. At sixty-two, Helen has already undergone a hip replacement, and her knee can't be far behind. But what she lacks in mobility, she more than makes up for in presence and personality.

"Ruby," Helen says, huffing and puffing a little as she smoothes her linen pantsuit. "I hope you don't mind that I brought along some company. I'll take the couch if there isn't room for all of us."

"You'll do no such thing," Ruby says, hurriedly kissing Helen on one cheek before moving on to Sunday, who whoops loudly as she throws her arms around Ruby's neck. "I have five bedrooms in this house, and as luck would have it, both Harlow and Athena are here right now. So we have just enough room for everyone."

"Oh, I'm so happy to see you!" Sunday says, squeezing Ruby as tightly as she can. "Why haven't you called?" She frowns and pushes back from Ruby, holding onto both of her arms as she admonishes her. "I've been worried about you, and you didn't answer my emails or texts."

Ruby doesn't have a good answer for that. Sunday has always been someone she trusts, and surely their bond runs deeper than the fact that their husbands worked side-by-side in the White House. In fact, there were times when Sunday's friendship was the only thing Ruby knew she could count on in a world of artifice and politics, and maybe it's the sense that she leaned too heavily on her friend towards the end, or that she revealed too much, that's kept Ruby away.

"I don't know…" Ruby says, looking out at the boat bobbing in the water. "I should have, but I got wrapped up in moving down here and getting the bookshop going, and I felt like I needed to do all of that on my own. I abused our friendship enough after Jack died, and—"

Helen clears her throat. "Let's reminisce later, ladies. I need a bathroom and a cup of coffee, in that order."

Helen shepherds them up the dock like a schoolteacher herding kids on a field trip. She's looking more relaxed than Ruby ever saw her look in the halls of the White House or in the Oval Office, but even though she's switched out her normal black or navy suit for a cream linen capri pants set, she still looks official and not fully on vacation. Which is a reminder to Ruby that they're *not* there on vacation.

"I'm just so happy to see you both," Ruby says, stepping back and offering a hand to each woman. Sunday takes her right hand and holds it excitedly; Helen clasps her left one, gives it a light squeeze, and then lets go. As the former Chief of Staff, Helen is pragmatic, reserved, and whip-smart. She is not given to overly emotional displays of affection, though it's no secret that she loves and admires Ruby.

"Honey, we're glad to see *you*. We've worried about you being alone down here, and I wanted to see you with my own eyes and make sure you hadn't completely gone off the deep end."

"I haven't," Ruby assures her. "And I don't plan to."

"So we won't catch you dressed up like a pirate or a wench and ladling out grog to island visitors?" Helen asks as she waddles up the dock to the golf cart that Banks is driving.

"Oh, I don't know about that," Ruby says with a laugh. "My wench costume is at the dry cleaners at the moment, but I wouldn't mind forcing mugs of grog on unsuspecting strangers."

Sunday is carrying both her own overnight bag and Helen's, and she drops them easily onto the backseat of the golf cart, sliding over to make room for Ruby. Helen takes the front passenger seat next to Banks.

"Lovely to see you, Banks," Helen says, giving the Secret Service agent a crisp nod.

"You as well, ma'am," he says, then flicks his eyes to the rearview mirror. "And you, Mrs. Bond."

Sunday busies herself with the leather duffel bag that she's brought along for the trip, but she glances up at the rearview mirror and catches Banks' eye. "Thank you," she says, before turning to face Ruby. "Okay," she says, nearly bouncing up and down on her side of the bench seat. "Now tell me *everything* about this island. Everything. All the details—leave nothing out."

Ruby laughs again as Banks pulls away from the dock, swinging the cart towards home. "Everything?" she asks. "Okay, let me start at the beginning. In 1513, a ship called the *Flor de Azucar* wrecked just off the island, and there was only one survivor: a woman everyone calls Flora. They say that the ghosts of every man who died on the ship haunt Shipwreck Key, and I've had more than one person come into the bookstore to tell me to watch out for Flora wandering Seadog Lane after midnight —just in case I'm ever there alone that late."

"Seadog Lane?" Helen snorts, turning in her seat. "Are you kidding me with all this pirate twaddle?" She turns her wide upper body back around with some effort, muttering to herself as she does.

Sunday reaches over and laces her fingers through Ruby's, giving her hand another squeeze like they're co-conspirators and allies once again. Ruby squeezes right back. There's nothing better than the feeling of having another woman—a true and dedicated friend—right by her side.

* * *

It takes no time at all for Ruby to get Sunday and Helen both set up in rooms that have views of the sand and the sea. They eat a fresh fruit salad for lunch made with juicy cantelope, chunks of sweet, tart pineapple, strawberries, and grapes, and then take a long walk on the beach. All three women gather shells and let their bare feet sink into the warm sand as they stroll and chat about their children, their marriages, and the people they know in Washington. There is an agreed upon rule between the three of them that anything they talk about while not wearing shoes is completely off the record (they invented this rule one late night on the campaign trail as they kicked off their heels in Helen's hotel room and shared a bottle of wine).

"God love him," Helen says, her pale, white feet sticking out below the loose pink cotton pants she's changed into. "Kent tries. But look at me." She touches the brim of the oversized sun hat on her head. "I'm no Victoria's Secret model—at least not anymore."

"But I bet you were," Sunday says loyally. She's the biggest supporter of other women that Ruby has ever met, and it's one of the things she loves most about Sunday.

Helen chuckles. "I was never runway material, but I wasn't too shabby in a bathing suit back in my day."

"Kent loves you," Ruby assures her, and she means it from the bottom of her heart. She's never seen a couple more in tune than Helen and Kent, and even though they've been married for thirty-five years, they still look at one another adoringly when they think no one is watching.

"He does," Helen says, nodding and looking out at the sky in front of them. "But love alone doesn't always help a man when it's time to lift the old flag, if you know what I mean. Sometimes it takes a little extra help."

Ruby looks at her hot pink toenails digging into the sand. "Oh," she says, nodding sagely. There is still a part of her that feels as if she can't speak freely about her sex life with Jack—after all, her husband was the president, and even though most of the free world seems to have some knowledge of his secret life with Etienne, she still can't bring herself to discuss anything that happened in her marriage.

The ocean roars just feet from them and Sunday throws her hands in the air, her diamond tennis bracelet catching the light as she laughs with abandon. "Men!" she shouts. "Why are they so complicated?" Her hands fall to her sides and her voice gets quieter. "We all know that my husband is no picnic between the sheets."

Ruby glances in Sunday's direction, as does Helen. Neither of them says anything, instead letting the moment hang there until Sunday turns around so that she's walking backward and looking at the two of them.

"But hey, what do I know. Maybe he *is* a picnic between the sheets —you'd just have to ask every gay man in Washington to find out!"

With a playful *whoop* that is pure Sunday Bond, she turns back around and starts to run toward Ruby's house. "Last one to the front porch uncorks the first bottle of wine!" she yells over her shoulder.

Helen shakes her head as they watch Sunday pull away from them, sand kicking up behind her as she goes. "She's a doozy, that girl. Fifty-four years old and running across the beach like a teenager on the way to meet her crush."

"I wish she'd find someone to have a crush on," Ruby says wistfully. She readjusts her baseball cap, pulling her hair from her neck and twisting it up so that she can tuck it into her hat. "She's put up with a lot over the years."

"She has," Helen agrees, nodding once. "And he just keeps stringing her along."

"How? The kids are grown. He's not making a run for the White House again—or is he?"

Helen lifts her shoulders and lets them fall. "Not officially. I've heard rumors. But he has her believing that she owes him more."

"More than thirty years of her life spent married to a man who—"

Helen holds up a hand. "I know. But honey, people make all kinds of bargains and arrangements. You know Sunday as well as anyone, and why she's tolerated it all these years is beyond us. But she has, and she does. So there must be a reason."

By the time Ruby and Helen get to the porch, Sunday is already out there with a chilled bottle of rosé and three glasses. She's sitting in one of the Adirondack chairs with her feet tucked under her, smiling up at them gleefully.

"It's so beautiful here," Sunday says, handing each woman an empty glass as she pulls the cork out with a corkscrew. "I don't ever want to leave."

Without thinking, Ruby says: "Then don't. You can afford a place here, Sun, and until you find one, you can just stay with me."

Helen has just gotten herself settled in a white-painted Adirondack of her own, and she looks up at Ruby with wide eyes.

Sunday's gaze sweeps the beach and the horizon. She frowns and pours herself a glass of wine before passing the bottle to Helen. "I could," she says, narrowing her eyes again as she considers it. "I really could. You started over, Rubes. I could too."

"Of course you could," Ruby presses. She can feel Helen giving her a sharp look, so she backs off a hair. "If you wanted to. If the timing was right."

"When is the timing ever right?" Sunday asks, looking up at Ruby, who takes the bottle from Helen, fills her own glass, and sits in a third chair.

They're all in a line, staring out at the sand. Ruby puts her bare feet up on the railing of the porch and sips her rosé.

"That's true for so many things," Ruby agrees, pausing as a wave crashes on shore. "If you always wait until the time is right, you might miss out on some of life's most wonderful moments."

"I was definitely not ready to have kids when Kent and I found out that Abigail was coming," Helen admits. "I'd just started a job, and he was working on his master's degree. We lived in a tiny apartment, and I knew money would be tight. But not having Abigail would have been terrible. We jumped in with both feet. Best decision ever." Helen knocks back a sip of wine like a punctuation mark at the end of her sentence.

"I wasn't ready to walk in on Peter with William," Sunday says, holding her glass out to Ruby for a top-off. "But when is the timing ever right to catch your husband in bed with a twenty-three-year-old congressional aide?"

Ruby pulls a face; she knows that Sunday has to joke about things in order to cope, but there are times when she feels like her friend might be pouring salt on her own wounds. Instead of saying so, she reaches over and takes Sunday's hand in hers.

"And to bring it back to the matter at hand," Ruby says, "moving somewhere new only has to feel right in your heart. But could you actually make it work? Would Peter be okay with you moving down here, or...?"

Sunday pulls her hand from Ruby's and runs her long fingers through her windswept hair. "That's partially why I wanted to come down here with Helen," she says, turning her flashing eyes on Ruby. She's obviously gathering as much confidence as possible for her big declaration. "I'm leaving Peter, and I wanted you to hear it from me before you heard it anywhere else."

Ruby's mouth falls open. She's always hated when characters in books are so stunned that their jaws drop, but hers truly does. She stares at Sunday for a long moment.

"You are? You're truly leaving him? Like, publicly, or just privately?" Ruby knows there's a difference. Throughout her years in Washington with Jack, she's known many couples who are only together publicly or on paper. At least half of the biggest "power couples" she knows are actually two totally separate individuals living their own lives in private, then coming together to make appearances and to present a united front. The reasons vary, but in many cases it serves one or both parties to be seen as a traditional, solid unit.

Sunday lifts her chin defiantly. "Publicly. He's being served with papers while I'm down here."

It's Helen's turn to have her jaw dislocated by a piece of stunning news. "Sunday Bond!" she shouts, reaching over and slapping Sunday's thigh. "I didn't know you had that kind of get-up-and-go, girl."

Sunday frowns at her. "You didn't?"

Helen tips her head from side to side. "Okay, I hoped you did, but there have been a lot of times over the years when you've stuck by that man's side and I truly didn't think he deserved it."

"That's true," Sunday says. Her eyes fall as she thinks for a minute. "There have been so many times that I've felt humiliated by things Peter's said or done, but I do have to say that he's been a wonderful father. I'll give him that much."

The three women look out at the ocean again, each pondering the image they have of Peter with the two little girls that he and Sunday adopted as infants. Olive was born in China and Cameron in Guatemala, and Peter has always been completely besotted by his little girls, who are actually grown women now.

"Well, credit where credit is due," Helen allows, nodding firmly. "But it's high time you pulled yourself up and got the chance to be your own woman. You stuck with him while the girls were young, you stood by his side while he was VP, and you've never spoken an ill word of him in the press—not one. It's admirable."

"Thank you, Helen," Sunday says softly. She turns to Ruby. "And if I won't be cramping your style, I think I really want to move down here. At least part-time."

A rush of joy fills Ruby's chest. "God, Sun. You won't cramp my style at all. It'll be wonderful to have you here—even part-time."

A huge grin spreads across Sunday's face. "Then you're getting yourself a new neighbor."

Ruby leans over and puts an arm around Sunday's neck, pulling her in for a quick hug.

"Now, I hate to break up this happy moment," Helen says, her voice taking on the *let's get down to business* tone she's famous for. "But the real reason for my visit was not to deliver this runaway bride to a far-flung island." She presses her lips together and looks at Ruby with a straight face. "You've got a big problem, and it's incoming."

Ruby frowns. "What are you saying?"

"Ever heard of Dexter North?" Helen drains her rosé and sets the empty glass on the wide armrest of her wooden chair. "The author?"

Ruby racks her brain. "The guy who wrote the book about Monica Lewinsky?"

Sunday makes a face. "Oooh. It was good. I stayed up all night finishing that book."

"Same," Helen agrees. "He really has a way of getting into the darkest corners of his subject's mind and heart."

Ruby feels impatient. "Okay, I know who he is. I have the book in the shop, but frankly, I didn't get around to reading it yet because I'm tired of stories about the women who unravel powerful men."

Helen and Sunday make fleeting eye contact. "He's coming for you," Helen says flatly, not pulling any punches.

Ruby splutters and stands up, walking over to the railing. She spins around so that she's facing the women and her back is to the ocean. "He's coming for *me*? But why? There's no story here. I'm a widow. If anything—"

"No," Helen says, holding up a hand. "You misunderstand me. He wants to talk to you and get your input, but he's writing a book about—"

It's Ruby's turn to hold up her hand. As she does, she closes her eyes tightly as if blocking out Helen and her words will make them stop. "No," she says in a whisper that sounds like she's begging. "No. Please do not tell me that he's writing a book about...Jack's death. Can't somebody wait another forty or fifty years to do that? Can't they wait until I'm long gone?"

When she opens her eyes again, Helen and Sunday are both watching her with concern.

"Honey," Helen says, her voice rough and ragged. "There's a story there. And if anyone is going to tell it and make it compelling, it's Dexter North. I really think you should talk to him, because you're not going to stop him. And if the story isn't written by him, then some talentless hack might get to it first."

Ruby's heart is beating wildly in her chest and her wine glass is shaking in her hand. She turns back to the water to hide her emotions from two of the women who know her better than anyone.

Helen is right: she probably won't be able to stop Dexter North and his freight train of words. But that doesn't mean she has to cooperate. It absolutely does not mean that she has to speak to him.

She has a house to manage, a bookstore to run, and a new life to live. If she can just avoid him and refuse to talk to him, then maybe the story will die out and no one will care about Jack and Etienne and any of it.

But even as she thinks this, she knows it's not true. The public will be insatiable for a book by Dexter North about the late president and his private romantic affairs and ensuing death. They will chew Ruby up and spit her out as they sharpen their teeth on the gory details of her husband's life and indiscretions. Ruby will not be able to avoid it, and saying nothing won't keep her out of the story.

But what she *can* do is decide how to do damage control before Dexter shows up on her doorstep. She can take control of her own narrative and hold her head high, because Ruby knows that she's done nothing wrong.

Sunday stands up and walks over to Ruby, putting her arms around her taller friend from behind and resting her cheek on Ruby's back. Even though Sunday is five years older than Ruby, their personalities have dictated their relationship for years, and it's very much been one where Ruby acts as the stoic big sister, while Sunday is the fun-loving kid sister who wears her heart on her sleeve.

"We got you, Rubes," Sunday says gently. "No matter what, okay?"

Ruby smiles at the ocean as tears fall down her cheeks, because there's only one thing she knows for sure right then: having both Sunday and her girls with her on Shipwreck Key is going to make everything better, even as some man she doesn't know starts digging through the wreckage of what's left of her marriage.

Harlow

A full month after the bar shooting, Harlow's mental state has improved, but she's still not feeling like herself. As promised, Ruby helped her to find a therapist and she's been talking to her once a week by Zoom call, but what Harlow is discovering is that she only *thought* she was living a full life in New York. She'd been under the impression that having her own apartment, working at the marketing firm, and going out with friends at night was enough to make a life, when truly, it was only the beginnings of a life.

On Shipwreck Key she's had time to think. Harlow has kicked around everything in her brain, turning it over like a pebble in her hand as she walks the beach alone, with Eldrick trailing after her at a discreet distance. His presence has always made her feel safe, and while three Secret Service agents on Shipwreck Key feels like overkill sometimes, Harlow is more aware than ever that it's necessary to have someone watching your back. Going home to New York feels less and less like something she wants to do, and with every passing day, Harlow is integrating herself more into Ruby's life on the island.

It started with dropping in some mornings to bring her mom a cup of coffee from The Scuttlebutt, the coffee shop on Seadog Lane with the owner who seems like she could make you a cup of coffee and then go out back and gut a fish that she's just caught with her bare hands, and before she knew it, Harlow was pitching in with shelving books and picking up a shift here and there at Marooned With a Book.

She's there now, standing behind the front counter with Tilly, who is a constant source of entertainment for Harlow.

How her mother ever interviewed a nineteen-year-old goth girl in Doc Marten boots with a four-inch sole and decided she was perfect for a bookstore that looks like a cottage in the Cotswolds is beyond Harlow, but everything that comes out of Tilly's mouth is pure gold.

"I can strike a match on my teeth," Tilly says right then as she's scanning the barcodes of books and inputting them into the system.

And okay, so Harlow isn't into wearing chains and leather and dying her hair until it's a jet-black pageboy, but come on, Tilly is only three years younger than her, and Harlow just spent the last year living in Manhattan. It's not like she's intimidated by a teenager who thinks she discovered The Cure, though she's spied some interesting looks on the faces of the bookstore's customers whenever Tilly is around.

"Must come in handy when you're setting fire to yet another man's heart," Harlow says as she organizes bookmarks and business cards.

"Ha," Tilly says, her perfectly outlined blood red lips pulling into a pout. "Why are men even a thing?"

Two women with white hair like clouds of cotton candy enter the store, their purses strapped across their bodies.

"Good morning," Harlow says, hoping to greet them before Tilly does. "Welcome to Marooned With a Book."

Every so often Tilly just stares at the people who walk through the door, giving them a long, appraising look like a cat roused from a nap. If she decides they're worth the effort, she'll say hello.

"Oh my," one of the women says, putting a hand to her chest. "Aren't you—"

Her companion rushes to her side and grabs her elbow. "Don't gawk, Diane," she hisses. She turns a smile at Harlow. "Good morning. We're just day-trippers visiting the island."

From the way they look around the store, Harlow can tell that they want to catch a glimpse of her mom, who is actually out roaming the island today with some real estate agent from Destin who'd come to the bookstore opening. Before Sunday and Helen had even left Shipwreck Key, Ruby had already made an appointment to check out the available properties for Sunday and send her the best options.

"Well, have a look around, and let me know if you have any other questions." The women walk to the back of the store together, leaving Harlow and Tilly alone again.

"I wonder if old people think about how close they are to dying all the time," Tilly says. Every statement that comes out of her mouth is apropos of nothing, in Harlow's opinion, and she stifles the urge to point that out. In the end she doesn't though, because putting a gag on Tilly would be like cutting off her main source of entertainment on Shipwreck Key.

"They probably think more about stuff like what they're going to make for dinner, or whether they remembered to send their grandkid a birthday card. You know—normal stuff," Harlow says. She's pretty sure that Tilly is always trying to sound shocking, so she intentionally refuses to give the girl what she wants. "Hey, did you hear that the star of the new season of *The Bachelor* is that guy who donated his kidney to save a little girl he didn't even know?"

Tilly's upper lip curls in distaste; *The Bachelor* is not something she would ever deign to watch, and Harlow knows this, hence the question.

"I'm not into that show," Tilly says. "I'd rather watch snakes eat mice on YouTube. I love it when they swallow them whole and you can hear the mice screaming."

Okay, this one does kind of get under Harlow's skin, but she shrugs and tries to act like Tilly isn't freaking her out. "Yeah. Sounds cool. Hey," she says, shifting gears. "Speaking of snacks, I'm going to take my break now and run over to The Scuttlebutt to see if they have fresh scones. Want one?"

Tilly is inspecting her artfully chipped black nail polish. "No thanks. I'm on a red meat only diet right now."

"Sounds healthy," Harlow says with a sunny smile. "I'll be right back!"

She's out the front door with her wallet in hand when Athena walks up, wearing a wrinkled sundress and a pair of dark black sunglasses. She looks pale and wan.

"Hey, Bean," Harlow says to her sister, using her nickname in hopes of making Athena smile. "What's up?"

Athena lifts one shoulder listlessly and lets it fall. Both Eldrick and Corbin are now on Seadog Lane, and Harlow nearly points out that they're on the safest street in the world, given that two highly trained Secret Service agents are within arms' reach. But her sister looks distracted, so instead she loops her arm through Athena's and guides her toward the coffee shop.

Athena sighs. "I don't know what to do with my life," she says as they walk down the sidewalk.

"You're only twenty-three," Harlow says, frowning. "And you have your life together more than anyone I know."

Athena stops walking. She's clearly agitated—more so than Harlow has ever seen her.

"I *don't* have my life together. You have no idea what a mess I've made of it." She looks around, pushing the sunglasses up into the pile of curly hair that she's just washed and let dry. "I don't think I can ever go back to D.C. and show my face again."

Harlow takes her sister's hand and drags her across the street so that they can sit on a bench that looks out at the water. The sun is climbing higher in the sky, and the heat and humidity are ratcheting up in tandem.

"Hey," Harlow says, tugging Athena's hand so that she snaps out of her trance. "What's the deal here? So you fell for some guy who dumped you? That happens to all of us at some point. Seriously."

Athena shakes her head sadly. Harlow has heard her mumbling to Ruby quietly as they sit in a different room, but so far her sister hasn't told her much about the guy who sent her running down to Shipwreck Key. But seriously, getting dumped isn't nearly as bad as almost getting shot in a bar. Not that she's trying to say she has it worse than her sister, she just doesn't understand why Athena can't pull it together when she herself is soldiering on after real tragedy.

Athena bends forward at the waist, resting her forehead on her knees. This is alarming.

"He didn't dump me," Athena says quietly. Harlow puts a hand on her sister's back and rubs it slowly. "And it was my first time."

"Your first time going out with him?" Harlow's eyes drift out to the water; the sun is dancing on the waves.

"No, my first time...ever. I was a virgin."

"Wait, what?" Harlow's attention snaps back instantly. "You were seriously still a virgin at twenty-three?" Athena turns her head and looks up at Harlow, her eyes as wounded and sad as they've ever been. "Sorry, sorry—I didn't mean it that way," Harlow says quickly, trying to cover her surprise so that it doesn't sound judgmental. "I just didn't know." She goes back to rubbing her sister's back in slow circles.

"Yeah," Athena croaks, hiding her face between her knees again. Her hands dangle toward the ground next to her calves. She looks like a broken rag doll. "I got in over my head."

"Okay, okay." Harlow's mind is racing. A guy ghosting a girl after a one night stand isn't unheard of, but the way her sister is taking it is completely heartbreaking. "So then can you just chalk it up to a mistake? I mean, if it wasn't horrible in the moment, then that's something. Of course it's bad that he didn't want to go out with you again, but—"

Athena lifts her head from her knees and sits bolt upright, turning to face her sister with sad, wild eyes. "It's not that, Lo," she says. "It's worse than that."

"Did he say rude things about you to a mutual friend?"

Athena shakes her head. "Worse."

"Told everyone you work with that you guys did the deed?"

Another shake of the head from Athena. She puts her hands over her eyes and keeps them covered when she finally reveals the truth: "He's married."

"WHAT?" Harlow stands up. She feels a rush of indignation on her sister's behalf. "No freaking way, Athena. You didn't know, of course—I know you, and you'd never sleep with a married man. Unless you were drunk—did he get you drunk?" She's angry and in a rage just thinking of some jack-hole intentionally getting her naïve sister tipsy just to take advantage of her. Harlow paces back and forth as Athena sits on the bench, watching her. "I'll kill him."

"Actually, he got married the week after I slept with him. In Bali. We don't work in the same department, and I didn't know until I went looking for him the morning after. His secretary had to tell me that he'd be out for a week for his wedding."

"That's not your fault," Harlow says quickly, standing right in front of Athena so that she has to look up and shield her eyes from the sun. "This is one thousand percent his fault."

Athena sighs. "I know. It just hurts."

"Of course it does. Do you want me to stalk him on social media and find his new wife and tell her?"

"No," Athena says sadly. "That won't make me feel any better. It's not her fault either—it's his."

Harlow shrugs. "But maybe she needs to know what kind of guy she just married..."

Athena waves her hands adamantly. "No, no, no. I need to worry about me right now, and messing up a whole relationship just to get revenge is not going to help me in any way."

Grudgingly, Harlow tilts her head to one side and lets her eyes roll up like she's agreeing—but only barely. "Okay. I hear you. So how can we make *you* better?" She sits back down on the bench so that she and Athena's arms are touching as they face the water.

"I think just being here is helping, to be perfectly honest. I love my job, but...I don't really want to go back. Is that weird?"

Harlow gives a soft laugh. "I feel the exact same way, so no, it's not weird." They're quiet for a long moment. "Hey, how long do you think Mom will let us stay down here? And how long can we be away from our jobs and apartments without losing everything?"

Athena thinks about this for the time it takes three different waves to roll in, crash, and retreat again. "Ummm, I'm not sure. But to be honest, Lo, I don't really care right now. We're both just out of college. Life handed us both lemons, and we're down here—"

"Don't say making lemonade!" Harlow puts both hands to her own throat and pretends to gag.

A huge grin spreads across Athena's face for the first time since she got to Shipwreck Key. "I was going to say 'squeezing the shit out of them,' but maybe we *should* just make lemonade."

"You were not going to say that," Harlow protests, shaking her head fervently. "You never swear, which is why Dad always trusted you to go to events with him and not me."

This makes Athena giggle, and Harlow instantly knows what she's thinking of.

"Remember the time you said that Dad wanted to bitch-slap that guy from the protest who threw rocks at the motorcade and that lady from the *Wall Street Journal* heard you?" Athena is full-on laughing now. "Dad was so mad."

"Hey, I'm the kind of girl who says what she feels." Harlow tosses her hair haughtily, but she's not lying: she absolutely *is* the kind of girl who has a hard time censoring herself when she gets worked up about something.

"I love that about you, Lo."

"Dad didn't."

Athena reaches over and rests a hand on her sister's knee. "I think he did love it, but it reminded him of himself, and no parent likes to see their own worst traits reflected in their children."

"You sound like a therapist," Harlow says, leaning over and bumping Athena's shoulder with hers.

"Maybe I'll go back to school and get my degree in clinical psychology or something."

"You mean give up the fast-paced, exciting life of a librarian?" Harlow jokes.

Athena shoots her a serious look. "Yeah. Maybe I need something more tame."

"Like a lion trainer?"

"More like one of those people who works on skyscrapers and walks on the metal structure a million feet from the ground with just a harness and a hardhat."

"Or you could just stay here and help Mom with the bookstore." Harlow throws her sister a glance.

"Hey, so could you."

"Let's see how long she'll let us stay before she kicks us out," Harlow says. "Just keep your nose clean so we both look good, okay?"

The girls giggle at the ridiculousness of Athena misbehaving. They lace their fingers together, then sit and watch the waves as they let the idea of staying on Shipwreck Key percolate between them.

Ruby

Ruby wakes up to a text from Harlow in the group chat she shares with both of her girls. The fact that they're currently sharing a house doesn't stop them from regularly dropping stories, pictures, and links to news articles in their group chat as if they're still living in three separate cities, and carrying on conversations from their respective bedrooms either late at night or first thing in the morning. Ruby reaches for her reading glasses on her nightstand and sits up in bed. Outside, the sky is blue and the seagulls are already swooping and diving for breakfast in the clear water.

Harlow: Mom, you have to watch this. It seems like a million years ago!

There's a YouTube link below this message with a tiny thumbnail picture of a younger Ruby sitting on a couch.

Athena: When is this, and where did you find it, Lo?

Harlow: Oprah reposted it on Insta this year for National First Ladies Day and I saved it but forgot to send it. Apparently Mom is ranked the number one favorite First Lady in the past hundred years.

Ruby: I would question who took part in that particular poll. Seriously, girls. No one is voting me as a favorite over Michelle Obama.

Athena: And not to crack on Mom, but what about Jackie O?

Ruby: Thank you, Bean. Exactly NO ONE is going to favor me in my Converse high tops and cargo pants over Jackie in her pillbox hats and gloves. At least no one with any fashion sense.

Athena: Definitely not what I meant, Mom.

Ruby: I know, honey.

Harlow: Isn't today the first day of book club?

Athena: It is the first day of her book club, and I can't wait. You all ready for the big event, Mom?

Ruby: I think so. Are you both coming? I want you girls to be there!

Harlow: I'm excited for you, Mamacita. I hope all the chicks who show up are as cool as you. And can we come even if we haven't read the book? Because I definitely haven't read the book.

Ruby: No one has—we're choosing the first one this evening.

Athena: I'll be there. You had me at "book club."

Harlow: [attaches photo of herself laying in bed, sticking out her tongue] Fine. I'll be there too, but mostly because I heard there'll be wine and cake.

Ruby smiles at her early morning chat with her daughters. It seems like five minutes ago they were little girls running around and shouting for her to please braid their hair! Find their sandals! Help them make cookies! And then suddenly they were teenagers in the White House, trying to date and fight acne and learn how to be young women in front of the entire world. There'd been a few mean-spirited internet posts (about Athena, in particular, and her awkwardness), and this had angered Ruby beyond words. After all, which of us would ever fare well if we were forced to grow up on a public stage? To display our changing bodies and gawkiness in front of the world? But Athena had bowed her head and pushed through it, maintaining all along the calm sense of self that Ruby has always loved about her.

And Harlow...her wild child. She smiles now remembering the way the press—in particular the outlets who loved to highlight fashion hits and misses—would follow her around, cataloguing the way her sartorial choices matched her incandescent personality. Harlow wore her clothes the way she wore her skin: with ease. She never hit a rocky patch as a teenager, instead preferring to look directly into any camera and show the world that she wouldn't be tripped up by its steady gaze. As much as Ruby has always loved Athena's steady, wise sense of self, she's also always admired Harlow's "no one owns me, and I don't owe the world a dime" insouciance. Her girls are like night and day. Ocean and desert. Sun and moon. Winter and summer. And Ruby is endlessly fascinated by them. She desperately wants them both to regain their footing and to feel like their old selves again.

Instead of jumping right out of bed, Ruby scrolls back through their text messages and clicks on the video that Harlow sent. Her screen fills with an image of herself from just over a decade ago. Her hair is blonder and blown out into soft waves; her forehead and eyes lack some of the lightly etched lines she now wears on her face permanently. She can look at this image of herself and remember everything that was going on: her girls were eleven and twelve, and she was thirty-eight. Jack was still a senator and incredibly dashing at forty-nine...coincidentally, the same age that Ruby is now.

The studio audience quiets down as their applause tapers off, and the camera pans out to show Ruby sitting across from Oprah Winfrey.

"Thank you for joining me, Ruby Hudson," Oprah says, reaching over and putting a hand on Ruby's knee as she gives her a warm smile. "I don't do a lot of sit-down interviews anymore, but there was no way I was going to miss the chance to talk with the wife of the future president."

The audience goes wild, their cheers and clapping drowning out any words that Ruby might say.

When they finally calm down again, Ruby turns to the crowd, smiling and laughing. Oprah lobs her a few softballs: *Tell us about your role as a senator's wife.* (Lots of travel, making sure Jack knows who he's meeting and anything important about the city they're in, and being available for any events that Jack wants her to attend.) *If you could choose the perfect platform for yourself as a First Lady, what would it be?* (Children's literacy, hands-down. Getting books into every elementary school, and making sure that reading materials are accessible to everyone.) *What are you most proud of?* (Her girls. Her beautiful, smart, funny, precocious, wonderful little girls.)

And then finally, as if Oprah has a crystal ball and knows that some future version of Ruby will be watching this video almost exactly ten years later, she centers her gaze on Ruby's face, waits for a moment of complete silence from the audience, and asks the million dollar question: "Where do you see yourself in ten years?"

Present Day Ruby watches her little phone screen intently, her eyes wide as she remembers her own words on that day that now feels like a lifetime ago. "In ten years?" The Ruby on the screen turns and glances out at the cameras. "We'll be serving a second term in the White House, and Jack will have solidified some of the most successful and strong political ties this country has ever seen. We'll be economically prosperous, and the American people will feel the kind of pride in their government that they haven't felt in years." Again, the audience breaks into a loud round of applause, and Ruby grins at them, crossing her nylon-clad legs. "Oh, and my amazing daughters will both be happy and successful at whatever they decide to do with their lives." She puts both hands to her cheeks. "I can't believe that in ten years my girls will be in their twenties!"

Oprah laughs along with her, clapping and nodding.

Ruby's eyes tear up now as she sits in her bed, watching it all on the screen. She'd been right about one thing: her girls *are* successful, and they *will* be happy again. As for the rest of it...well, much of that was out of her control. She wishes that her beloved country was in a better place economically, and that things weren't so divided. A lot has happened in ten years for everyone in America, but for her personally, this chunk of time has changed everything. She's experienced life as a First Lady, and she's fully raised her children. She got to travel the world and support the man she loved, and then she lost him—completely and totally, and in so many ways.

America's favorite First Lady? she thinks, shaking her head. *There's no way.*

Ruby clicks off her phone and sets it on her nightstand along with her reading glasses. She climbs out of bed and stretches her arms high overhead, looking out at the beach from her second-story bedroom window. It's going to be a beautiful day, and she has a lot going on.

But it's jarring to look back at a less jaded, more hopeful version of herself. A former Ruby who had no idea what was coming her way, and a younger, more trusting woman who believed that only good things would happen to her and her little family.

She lets her arms fall to her sides as she watches a boat moving across the water in the distance. As it speeds on and gets smaller, Ruby realizes that the version of herself who sat on stage with Oprah ten years ago is just like that boat: going, going, gone.

* * *

"Good morning, boss!" Vanessa walks into the bookstore with an oversized purse, a cup of coffee from The Scuttlebutt, and her cell phone in hand. She's in her early twenties, and in the short time Ruby has known her, she's discovered that Vanessa is like a much older woman stuck in a younger woman's body. She has already told Ruby that she'd love nothing more than to marry, settle down, and have kids, but there's no one on Shipwreck Key who she sees as a potential prospect.

"Hi, Ness," Ruby says, feeling mildly distracted. She's got a pile of books next to the register that she's entering into the system, and the first book club meeting is on her mind. "I'm glad you're here today. I'll be running in and out, so if you don't mind holding down the fort—"

"I never do!" Vanessa says cheerfully, bending at the waist and sliding her purse and cell phone into the drawer behind the counter. She's wearing a long, stretchy dress that hugs an ample, curvaceous figure, and her lovely, dimpled smile is highlighted by perfectly applied red lipstick. Vanessa has dark, groomed eyebrows, and the kind of thick hair that spills in waves down her back.

With a smile, Ruby takes a stack of books from the counter and walks toward the center of the store. "I'm just going to do a little inventory," she says, sliding the new Stephen King novel onto a display rack that's facing out. Behind it, she puts several copies of the book.

In the next room, Ruby seeks out the biographies and memoirs. Sure enough, she has two copies on hand of Dexter North's Monica Lewinsky book, and she glances over her shoulder to make sure that Vanessa is otherwise occupied before pulling the hardcover book off the shelf and flipping to the back jacket.

Dexter North is a best-selling biographer. His works have been published in The Atlantic, The New Yorker, and the Harvard Review. This biography of Monica Lewinsky is his first full-length title. Dexter splits his time between New York City and Christmas Key, Florida.

"Christmas Key," Ruby says under her breath, closing the book. Of course Dexter North spends part of his time in Florida. She's never been to Christmas Key, but she knows it's a cute, rustic island located out in the Gulf of Mexico on the way to the Dry Tortugas, and apparently it's decorated for Christmas all year long. Oddly, she wouldn't picture a serious, hard-hitting journalist like Dexter North spending time there, but what does she know? Maybe he's less of a hard-hitting journalist and more of a beach bum with a laptop?

"Hey, boss?" Vanessa calls out, her hips swaying as she walks through the store holding a piece of paper. "Is this a list of things you need for tonight?"

Ruby slides the book back onto the shelf and reaches for the paper, glancing at it. "Yes. I have most of it, but I was going to run out and grab a few things."

"I can do this on my lunch, if you want."

"No, no. I've got it. Thank you though." Ruby folds the paper in half and hands Vanessa the last few books she was going to put on shelves. "But if you wouldn't mind finding homes for these, I think I'll step out now."

"Sure. No problem."

The rest of the day passes in a blur as Ruby walks up and down Seadog Lane with Banks at a slight distance. Truth be told, when she's preoccupied and thinking of other things, Ruby hardly even notices he's around. Which, she supposes, is the sign of a good Secret Service agent, but it's still mildly unnerving when she realizes once again that she's the only woman on the island with her own personal security guard.

For instance, when she stops in at The Scuttlebutt two doors down from Marooned With a Book, Molly, the owner of the shop, rings up the boxes of pastry for Ruby with an eye on the door. When Ruby glances in that direction, she sees Banks standing there, his wide, muscular back nearly touching the window of the coffee shop as he looks out at the street, standing sentry.

"How is that?" Molly asks, lifting her chin in Banks's direction.

"Having a handsome specimen of manhood follow you to and fro all day, with nothing to do but guarantee your safety?"

Ruby frowns just slightly. "It's weird," she says honestly. "At first I kept wanting to tell whoever was on my detail that they could just go have a cup of coffee or something because no one was going to bother me, but I was wrong."

"People bother you?" Molly's eyes cut back and forth between Ruby and Banks as she ties a piece of white string around the pink pastry box.

Molly is sixty, if she's a day, and she gives the distinct impression of a woman who has spent her entire life on the ocean in one way or another. In fact, Ruby knows from their interactions thus far that Molly is one of just a handful of life-long Shipwreck Key residents, and that her husband died in a boating accident in 1982. Her hands and her skin have the weathered appearance of a woman who knows how to tie a knot in a thick piece of rope under the hot sun, and her hair—far more salt than pepper at this point—is short and windswept. Her blue eyes dance above pink cheeks, and she is no stranger to colorful language or sarcasm.

Ruby tries to choose her words carefully. "People have bothered me on occasion, yes. But mainly they mean well. I think a lot of people are unaware just how unsettling it can be to have strangers following you with cameras out, or to have men shouting your name angrily simply because they disagree with your husband's economic policies."

"I hear that," Molly says, slicing the string with a pair of scissors and sliding the box across the counter to Ruby. "Men are always running off at the mouth. It's one of the reasons I never bothered to find myself another one after Rodney went on his permanent fishing trip in the sky."

Under other circumstances Ruby might have laughed in disbelief; after all, making jokes about your husband's untimely death could come across as distasteful, but Ruby already understands the need to find a way to cope with loss, and laughter and jokes are both huge stress relievers. Not to mention the fact that Molly has been a widow for over forty years, so she's certainly got a handle on how she deals with her own grief.

"Are you coming to the book club meeting tonight?" Ruby asks her, tapping her credit card on the screen next to the register to pay for the pastries.

Molly looks at her with surprise. "You want an old barnacle like me to crash your cookies and tea book club?" She runs a rough hand through her unstyled hair.

Ruby laughs. "Of course I do. I want a book club filled with people who love to read. I want varied life experience and different personalities and—"

"Okay, madam, I'll show up." Molly gives her a half-smile. "But can I bring a bottle of wine? I'm not much for dainty little hors d'oeuvres and chamomile."

"No need," Ruby assures her, picking up the box. "I've got wine already chilling. Six-thirty, just bring yourself."

She walks to the door and pauses. Almost as if he's got a sixth sense that's finely attuned to Ruby's whereabouts, Banks steps away from the window to hold the door for her wordlessly.

* * *

The back room of the bookstore is filled with chairs and a table is set along one wall with drinks at one end (wine, bottled water, sodas), and hors d'oeuvres at the other (a variety of cheeses, crackers of varying shapes and colors, grapes and strawberries, Molly's flaky pastries, and tiny bits of prosciutto wrapped around herbed ricotta on toothpicks.

At six-thirty, Molly strolls in, picks up a wine glass, and serves herself a generous pour of Chardonnay as she scans the chairs. Vanessa and Tilly are there to greet people as they walk in, and Ruby is standing with Marigold Pim and Heather Charleton-Bicks. Ruby eyes Tilly's short tartan skirt and ripped fishnet stockings with mild disapproval, but in the short time that Ruby has known her, Tilly has stayed completely on-brand. These getups aren't just to make a point; Tilly is clearly committed to this gothic lifestyle, and Ruby does admire commitment.

"Ladies," Ruby says with a big smile for Marigold and Heather as she walks by them. Harlow and Athena are seated next to one another across the room, each with a glass of wine in hand as they watch their mother with pride. They've been so supportive of her with the entire move and with the bookstore, and a tiny part of her is secretly thrilled that they're here, regardless of the life circumstances that have delivered them to her doorstep.

Ruby smiles at Molly warmly; she's happy to see her there. Her real intention for these book club meetings is to build a bond with the other women in her community. And she isn't trying to be sexist or exclusionary—men are certainly welcome if they choose to join—but Ruby knows that a safe, accepting place for women to congregate, talk, and break bread is nothing to sneeze at. It's something she wants to create on Shipwreck Key, and it's something she desperately wants for herself.

"So this guy was basically ripping you apart on your own Instagram post?" Heather asks Marigold in a hushed whisper as everyone waits to get started. "Who the hell does he think he is?"

Marigold shrugs a narrow shoulder and lifts an eyebrow like the guy in question isn't worth the effort of raising two shoulders or two eyebrows. "Who do any of them think they are?"

"Goldie," Heather says, lifting her wine glass to her lips. "You are a wonder to me. A woman as gorgeous as you should not have to put up with that kind of BS when it comes to men."

Marigold shakes her head emphatically. "It has nothing to do with beauty," she insists, holding up an elegant hand with long, tapered fingers. "No woman should have to deal with the scrutiny of a man on social media when it comes to her looks. No woman should have complete strangers feeling comfortable enough that they can voice their opinions about her aging, her place in society, or her value. That is one hill I will absolutely die on, and I'm already halfway there." She laughs at her own joke.

Heather bows her head slightly in deference. "Thank you for giving a voice to this. Seriously. Every time I post a picture of myself in a bikini on my Instagram, I have some creep sliding into my DMs, or commenting on how I need to give up and stop being so thirsty for attention."

Ruby is listening to their conversation, but this is where she excuses herself. It's not that the topic doesn't fascinate her—it does. As a woman aging very publicly and as someone who has had her appearance dissected by strangers, Ruby knows that this matters. But she needs to get the ball rolling here, so she steps over to the table where the food is and turns to face the small gathering of women.

"Ladies," Ruby says, clapping her hands together. "Thank you so much for coming this evening, and I want to welcome you to the first of what I hope will be many meetings of the Marooned With a Book Club. I know we haven't officially chosen our first book, so tonight I'm hoping we can just chat, get to know one another, and vote on our first pick."

Molly leans back in her chair, looking around at the other women. "Uh, Ruby?" she interrupts, raising the hand that isn't holding a wine glass. "I think we all basically know each other. This island isn't much bigger than your fist."

Ruby should have counted on this, given that Shipwreck Key isn't exactly a booming metropolis, but she still pauses and glances at everyone briefly. "Okay, then how about we just mingle a bit more, and you can vote on the three books I've selected as possibilities for our next meeting. I have them all there to browse on that table," she says, pointing to where she's chosen three books and laid them out next to scraps of paper and pencils. "And if you want to leave your vote in that little box there, then I'll email you all later with the book that we select."

"I see you went with the Monica Lewinsky book," Molly says loudly and to the room at large. She really is a woman who just presents herself exactly as she is at all times without fear or shame, and Ruby loves this about her. "Any particular reason?"

Ruby tries to keep her face neutral. "No," she says, "no reason." Though this is untrue. Dexter North has gotten into her head, and if she's being honest, she wants to read his work--but only if some other force is pushing her to do it. It makes no sense, even in her own mind, but if the book club is reading it and discussing it, then it's not just her picking it up and forcing herself to turn the pages as she gags at the way Dexter peels back the layers of a former president's love life. "I just thought it might be a compelling read."

Heather and Marigold have moved down the length of the table, filling their small paper plates with bites and nibbles, and now they perch on the edge of two chairs, their eyes on Ruby.

"Are we comfortable with that topic?" Heather asks boldly, her plate balanced in one hand and her clear plastic wine cup in the other. "The whole 'president's mistress' trope?"

Ruby can't help it: she laughs. "Thank you for calling it a trope, Heather," she says, feeling her guard drop like a curtain at the end of a play. "You have no idea how much that lightens my mood and endears you to me."

Heather winks at her conspiratorially, and Ruby knows that this is just the beginning of new and interesting friendships with all of these women.

Ruby takes a deep breath. "I think this is a place for honesty," she says. "At least I want it to be."

"Well, I'm always going to tell you how it is," Molly says, crossing one denim clad leg over the other and letting her Birkenstock sandal dangle from her bare foot. "I've been called a lot of things, but 'pussy-foot' isn't one of 'em."

Heather laughs. "Truer words were never spoken."

"Remember when you brought that last husband into my shop?" Molly asks, nodding at Heather. "And I told you he looked like he could handle either a pacemaker or Viagra, but not both?"

Marigold sputters and the wine she's sipping spews out everywhere.

Flustered, Vanessa stands up and reaches for a stack of napkins, handing one to each book club member for good measure. Tilly sits in her chair next to Vanessa's, looking slightly bored.

"How could I forget?" Heather laughs, tears coming to her eyes as she tries not to knock her plate off her lap. "And you weren't wrong, sadly. Rest in peace, Jacob Edwin Polymer the third." She bows her head in a moment of reverence.

"So which was it?" Marigold nudges her with an elbow. "Did the pacemaker or the Viagra finally do him in?"

"Let's just say that he took a lickin', but he couldn't keep tickin'," Heather says with a smirk. The women all roar with laughter and Heather shakes her head. "I tease, I tease," she shouts over the laughter. "Jacob was a wonderful man. Of course we were only married for eighty-six days, and I would imagine he was far more lively in the years before WWII, but..."

"Oh, stop!" Marigold says, wiping away the tears from her own eyes. "You've seriously married a man old enough to be your grandfather?"

Heather pauses and shoots Marigold a serious look before cracking and breaking into laughter again. "More often than the Kardashians have gotten plastic surgery!"

Even Molly is chuckling at this exchange, though she looks a little scandalized. "Listen, ladies," she finally says, sweeping her hand through her unkempt graying hair—a habit Ruby has noticed. "I'm not sure I'm going to be able to keep up with you lot. I married Rodney in 1975 and he was the love of my life." The room gets quiet and Molly clears her throat, leaning forward and putting her elbows on her splayed knees. "When he was killed on the water seven years later, I thought I wouldn't go on. But I did. And I never found love again. I don't read romances, and I don't believe in spewing hogwash. I won't be hornswoggled or bamboozled, and I don't suffer fools."

Heather looks appropriately chagrined. There is no way that she and Molly would ever move in the same circles outside of this room, and anyone can see that of all the women, Molly is the least polished—at least on the outside. Marigold, with her long, yoga-toned limbs and strong bone structure, is more cosmopolitan and worldly than most of them, and even Ruby's daughters have traveled the world and been exposed to fashion, food, human nature, different cultures, and life. But there's a balance to this small gathering of women sitting together in the bookstore: Ruby, well-traveled and known around the world. Vanessa and Tilly, one quiet and sweet, the other quiet and brooding, but both observing the goings on around them without imposing their own personalities on the group just yet. Heather, bombastic in speech, but obviously vulnerable in ways that she doesn't like to show. Marigold, serious, sharp-eyed and determined to be heard, regardless of whether people still want to hear what she has to say now that she's not just a pretty face. And Molly, salt of the earth, honest to a fault, and completely guileless.

Ruby smiles at them. Already she is growing to love this group of faces, and the feeling of being amongst women who laugh, talk, and joke is thrilling to her. Aside from Sunday and Helen, most of the female friendships in her adult life have been ones that revolve around politics or the alliances of husbands who lead countries and governments, but this group is hers and hers alone.

"Okay, truth time. The real reason I wanted to nominate the Dexter North book is that I don't want to read it alone," Ruby says, her eyes landing on each of the women in turn. "I found out recently that he's doing a book about my husband and...some of his personal choices," she says, nearly choking on the words. "And obviously Mr. North will be coming for me. Either literally or metaphorically—maybe both."

Molly's face hardens as she listens. "So we're reading him to find out what kind of dirt he likes to put in his books?"

Ruby sandwiches her hands between her knees and nods. "Essentially. I want to know what's coming."

"Then we'll read it," Heather says with a firm nod. "Easy-peasy, that's our choice. We'll read this guy's book, and by the time he gets here —if he comes to Shipwreck Key—*he* won't know what's coming."

"In my experience, they rarely do," Marigold adds, inspecting her cuticles.

"So should we order more copies of that particular book?" Vanessa asks softly, her voice floating through the room like the tinkling of wind chimes.

"I think the peanut gallery has spoken," Molly says, standing up. "Order me a copy, if you will, and I'll swing by to pay for it. Now, if you all don't mind, I should call it a night. I'm up at three o'clock to get my baking in before The Scuttlebutt opens."

Ruby stands up and walks over to Molly, reaching out for her. The women clasp one another's hands briefly and then Molly nods at everyone else before making a beeline for the front door.

"I'm going to order ten copies of Dexter North's book right now." Vanessa stands up and gathers her long dress in both hands, stepping around the chairs as she goes.

That leaves Ruby alone with Heather, Marigold, Tilly, Athena, and Harlow. On the table are three bottles of wine and plenty of bite size hors d'oeuvres.

Heather and Marigold look at one another.

"Real question time," Heather says, waiting for Ruby to sit down again. "This book—if and when it comes out—how are you going to feel about everyone knowing the ins and outs of your marriage? Because I've seen a couple of interviews with Dexter North, and he does not give up. That man will take a deep dive into the vault of your soul."

Marigold bumps Heather with her elbow, much as she had earlier, only this time it's a warning nudge.

Ruby nods, considering the question. "Well," she says, biting her lower lip. Her eyes skitter across the room to where Banks is standing, looking as though he's not listening to a word that's being said, though she's more than certain that he is. "I think that whether I'm ready for the world to hear it all or not, they're eventually going to. I can cooperate, or I can bury my head in the sand and have no say in what Dexter North writes about me or my husband or our life. And I don't think I want that."

"Exactly," Marigold says, slapping her own thigh. "Control your own narrative, or the rest of the world will do it for you. I'm a huge proponent of not letting anyone put words in your mouth."

Ruby shrugs. "I don't know what I'll say. I don't always know what I feel...but Jack has been gone for over a year now, and it's time for me to start untangling the mess he left behind."

"That's incredibly brave, Ruby." Marigold nods as she watches Ruby's pained expression. "You never asked to share your trauma with the world, the world just decided it had a right to know every last detail."

Ruby gives a soft laugh. "There are plenty of things we never ask for, and unfortunately, we don't have any say about how we work through them. I'm just one of many going through something ugly while people watch."

"Well," Heather says decisively, giving Marigold a quick glance. "You won't go through it alone. We're not a mighty book club just yet, but we are a gang of gals with some history behind us, and we'll be right here while you sort things out--if you want us to be here."

Ruby nods quickly and emphatically, tears filling her green eyes. "I do." She looks at the other women, her daughters included, and thinks of Molly and the four decades she's spent living a romance-free, no nonsense life on this island after losing her husband. The sound of Vanessa and Athena (who has gone up front to talk books with Vanessa) chatting at the computer at the front of the store filters back to her, and in that moment, there is nothing sweeter to Ruby than the sound of women's voices. She loves seeing women work together, and she adores everything about female companionship. Her heart is warm just being surrounded by these strong, funny, interesting women. "I absolutely want you all to be here while I sort things out," Ruby says, feeling certain that this book club is going to be the best thing that's happened to her in years. "One thousand percent."

Ruby

Ruby is halfway through reading Dexter North's book when her assistant gets a message from his assistant requesting a time and place to meet. Ruby has spent some time mentally preparing herself to sit down with the man who intends to turn over every leaf and look under every rock as he examines her life--or Jack's life, rather—but in essence, what's left of her marriage. He's going to sift through the detritus and see what remains to find out if there's anything worth massaging and turning into word gold.

Marigold Pim walks into Marooned With a Book, holding Dexter North's tome under one arm.

"I finished it," she says, slapping the hardcover book on the front counter. "And you know what? It's damn good."

Ruby nods. "I know. I'd be completely done with it myself, but I've been busy with my girls and with running the shop, and whenever I climb into bed with Dexter North—"

Marigold moans and makes a blissed-out face. "I should be so lucky."

Ruby laughs, realizing what she's said. "Okay, whenever I climb into bed *with his book*, I pass out after a page or two. My only reading time is early in the morning over coffee."

Marigold pulls her phone out of her crossbody bag and starts tapping away. "But have you seen this man? Good god, Ruby. He's gorgeous."

Naturally, Dexter North is handsome. Of course he is. She's seen his black-and-white photo on the book jacket, and she knows he's good looking.

"Do you think there's any way I'll be able to, like," Ruby pushes the air with her hand like she's shoving something out of the way, "just move *past* the fact that he's extremely attractive and feel unselfconscious as he pokes and prods around in my personal life?"

Marigold frowns. She's still holding her phone in her hand, which she turns around to show Ruby. On the screen is Dexter North in a cream-colored linen blazer and a tight black t-shirt. His sandy blonde hair is blown up and away from his chiseled face, which is covered by a dusting of five o'clock shadow. He's standing outside on a street corner, and his eyes are focused on something in the distance.

"If you can look past this level of hotness, then you're a stronger woman than most," Marigold says, swiping at the phone screen and coming up with another photo, which she shows Ruby. "It's hard to find fault with a man who looks like he's spent time on a runway and who can sit down and write a book that keeps you up all night, turning pages."

"Smart and attractive *are* quite the combo," Ruby says, feeling her heart sink. Why can't the person writing the book that's going to blow the doors off her heart be a woman? Or at least a completely unappealing man? It would be so much easier to put the whole thing in a box and handle it at a distance if she wasn't going to have to sit across from someone who looks like a young Robert Redford.

Marigold puts her phone back into her purse and leans on the counter with both elbows, leveling her gaze at Ruby. From the side of the room, Banks flicks a gaze in their direction, clearly deems this close and quiet discussion as nothing noteworthy, and continues his silent vigil.

"Listen," Marigold says, tapping the counter with one short, red nail. "You need to stay ahead of this. Since the beginning of time, women have used their looks to cast a spell over men and get what they want. You know how that game works—you're a stunning woman."

Ruby starts to demur, but she knows that Marigold isn't just blowing hot air up her skirt. Women *do* know how to use what's been given to them, and Ruby perhaps better than most. After all, she'd parlayed sunny, all-American good looks into a career in commercials and then into a life as a First Lady, so to act like she had no awareness of her fine features, her long, graceful neck, or her innate composure would be disingenuous.

"So you're saying I should use my looks to manipulate him?"

Marigold gives a shake of her loose, auburn hair. "No. I'm saying that you understand how the game works. Don't let *him* use the power of his good looks to loosen your lips—either pair."

Ruby guffaws; she wasn't expecting Marigold to be so forward, but she's not complaining. One of the qualities that's served her well in every area of her life is a solid—and sometimes bawdy—sense of humor. She recalls one time in Mexico City where she and the First Lady of Mexico shared too much tequila and told the filthiest jokes they could think of. Even the Secret Service agents on duty had cracked smiles as they tried to appear detached and impartial to that conversation.

"Got it," Ruby says, patting the counter with both hands. "Don't tell him my secrets and don't drop my drawers just because he's hot."

The women lock eyes and start giggling like teenagers.

"We've all been there," Marigold says, shaking her head. "Lord have mercy. I've made some terrible choices in the presence of extremely fine men. And when they're brilliant *on top* of looking like a dessert buffet..." She drops her chin like she's in prayer, then lifts her head quickly, tossing her hair back as she looks right into Ruby's eyes with laser-like focus. "All I'm saying is you know his game. You've played it. No need to give him everything—or anything—he wants. Decide before you meet him what you're willing to talk about, and then stick to it."

There is a moment as Ruby stands there, listening to the ocean in the distance, which is barely audible above the 80s Spotify playlist that she has playing over the shop's speakers, that she realizes she's a former First Lady taking advice from a former supermodel. The whole thing tickles her that, at their age, they're still standing around, sharing age-old wisdom like a couple of young girls. It's one of the things she loves most and has missed the most over the past couple of decades about having a group of girlfriends, and though she and Marigold haven't known each other long, she feels a rush of warmth towards the woman.

"You're right," Ruby says. "My assistant has already heard from his assistant, and we're trying to set up a time to talk."

Marigold's groomed brow lifts just a hair. "You have an assistant?" She stands up straight and looks around the shop. "I want one of those. Do they organize your life and answer your emails and stuff?"

"In fact, she pretty much does. I've never met her in person, but Ursula is in New York. She sifts through my emails and answers a lot of them herself, but she also lets me know of any invitations to dinners, banquets, events, etcetera. And she doesn't plan my day-to-day life— obviously things are pretty laid-back here on Shipwreck Key, plus I can manage getting up, making my own coffee, and dragging my tired butt into the bookstore, but she coordinates dates and plans and whatnot. Having an assistant is a luxury, but for now it's nice to have her."

"A virtual assistant..." Marigold says, twisting her long hair with one hand and letting it unravel down her back. "I could use someone to weed out the trolls on my Instagram posts." She rolls her eyes. "Sometimes that takes half my day, just deleting and responding to stupid posts. But we're talking about you. Let's get you ready to meet this guy. Do you want him to come here, or are you going to him?"

Ruby thinks about this. Having him on Shipwreck Key feels weirdly invasive. She isn't keen on watching him walk up and down Seadog Lane, stopping people to ask them what they think of having a former First Lady on the island. *Nope, nope, nope.* She doesn't want that.

"Maybe I could go to New York?" Ruby says, but it sounds like a question. Then an idea hits her. "Wait, it says in the back of his book that he splits his time between New York and Christmas Key."

Marigold does the eyebrow lift thing again. "As in the Christmas Key that's just a short boat ride away?"

"The very one."

"That could be a neutral meeting ground. I'm just saying."

Ruby nods. "You're right. I need to call Ursula."

* * *

Ursula is a voice on the phone. She is words typed in an email. And occasionally she is even a floating head on a Zoom call, but most importantly, she is cheerful, capable, and handles the details that pertain to Ruby's life *off* the island.

"Christmas Key," Ursula says. The tapping of her computer keys is audible in the background. "We're talking about a trip that's basically south—well, kind of south and a jog to the west—and I can hire you a boat to pick you up at Shipwreck Key and deliver you there to their dock. There's a B&B on the island if you want to make it an overnight trip, and honestly, Mrs. Hudson, these pictures are gorgeous. It's a super cute place."

Ruby is chewing on a pencil as she looks out the window of the bookstore. On Seadog Lane, she spots Bev Byer pulling a dolly up onto the sidewalk and into the front door of The Frog's Grog. He's got a red bandanna tied around his gray hair, and his arms are muscular and strong.

"I think that's my best option," Ruby says, setting the pencil on the counter and standing up straight. "Could you possibly arrange a date and time with Dexter North's assistant? I have no idea if he's even down here in Florida at the moment, but I'm sure he'll be willing to make it happen. He probably expected this to be more of a challenge to set up, but I want to get it on the calendar and just get this first meeting out of the way."

"Certainly," Ursula says, still tapping away. "I'm composing an email to his assistant as we speak, and I'll let you know as soon as I hear anything."

"Ursula, you're the best." Ruby thanks her and ends the call, walking out the front door distractedly.

Banks is stationed in the sun this morning, and he's finally given in to the harsh change of seasons, switching from black pants and a button up shirt to a pair of sharply creased khaki shorts and a golf shirt. Florida in May is no place for black pants, and Ruby is glad that he's not going to die of a heatstroke on her watch.

"Hey, Bev!" Ruby calls out, looking both ways as she crosses the street.

"Lady Hudson," Bev says with a deep, dramatic bow. He sets his dolly upright and leans against it as she approaches. "To what do I owe this honor?"

"Hey," Ruby says, breathless as she reaches him. "I wanted to know if you've ever been to Christmas Key."

"Oy," he says, giving her a nod. "Of course. One of my cousins lives on Christmas Key, and I took a lady friend there once for a long weekend. She loved Christmas, and while the holiday is a bit overdone for my taste, I fancied the pants off of this girl, so I went. Was lovely. You been?"

Ruby shakes her head, pushing a stray lock of hair behind one ear. "Never. But I'm thinking of making a quick trip. Maybe two days. Apparently I can hire a boat to come pick me up and take me there, but I thought you might know of someone here I could pay for the trip instead."

"No need," Bev says, adjusting his bandanna with one meaty hand. "I'll take you. When would you like to go?"

"Oh," Ruby says, surprised. "I can pay you. I would never ask for a favor that big."

"Don't even think of it as a favor--think of it as repayment for hiring my sullen and sometimes petulant granddaughter to sit around Marooned With a Book like the unofficial store cat," he says, referring to Tilly, who he's raised on his own since she was only six years old. "I should visit my cousin anyhow. Just give me a heads-up on when, alright? With twenty-four hours notice, I can make sure I'm fully staffed here. If you're wanting to stay over, I'll bunk with my cousin Bonnie, and there's a real nice B&B there you can book."

"Oh, Tilly is a joy to have around the shop," Ruby says, and she means it. Her hilarious asides and non sequiturs are exactly what Ruby would have expected from a slightly younger teenager, and truth be told, having Tilly around sometimes makes her feel like a high school teacher, which is the one thing she feels like she missed out on doing in life. "And thank you so much for the offer to take me over, Bev," Ruby says, feeling a rush of gratitude. "I'll get back to you as soon as I know more."

* * *

The water is smooth and the ride is fast. Bev steers them deftly across the open Gulf of Mexico four days later, the bow of his boat pointed toward Christmas Key.

From her seat near the stern, Ruby holds her hat in place against the wind, watching the horizon through a pair of dark sunglasses. Banks is there next to her, for once relaxed and seemingly at ease. He sits with his elbows on his knees, talking loudly to be heard over the motor every time Bev turns to him to say something about the boat, the water, or the abundance of grouper to be caught in the Keys. It makes Ruby smile to listen to them; she's always charmed by the way other people make small talk—particularly men. In her experience, they start with finding some common ground: sports, fishing, golf, politics, and, if all else fails, the weather. Jack had been a master at that, talking just as easily to the man shining his shoes as to a visiting dignitary. He always had a seemingly endless stream of topics on hand to talk about, and it had amazed Ruby the way he put everyone at ease.

It takes about an hour to reach Christmas Key, and as they approach the small tropical island, Ruby feels a sense of anticipation. Banks draws himself to attention, scanning the shoreline, and Bev slows the motor, cutting it altogether as they drift right up to the small dock. Banks steps off first and takes a walk up the dock and onto Main Street, where he looks back and forth. As soon as he feels sure about their surroundings, he gives Bev a nod. Bev ties them up and then helps Ruby onto shore.

"Hello! Welcome!" A brunette in her thirties with a huge smile and a toddler on one hip approaches. She's got her long hair pulled back into a braid that spills out from under a blue Yankees baseball hat, and she's wearing a sundress with a pair of flip-flops. Banks walks up to her and they chat briefly before the woman turns back to the dock and walks up to Ruby.

"I'm Holly Baxter-Cruz," the woman says, extending a hand to Ruby. "And this is my daughter, Stella."

Ruby shakes Holly's hand and then reaches out and takes Stella's small, soft hand in hers gently. The baby looks at her with wide eyes, though she's clearly just curious and not the least bit afraid. Stella's small dimpled hands and the way her dark, shiny hair sweeps gently over her little head sends a shock through Ruby's heart. It seems like only yesterday that her own girls were this size, and every time she sees a baby up close lately, she's reminded of how quickly time slips away, almost unnoticed.

"Thank you so much for having me," Ruby says, smiling at Holly, who she already knows is the mayor of Christmas Key and the owner of the island's B&B. "I've heard so much about the island, but this is my first visit."

Holly steps back as Bev hoists two bags from the boat and hands Banks a third piece of luggage.

"Well, we are absolutely thrilled to have you here," Holly says, turning to the men. "And you must be Mr. Banks," she says to Banks, nodding at him. "I have no idea how to greet a Secret Service agent." Her smile fades and she turns to Ruby with a frown. "Am I allowed to talk to him?"

For some reason this strikes Ruby as hilarious, and she laughs. "Of course you are."

Holly looks mortified. "Oh my god. I'm so sorry," she says, putting her free hand over her mouth and shifting her daughter to the other hip. "I didn't mean to treat you like a seeing eye dog. I just didn't know the protocol and I--"

Banks cuts her off with a friendly smile, and even takes off his sunglasses, which Ruby knows that he rarely does. "Ma'am, please don't worry about it," he says, wiggling his fingers at Stella and getting the first grin from the baby that she's given since their boat docked. "I know it's weird when you see a bunch of serious looking men and women in dark glasses, and a lot of people think we're like the guards at Buckingham Palace, but we can definitely talk to the public. And we do. But when things are hectic, we stay extremely focused."

Holly relaxes. "Oh, good. I was hoping that you were going to be able to enjoy the island and get to know us. I promise we're all friendly."

Holly is about to greet Bev when a woman who appears to be about eighty-five comes walking in their direction, waving both arms in the air. She looks like she's about to tell them her house is on fire, but when she gets closer, she breaks into a wide smile and claps her hands together.

"My goodness, if it isn't the First Lady," she says with just the slightest touch of an Italian accent. "You are so much prettier in person than you were in that magazine I saw you in. They did you no favors with that boring black suit, honey."

Again, Ruby laughs. Everything that's happened since her feet touched soil here on Christmas Key has tickled her. "Believe me, I told them the black suit was a mistake," she says, walking over to shake the woman's hand. "But when *Vogue* tells you to wear the black suit, you wear the black suit. I'm Ruby Hudson, by the way," she says, taking the woman's gnarled hand in her own.

"Maria Agnelli," the woman says firmly, wrapping both of her hands around Ruby's and holding on. "Listen," she says, starting to walk without letting go of Ruby, which forces Ruby to follow. "Let's have a cup of coffee—it's on me. I want to hear everything about the White House. Did you find out who killed Kennedy while you lived there? Is there anything there on the bookshelves about Eisenhower? Did he leave any family photo albums behind?"

"Oh," Ruby says, looking back at Holly for help. "I'm not sure..."

"What a cutie that man was," Mrs. Agnelli says, guiding Ruby towards the coffee shop. "I always had a bit of a crush on old Dwight, but my husband never liked to hear about it. He thought Eisenhower looked like a frog—can you believe that?"

Holly is stifling her own laughter behind one hand when a short, round, red-headed woman in her fifties comes out of the coffee shop that's right in front of them. She throws both hands in the air, and her face becomes an animated mask of joy.

"Well, if it isn't my favorite cousin!" she squeals, walking as quickly as she can on her little wedge sandals. Bev drops both bags and opens his arms. He scoops the woman up as they both laugh and cry. "It's been too long, darlin'—I was starting to worry about you something fierce!"

"Don't you even worry, Bonnie. I'm right as rain. Fit as a fiddle. Happy as a clam." Bev sets her down and they beam at one another.

"Holly," the redhead says, turning to the mayor. "This is my number one, all-time favorite cousin, Bev Byer. He runs a little shack of a beach bar on Shipwreck Key called The Frog's Grog. Quite the place. And he's an old pirate at heart, in case you can't tell."

Bev runs a hand over his graying mustache and winks at Holly. "Lovely to meet you, miss."

Bonnie looks at Ruby then with a stunned smile. "Holy crow, it's the First Lady."

"Former," Ruby clarifies, reaching out to shake Bonnie's hand.

"I'm Bonnie Lane. Resident bigmouth and life of the party. Welcome to Christmas Key!"

"And this is Banks," Ruby says, introducing him to Bonnie. "We don't want to be any trouble at all, so please just treat us like anyone who shows up to enjoy your beautiful island."

"Let's get you all checked into the B&B," Holly says, switching Stella to her other hip again and leading the way up the street. "This is Mistletoe Morning Brew here." She waves a hand as they walk past the coffee shop. "And we have a little bookstore right next door."

Ruby looks at the shop with interest. A Sleighful of Books is a long and narrow store, with a front window filled by a display of new releases. Next to it is the B&B, with three steps that lead up to a porch with a railing, and glass front doors that open into a light-filled lobby. Ruby stands on the porch and looks at the opposite side of the street, where Scissors & Ribbons salon looks out onto the paved road, and down near the end of the street—next to the dock where their boat is tied up—North Star Cigars sits with its front door propped open. The sounds of tropical steel drum music pour from a speaker over the door of the cigar shop.

"Our island's radio station is located just above the shop," Holly explains, looking back at North Star Cigars as she holds the door of the B&B open for Ruby. On Holly's hip, Stella kicks her bare feet and waves her arms in the air, making a happy gurgling noise. "Our resident deejay is seventeen and he keeps us entertained with all kinds of music."

Inside the lobby, Bonnie is behind the counter, tapping on the keyboard. She hands Ruby and Banks the keys to their respective rooms. Ruby had insisted that he didn't need to be right next to her—after all,

Christmas Key is a tiny island filled with residents whose average age is over seventy, but he insisted.

As Ruby picks up her travel bag and follows Holly, she can hear Bonnie and Bev chatting about family stuff and she smiles, secretly thrilled that her own trip to Christmas Key has afforded Bev the opportunity to visit with his cousin.

"I understand you're meeting with Dexter North," Holly says in a hushed voice as she walks Ruby to the door of her room. Banks swipes his key card and lets himself into his own room with a nod at the women, disappearing as the door closes behind him. Ruby knows the protocol: if she's ready to go anywhere, she'll call him.

"I am." Ruby smiles at Stella and reaches out again to touch the baby's bare toes. She's adorable, with deep dimples and bright eyes, and there's a yearning in Stella that she knows will someday soon manifest as a desire for grandchildren. But for the moment, she's still unwilling to admit that she's even old enough to be a grandmother.

"He's such an interesting character," Holly says, taking off her baseball cap and handing it to Stella so that she can fold the fabric in her hands and chew on the brim of the hat. "Dexter bought one of our tiny homes here about six months ago, and now he shows up on Christmas Key a few times a year and takes his laptop everywhere he goes. He's friendly enough, but he's always writing something, so we mostly just stay out of his way."

Ruby smiles and shifts her bag from one hand to the other, still holding onto the key card.

"I'm sorry," Holly says, looking at her feet as Stella throws the Yankees hat on the ground with a giggle. "I'm sure people meet you and just babble on and on. Please, go in and enjoy the room. Let me know if there's anything at all we can do to make your stay more comfortable."

Ruby bends at the waist and picks up the Yankees cap, handing it back to Stella. "You aren't babbling," she assures the younger woman truthfully. "We're just chatting. I can't wait to see the whole island, and I will definitely let you know if we need anything." She turns her attention to the baby. "And thank you for the personal escort to my room, Miss Stella."

Christmas Key is just as magical as Ruby has heard it is. After a short rest in her room, she and Banks borrow the B&B's golf cart for a few hours and drive around the outer edge of the island, along a street called December Drive, stopping to look at the beautiful, crystal clear water, and white sand. And on the north side of the island, they slow down to look at a cluster of "tiny homes" with little front porches, window boxes filled with colorful flowers, and views of the water. She assumes that this is where Dexter North lives.

Banks brings her all the way around to the island's only real restaurant, the Jingle Bell Bistro, and they park in the sandy, unpaved lot as the sun starts to inch lower in the sky.

As promised in his email, Dexter North is waiting at a table on the restaurant's huge porch at six o'clock; he stands as Ruby approaches.

"It's such a pleasure to meet you," Dexter says, shaking her hand as he holds her gaze. "And I so appreciate you making the trip to Christmas Key, which is my own private version of paradise—minus all the candy canes and tinsel." He gives her a lopsided grin. "I would have never dreamed of asking you to come all the way out here, but it's the perfect place to talk."

Dexter has already stepped around the table to pull out Ruby's chair and she sits as he slides it in. There are eyes on them, though the porch isn't full of diners or gawkers. Banks settles at a table about ten feet away with his back to the water.

"The trip was no problem at all," Ruby assures him, still measuring every word that comes out of her mouth. After all, she has no clue what Dexter is already formulating in his head. What's his angle? What information will he pry from her if she has a glass of wine and starts to feel comfortable? Instead of letting her guard down even an inch, Ruby puts her elbows on the table and leans forward, her eyes boring into his hotly. "I wanted to meet face to face and find out what you're after."

Just then, a woman with a deep Irish accent approaches holding two bottles of water, one a clear glass bottle of still water, the other a green glass bottle full of bubbly San Pellegrino.

"Welcome to the Jingle Bell Bistro," the woman says formally. "We're thrilled to have you here. Could I start you with a glass of water, or perhaps a bottle of wine?"

Dexter and Ruby both ask for San Pellegrino and a few minutes to decide, then pick up their menus like two cowboys at a shoot-out at high noon, each eyeing the other to see what the next move is.

Once they've both decided on the shrimp and grits—a pile of yellow corn grits covered in Key West pink shrimp, heirloom tomatoes, crispy bacon, mushrooms, and red gravy, and a bottle of chilled Prosecco, which Ruby promises herself she'll only sip—they eyeball one another again. It feels like a standoff.

"So," Dexter says, pausing so the sound of the surf and the crashing of the waves fills the silence between them. The Irish woman who took their order circles the patio, stopping by the few other tables to talk with her customers. Everyone is studiously ignoring Dexter and Ruby. "So," he begins again. "What's your life like now?"

Ruby blinks twice. "Now?" She isn't used to being asked about her own life. In fact, she's far more accustomed to being asked about what it was like living in the White House, how many of her outfits she got for free while she was First Lady, and what Jack liked to wear when he wasn't in the public eye (gym shorts, a beat-up Harvard t-shirt, and a pair of leather slippers, for the record, but Ruby would never share that).

"Yes," Dexter says, leaning back slightly as their server approaches with an uncorked bottle of Prosecco, which she pours into two large wine glasses.

"In a big glass, just like they serve it in Italy," the Irish woman says, pouring with a flourish. She sets down a basket of bread and butter. "And this is the soda bread my husband's grandmother made when he was a wee lad. Secret recipe," she says with a wink, walking away before either Dexter or Ruby can comment.

"My life now, is..." Ruby squints out at the water for a second, then looks back at him. "Quieter. I own a small bookshop on Shipwreck Key, and I bought a house there. My girls are both currently staying with me, and I fall asleep most nights reading a book."

"Mine?" An amused smile quirks at the corners of Dexter's full lips. He's even more handsome than in the photos Marigold pulled up on her phone, and for their meeting, he's chosen a pale blue button-up shirt with the sleeves rolled to the elbows and a pair of navy blue dress shorts. His hair is wind-swept, and he smells—even from across the table—deliciously like soap and aftershave.

"Yes, yours," Ruby admits. "I'm sorry to say that I did fall asleep while reading it, but not because it was boring."

"It's never a compliment when a lady falls asleep during your best work," Dexter says, looking entertained but also like a little boy who's getting away with saying a naughty word in front of a teacher.

"I'm sure it's a rare occurrence that a woman falls asleep with you on her chest," Ruby assures him, lifting her eyebrows just slightly as she reaches for her glass of Prosecco. *Dear God,* she thinks, *you've been in Dexter North's presence for ten minutes and already you've slipped into innuendos and doublespeak. Sip, sip, sip, Ruby,* she reminds herself, *don't guzzle.* She needs to not let the bubbles go to her head. "Or with your book open on her chest, that is," she adds after an intentional beat.

Dexter's face cracks and he laughs out loud. "Indeed. So you're living on Shipwreck Key, which I've yet to visit. Lots of pirates?"

Ruby tips her head from side to side. "A few. Mostly pirate-themed shops and pirate street names. Scallywag Street. Landlubber Lane. Very charming, and the people are wonderful. I'm making friends."

"With the pirates?"

"Yes. And with the women. I've formed a book club, and I'm building a little community for myself, which is what you do when you start over somewhere new, right? I mean, you kind of have to."

Dexter glances around as if he's seeing the Jingle Bell Bistro for the first time. "I suppose. When I come down here I usually keep to myself. I'm pretty self-sufficient when I'm here, holed up in my tiny home, and I like to keep it simple: a few books to read, a laptop to write, and as little time spent on my phone as possible. I deplore social media, hate answering emails, and refuse to text anyone the second my feet touch sand on Christmas Key."

"You don't hang out with the locals?"

"Here and there. I like the bar that's tucked away from Main Street. It's right on the beach, and the owner used to play guitar for some of the biggest rock bands of the seventies. Everyone gathers there and I've gotten to know a few people that way."

"Beer and music—the great equalizers."

Dexter chuckles. "I suppose so." He sips his wine and takes a piece of bread from the basket between them. The sun drops a few more inches, sending warm rays over the railing of the porch and bathing their white linen-covered table in golden light. "But I want to talk about the Ruby Hudson who is finding her way after life in the White House. After everything."

Ruby's heart beats faster. Of course he wants to talk about the big stuff: being married to the president, Jack's death, the affair, her life as a widow. She swallows hard and takes a piece of bread that she isn't sure she can even eat. Ruby casts a glance at Dexter's face and he's watching her intently.

"Before we talk at length, I want some things on the table up front," Ruby says, feeling her resolve strengthen. "I want to know what the exact angle is on this book. I want to have final say on which of my words and stories are included. I'm not going to sit here for two days and talk to you if, in the end, what you want is just to compile salacious tidbits about my late husband or our marriage. I don't want any part of that."

Dexter lowers his hazel eyes and nods for a long moment as if he's processing her words. When he looks back at her, it's with a piercing gaze. "My book is going to be about President Hudson...through your eyes."

Ruby is completely taken aback. "Through *my* eyes? But I'm not going to be interesting to your readers. You wrote about Monica Lewinsky and she herself is a point of interest—I'm nothing like that. I assumed that this book would be about, you know, about...my husband's..."

"*Side piece*, I think is what the kids are calling it these days." Dexter doesn't back down, but keeps his eyes locked on hers. "Sorry for being so crass."

Ruby gives a surprised laugh. "Wow. Right to it. Okay." Instead of sipping her Prosecco delicately, she takes a hard swig and sets the glass down. "So that topic will be covered?"

Dexter lifts a shoulder and lets it fall dispassionately. "Of course. I want to find out what makes Ruby Hudson tick. And through you, we'll get a totally different view of the White House, of the presidency, and of what life is like as the wife of the most powerful man in the free world."

"And as the widow of the most powerful man in the free world," Ruby adds softly, turning her wine glass around by its stem as she watches the bubbles dance.

"Of course," Dexter says. "I don't mean to be inconsiderate, Ruby. I started my career as an investigative reporter, and I pride myself on my ability to dive into a subject so deeply that I sometimes forget where I am. I become completely engrossed in, say, what you wore to the senior prom. Your thoughts as you were giving birth to your first child. The last fight you had with your husband and whether you resolved it before his death. I want the minutia, but also the intimate details. It helps me to paint a much stronger picture for my readers if I know what wattage the lightbulb is in the lamp on your nightstand as you fall asleep to my words at night."

This little attempt at humor brings Ruby back to the present and she looks right at him again. "I hear you. I'm still not sure that I'm the angle you want."

"*I'm* sure you're the angle I want."

Ruby frowns; she's confused. "What about me screams 'best selling book'?"

Picking up on the serious mood at the table, the restaurant owner sets down their plates of shrimp and grits and disappears without a word. Ruby picks up her fork.

"I want to take a good, hard look at womanhood. I want to find out what sacrifices you made to be the wife of a man who rose to the highest office in the land. I want to understand what made you a prime candidate to be the right-hand woman of a man with his eye on the White House."

"Wait," Ruby says, her fork halfway to her mouth. "You think he *picked* me to be his wife because I satisfied some sort of checklist?"

Dexter busies himself with pushing shrimp and vegetables around his plate. "Doesn't everyone pick a mate—on some deep level—based on a checklist of some sort?"

Ruby takes her first bite of food and chews thoughtfully, thinking about his question. "Okay," she says after swallowing. "I guess so. In some ways."

"What qualities did Jack satisfy for you?"

"Older, wiser, more settled, ready for a family, had goals, swept me off my feet," Ruby says, ticking each item off quickly. "Yeah," she says, shrugging. "I never really looked at it that way, but I guess you're right."

Dexter nods at her like he's glad that she can see his point. "It generally works that way. Every human has needs, either intrinsic or extrinsic —maybe both—and they choose a partner who satisfies as many of those needs as possible. So which did you cover for Jack?"

Ruby eats a bite of shrimp while she considers this. She washes it down with another sip of Prosecco. "Well," she says, setting her glass down. "I was a commercial actress with an English degree from UCLA, so I was reasonably attractive and had an education. I was young and single—no divorces or kids or baggage in that sense—so relatively uncomplicated. And being younger than him also meant that I was likely a good candidate to have his children, which I guess any good politician is probably interested in—either for personal reasons or for optics, but maybe both."

She pauses and lets her eyes fall to the table for a moment. Dismantling herself this way and looking at all of the separate pieces that made her marriageable in Jack's eyes is strange, but she's able to do it without any of the feelings of self-pity that usually accompany her thoughts about what made her *undesirable* enough to him that he wound up in the arms of another woman. Looking at her younger self this way is analytic and it feels honest; looking at herself as their marriage ended is painful and it still feels too close to see it all clearly. Maybe she's not ready for that, but she can handle delving into their early years and assessing the majority of their marriage with ease.

Dexter leans back in his chair and watches Ruby. It's clear that he'd like to ask her more follow-up questions, but they've moved rather quickly into a discussion about some very personal things, and she tries to shoot him a look to let him know that he needs to scale back so that he doesn't lose her.

"Tell me about your bookstore," he says, picking up on the message and changing gears as he forks a few bites of shrimp and grits into his mouth. "What's it called, and what made you go that direction?"

Ruby is ready for a change of subject, so this is an easy transition for her. "It's called 'Marooned With a Book,' and it's really a culmination of a life-long dream. When I was in college I desperately wanted to be a writer and to own a bookstore in the South of France—"

"Oh," Dexter says, looking surprised. "Okay. Do you speak French?"

"Not much," Ruby admits. "I took a few semesters of it and had a dream of moving there and learning the language as I traveled around the countryside, but you know how dreams go when you're twenty-one."

"They can crash pretty hard," Dexter says, reaching for a piece of bread from the basket, which he uses to scoop more grits onto his fork. "When I was twenty-one I wanted to write fiction by day and go to law school at night."

"Law school? Really?"

Dexter nods. "Really. My dad thought that being a novelist was a job for hacks and hucksters, and that I needed something to fall back on. So I thought criminal law would be the way to go."

"What happened?"

"My first book was garbage that no one wanted to read, and I realized that I'm not cut out to write fiction and I hate the law."

Ruby laughs. "Yes, dreams do fizzle when you're young. But honestly, how long ago was that for you...twenty years?" she ventures. It's obvious that Dexter is some years younger than her, she just can't tell how many years.

He gives her a long look. "It was fifteen years ago. I'm thirty-six."

Something in Ruby's heart constricts. It's been years—decades—since she's sought or desired the attention of a man other than Jack, and while Dexter North is incredibly handsome and rather dashing, she hasn't really been thinking of whether or not he finds her attractive or appealing. It's only now that she does the quick math in her head and realizes that he would probably be more interested in her daughters than he ever would be in her that Ruby feels the particular pang of loss that women everywhere start to experience at her age; it's the reminder that her beauty and her sex appeal aren't the first things that men see about her anymore. That they look at her and, if she's lucky, think things like: *Hmm, she looks good for her age.* Or, *Wow, I bet she was hot when she was younger.* Never in her younger years had Ruby imagined that she'd be washed up at the ripe old age of forty-nine, but she feels that way now as she watches the fading sunlight playing across the golden hairs on Dexter's forearms. He's young and vital and sexy, and she's...not. At least not in the eyes of the general public. An inner voice reminds her that she needs to take a page from Marigold Pim's book and embrace herself—at every age—but that's far easier said than done.

"What's on your mind, Ruby?" Dexter asks, his deep voice rubbing against her nerves like a piece of sandpaper brushing smoothly over rough wood. "You look lost in thought."

"Is the book going to tell the world everything that's on my mind, or will it just be about my life?" she asks, narrowing her eyes at him and hoping that her words sound more playful than biting.

In return, Dexter narrows his eyes right back at her. "I'm not sure. I guess it depends on whether what's on your mind will help sell books."

"To be honest, it might. Front page news, everyone," Ruby says jokingly, pretending to shout the headlines like a newsboy on a street corner as she cups her mouth. "The former First Lady is just a regular woman with regular woman problems and feelings! Read all about it!"

Dexter gives her an appreciative smile, but he's watching her the whole time, and Ruby knows he's parsing her facial expressions and words for meaning.

"I want to hear more," Dexter says. "Tell me all about your regular woman problems."

Ruby sighs. "Not over dinner here on the first night. I'll peel back the layers as we go. Maybe," she adds, picking up her wine glass and pointing the forefinger of that hand at him directly. "If you're lucky."

From the corner of her eye, Ruby spies Banks sitting at his table, sipping a beer. She's never seen him relaxed enough to drink a beer while he's on duty, but something about Christmas Key has made her feel loose-limbed and free, and she actually kind of hopes he feels the same way. There is no clear and present danger; there are no bad guys to watch out for.

Dexter clears his throat like he's about to say something and Ruby has a sobering thought: maybe *Dexter* is the clear and present danger. Maybe *he* is the guy she needs to watch out for.

The sun finally sinks below the horizon, and the golden sunlight falls away. Suddenly Ruby and Dexter are just as they are. Without the warm and flattering light, they are simply two people with agendas and fears and worries.

She shivers.

Ruby

Ruby wakes to find a text from Sunday: *Condo is sublet. Car in storage. Boxes packed. All I need is a bikini and some sunglasses and for my place on Shipwreck to be ready. Approximate move-in date is June 15. Tell the locals that they'll be living on the southern outpost of D.C. once we're both there.*

This makes Ruby smile because Sunday isn't wrong: with both the former First Lady and Second Lady and a Secret Service presence, they are essentially bringing D.C. down to the tropics. But Ruby never thinks of herself as part of the political machine, and when she and Sunday are together, forget about it—they're just two girlfriends laughing and drinking wine and doing their thing. Sure, they talk about their husbands and their lives amongst the elite of Washington D.C. the same way other women might talk about their peers on the PTA, but at heart, they're just living their lives and enjoying their friendship like anyone else might.

She sends a quick message back: *I'm so glad you liked the places I picked out. Can't wait for you to get down here!!!*

Dexter is waiting for her at Mistletoe Morning Brew when she arrives. Ruby walks into the small coffee shop at the end of Main Street and pauses to appreciate the decor, which is a riot of color in the form of bursting flowers. The walls are covered with flora and fauna made entirely of tissue paper in a rainbow of hues, and the chalkboard behind the front counter has been decorated with lilies and roses and daffodils in full bloom. On each table is a different colored glass vase filled with fresh-cut flowers, and on the giant front window someone with an abundance of talent has painted a tangled garden that teems with blossoms in every color. It's all quite beautiful.

"Good morning, Mrs. Hudson," a woman in a flowered shirt says from behind the front counter. "I'm Carrie-Anne, part-owner of Mistletoe Morning Brew. Welcome to Christmas Key."

It's all very polite and formal, and Ruby instantly wants to wipe it all away and start fresh. Here on this tiny, rustic island she feels more like herself than she has in ages, and she doesn't want to stand out because people are treating her with any special deference.

"It's wonderful to meet you. Please, call me Ruby." She smiles at Carrie-Anne and gestures at the inside of the coffee shop. "I was expecting more mistletoe than flowers," she admits.

"We decorate differently every month. Usually it's themed around a book or a song—something like that. Occasionally movies or seasons. This month is our 'garden' month. *A Secret Garden* and *A Tree Grows in Brooklyn*. Or *Midnight in the Garden of Good and Evil*, if you prefer something more in that vein." Carrie-Anne points to a stack of the novels next to her register. "We loan out copies, or you can just sit and read one while you have coffee if you like."

Ruby picks up a paperback copy of *A Secret Garden* and flips it over in her hands. The corners are well-worn and it's obviously been read and enjoyed a number of times. "Is it for a book club?" She frowns.

"No, just for fun. My wife, Ellen, and I are just huge fans of books and pop culture, and we thought it would be fun to do a different theme every month. It's kind of taken on a life of its own at this point though."

Ruby sets the book back on the pile. There's a homespun charm to Mistletoe Morning Brew that makes her feel warm inside, and as she glances back over her shoulder, she can see Dexter North approaching the front door. Sunlight spills in through the windows and onto the tile floor.

"Well, your shop is lovely. Truly. I've only been here since yesterday afternoon, but I'm already crazy about Christmas Key. What a special place."

"Morning," Dexter says as he walks in the door. He gives both Carrie-Anne and Ruby a brisk nod. "Sorry I'm late." Dexter adjusts the strap of his book bag as he looks up at the chalkboard menu.

"You're not late," Ruby assures him. "I'm just early." She turns to Carrie-Anne. "I'll drink whatever you recommend."

"Oh," Carrie-Anne sounds surprised. "Okay, let's see. I'm a big fan of the iced lavender latte, but the rose hip tea is wonderful, too."

"I'm definitely thinking coffee," Ruby says. "I'll try the iced lavender, please."

Dexter pulls his wallet from the back pocket of his shorts. "I'll do the same," he says. "Thanks, Carrie-Anne."

They take their cold drinks out the front door and Dexter leads them through the front door of the bookstore, which shares a wall with Mistletoe Morning Brew. Inside, a tall, Black man with a runner's build and stylish tortoiseshell eyeglasses is typing at a computer on the front counter.

"Hey, Dexter!" the man says, his face breaking into a huge, toothy grin. He walks out from behind the counter and extends a hand. "Welcome back."

Dexter shakes his hand. The two men appear to be close in age, and they both look bookish and cerebral in their dark-framed glasses.

"Ruby, this is Vance Guy, owner of A Sleighful of Books. Vance, this is Ruby Hudson."

Vance offers her a hand, looking awed. "I'm thrilled to meet you, Ruby—if I may call you that—and not for the reason you're thinking." Vance glances at Dexter excitedly and then back at Ruby. "I heard you opened a bookstore on Shipwreck Key, and I was hoping maybe we could talk about collaborating on events at some point."

Ruby feels a tingle in her toes; this is the first time in as long as she can remember that anyone expressed an interest in meeting her for any reason *other* than the fact that she's lived in the White House.

"That would actually be incredible," Ruby says. "I'd love to talk about that more. Did you have anything specific in mind?"

Dexter is holding his coffee in one hand, looking pleased as Ruby and Vance talk. A shaft of morning light beams through the front window of the narrow shop, falling on the wood floor just as it had fallen on the tile in the coffee shop. Christmas Key has the constant feeling of being bathed in soft sunlight, and Ruby loves it.

"I was thinking about possibly bringing authors here for readings." Vance folds his arms over his chest, rocking back on his heels. "Maybe having them do a tour of the Keys that includes Shipwreck and Christmas, in addition to the usual spots like Key West and Islamorada."

"I love that idea so much. I haven't even started thinking that far ahead yet," Ruby admits. "But I would love to get to the point where I host a stop on someone's book tour. Fabulous idea, Vance."

"Here," Vance says, stepping back behind the counter and plucking a business card from a small holder by the computer. He hands it to Ruby. "Let's share information and we'll make it happen. I think there are tons of things we could work together on, and I'd love to make a trip over to Shipwreck and check out your shop."

Ruby takes her wallet from her purse and pulls out a business card that she hands to Vance.

"Thank you," Vance says, holding the card with both hands reverently. "I'm really excited about this."

"Now, if you don't mind," Dexter says, shaking the ice in his plastic cup. "Ruby and I were going to borrow your back deck and talk for a bit. Is that cool, Vance?"

Vance sweeps a hand toward the back door of the shop. "Absolutely. Enjoy, and let me know if you need anything."

Ruby nods at Vance with a smile and follows Dexter onto a wooden deck that's surrounded by palm trees and smaller bushes. There are three round tables with umbrellas on the patio, and Dexter chooses one, sitting down in a chair and placing his iced coffee, a notebook and pen, and a small recorder on the table. Ruby pulls out a chair opposite.

"Mind if I record a bit today?" Dexter asks, glancing up at her as he jots something in his notebook. He looks freshly showered, and he's wearing cargo shorts and a collared, short-sleeved shirt with Converse. His hair is still slightly damp.

"No, not at all," Ruby says, though she does mind. Or rather, she's nervous—at least a little bit. Dexter did say that anything he puts in the book will have her final approval, but the fear that she'll slip up and say something too revealing is there. Ruby doesn't want to have to backpedal or demand that he leave something out of the book just because she messed up and let her tongue get too loose. She clears her throat and wipes the cold condensation from her coffee off her palms and onto her bare thighs.

Dexter takes a moment getting ready, then leans back in his chair as he gives Ruby a long look.

"I think we should start with the hard stuff today and work backwards, even if we don't get it all covered during this visit." His words land in her gut like a heavy stone in the bottom of a pond. They both sit there for a long moment, well aware of what he's getting at.

"Fine," Ruby says, her voice neutral. She knows where this is going.

Dexter clears his throat. A gecko skitters across the table next to theirs and they both glance at it. Small blooms of hot pink hibiscus dot the low shrubbery around the deck and a slight breeze off the ocean blows the leaves and petals around ever so slightly.

"Etienne Boucher," Dexter says, biting on the end of his pen as he watches Ruby's face. He's switched on his recorder and Ruby can almost feel the device capturing every irregular beat of her heart.

She nods. "Jack's mistress," she says firmly, trying to own this conversation before it owns her. "I'm aware of her."

"Can you tell me how you felt when you found out about her existence?"

This seems straightforward enough, and Ruby doesn't censor herself. "Betrayed. Confused. Lost. Annihilated. Lied to. Alone."

Dexter doesn't write anything, and his eyes never leave her face. "How did you become aware that Jack had been unfaithful?"

"My daughter, Harlow, bought one of those DNA kits for a college class she was taking. It was supposed to be straightforward, but the results suggested a potential sibling in France." Ruby sets her elbows on the table and laces her hands together. She rests her chin on the hammock that her fingers make and she looks directly into Dexter's intense gaze. "As you can imagine, I was floored. At first I thought it was a mistake—maybe they'd mixed up Harlow's results with someone else's. Jack had never been married before we met, and he'd never mentioned anything of the sort. And obviously I knew that I only had two children," she says, closing her eyes for a long beat and keeping them that way. "So I thought it had to be a mistake."

Ruby opens her eyes again and looks at the flowers just over Jack's right shoulder. "But then I did a little digging, and found out that this child was twelve years old and that his mother was the sister of one of Jack's closest friends, Yannik Boucher. Every time Jack had gone to France for diplomatic reasons, or to visit Yannik, he'd truly been going to see Etienne and the child."

"Julien."

"Yes," Ruby says, her voice nearly a whisper. "Julien."

Finding out about him had been particularly hard for her, as she'd always held a secret wish in her heart that she might someday give Jack the son he so dearly wanted. Of course he'd loved his girls with all his heart, but she knew that he saw himself with a son, and so after Harlow, she'd tried again and again to get pregnant, but after three miscarriages in a row, she'd never again been successful, and that part of her life had unceremoniously ended. So to find out that another woman—a secret mistress—had given Jack what his heart had truly desired had gutted Ruby. It brought her to her knees.

"How did you approach Jack when this information came to light?"

Ruby inhales sharply and leans back in her chair, no longer resting on her elbows. She tries to remember something that she's always worked so hard to forget: her husband's face as he continued to try and lie to her. After all the years she'd known and loved him, Jack had thought that he still might be able to wiggle out of the truth of what he'd done, and it had infuriated her.

"I didn't approach him. Harlow did."

She goes back to another memory that she generally keeps tucked away in her mind: she, Jack, and the girls were in Palm Beach for a golf tournament at which Jack had agreed to appear, and Harlow had opened the email results over brunch on the balcony of their hotel that overlooked the water. What had ensued was a ridiculous farce—Jack insisting that DNA kits were an inexact science, and that most likely the potential match was a cousin of some sort. He'd brushed it all off, smiling at Ruby across the table calmly as he asked her to pass the cream and sugar.

"And what happened?" Dexter's damp hair has dried in the warmth of the tropical morning, and his brow is furrowed as he tries to make sense of one of the hardest times in Ruby's life. "Did he deny it?"

"He absolutely did. He shrugged it off, told Harlow it was probably wrong, left us to finish our brunch together at the hotel where we were staying, and was whisked away in a limo to the golf tournament we'd gone to Palm Beach to attend. Later that night, on Air Force One, he locked himself in his private office and stayed busy with who knows what so that we wouldn't have time to talk. The next morning he was off again on some trip, and he absolutely denied the possibility of his children having a sibling." Ruby chews on her lower lip as she reaches over and plays with the straw of her iced coffee absent-mindedly.

"How did the truth finally come out?" Dexter moves them forward, pulling Ruby out of her thoughts.

"I hired someone to look into it." Ruby straightens her shoulders and looks at Dexter across the table. "I wanted answers, and I knew Jack was never going to give them, so I paid a private investigator to get to the bottom of it."

Dexter looks up from his notes and blinks repeatedly in disbelief. "The First Lady of the United States just hired a P.I. to uncover her husband's love child?"

A smirk tugs at the corners of Ruby's mouth as Dexter realizes how tacky it is to call Jack's son his "love child." But he'd called Etienne her husband's "side piece" the night before, so rather than feeling affronted, she laughs and after a few seconds, Dexter does too.

"I'm sorry," he says, shaking his head. "You just caught me off guard there."

"For what it's worth, Sunday Bond is one of my best friends, and she had her sister hire the P.I. So it wasn't terribly far removed from me, but no, I didn't show up and knock on the frosted glass door of a private detective, wearing a trench coat and a fedora and a fake mustache."

"Although that would have been a really amazing story." The smile lingers on Dexter's face for a moment, and then fades. "So what happened next?"

"Oh," Ruby says, waving a hand dismissively. "It took him less than forty-eight hours. The DNA results pointed at Julien Boucher, a young boy living in France with his mother. The P.I. approached Julien's mother, Etienne, who had no idea her son had even taken a DNA test. She was appalled, because obviously Jack would have forbidden such a thing. Apparently Julien had some questions about his father, who had always confused him with his comings and goings from their lives, so he and a friend ordered the kit and did it all as a science project for school."

"Wow."

"Yeah, big wow. Surprise, young Julien—your father is the President of the United States of America!" Ruby throws her hands wide like she's on a stage and makes an exaggerated face that she drops immediately. "He would have stumbled on this information for himself at some point in his life, but I'm assuming that Etienne kept him fairly isolated from the news and such. He'd been homeschooled and his friends hand-selected, but she couldn't have kept it from him forever anyway."

"So once you were armed with that information..."

"Armed with that information, I was ready to kick Jack's butt from here to next week." Ruby looks out at the palm trees and the sand behind the bookstore, remembering. Her eyes fill with tears. "But he never came home."

Dexter gives her a second to compose herself, busying himself with jotting notes. When he lifts his pen from the paper, he takes a beat to carefully formulate his next question, which hangs between them as Ruby glazes over. "Do you know what happened to him?"

"I know the basic details just like everybody else. But when it comes down to it, I know as much about what really happened to Jack Hudson as I do about what really happened to Jack Kennedy."

* * *

The morning's line of questioning takes it out of Ruby, but she's game to keep talking. She needs to do this, and oddly, sharing her own thoughts and feelings with Dexter is proving oddly cathartic.

After their iced coffees and following his hard questions about Jack's death, Dexter suggests a tour of the island and Ruby readily agrees to go along, even though she and Banks did the full drive the day before when they arrived. She hops into his golf cart, which is parked on Main Street right in front of an open air restaurant and bar called Jack Frosty's. Dexter pulls away from the curb, taking the corner onto December Drive so quickly that Ruby whoops in surprise and reaches out for something to hang onto.

"You trying to knock me loose?" she shouts over the sound of the wheels crunching on sand and shells. She's given Banks the morning off, and shockingly, he's accepted it. Apparently he's finding Christmas Key to be a relatively safe place with very few surprises, and Ruby is thrilled for the space to breathe. For the first time in more years than she cares to think about, she's on her own, no Secret Service, no planned meetings, no one to report to. And it feels amazing.

"Sorry, boss," Dexter says, leaning forward in his seat and resting his forearm on the steering wheel.

The wind whips through the open cart, lifting his shirt away from his body and blowing his hair back. It would be hard not to notice how handsome he looks with the blue of the ocean as his backdrop.

Ruby looks around at what feels like miles of untouched white sand and sea as Dexter nods up ahead of them. "Right around that bend is the cluster of tiny homes that Holly, the mayor, had built here. Did you hear about that project?" he asks.

Ruby shakes her head. "Banks and I drove past them, but I don't know the story."

"HGTV came out here and they did a reality show while the houses were being built. I bought one, and the other nine are all owned by various part-time residents."

"How tiny are we talking?" Ruby looks at the perfect little houses that she'd only glimpsed the day before as they approach the miniature community.

"Mine is three hundred square feet," he says, rolling to a stop in front of a white, two-story cottage with a silver light fixture hanging next to the door. "Wanna see?"

Ruby is tempted to make a smart comment about not being the

kind of girl who goes into a man's house on the first date, but she catches herself before it escapes her lips. There's a freedom to being on Christmas Key and to talking about her life and her secrets, but Ruby doesn't want to get too carried away.

"I'd love to see how a whole house fits into three hundred square feet," she says, climbing out of the cart and smoothing her hair.

Even back here, on the quiet side of the island, there are obvious nods to the Christmas season. Each of the tiny homes bears a hand-painted wooden shingle with a holiday name on it. For instance, Dexter's says Cocoa Cottage, and the one right next to his has a sign that designates it as Peppermint Palace.

"Cute," Ruby says, tapping the sign with her fingertips as Dexter opens his front door to let her in.

"I did *not* choose that name," he says, looking at her with mild disdain from under his brow.

"I'm going to pretend that you did," she jokes as she steps into the tiny foyer.

The little house stops Ruby in her tracks; it's adorable. The front room is white with navy blue accents, the couch a comfy looking denim loveseat. The room merges right into a small but functional kitchen with white marble counters. The sink is a stainless steel farm sink that's about half the size of a normal kitchen sink, and instead of cupboards with doors, dishes rest on open shelving with nautical ropes running the length of the shelves to hold plates and glasses in place.

In fact, there are nautical touches everywhere Ruby looks, including a rope handrail running up the stairs to the second floor loft, a rusty anchor hanging from the wall next to the bathroom door, and a small desk made of wood from a boat that folds down from the wall and holds a laptop and a few books. The slab of wood that forms the desk is covered in blistered paint and bears the stencil of a boat's name: *The Nickel and Dime.* Everything feels just right, and Ruby loves seeing where the man who is digging so deeply into her life lives his own life—it gives her some insight into who he is and how he functions.

"This place is incredible," Ruby says, walking over to the bathroom door. "May I?"

Dexter shrugs. "I brought you in and offered to show you around, so I guess that's on me. Go ahead. Explore."

Ruby takes him at his word, checking out the marble shower and the small sink with a cabinet beneath it. The mirror over the sink is ringed in seashells ("The whole place came decorated," Dexter says loudly and somewhat defensively as she runs her fingers over the wainscoting in the front room), and there are small, hand-painted pictures of sailboats running up the wall next to the stairs. As she pokes her head into the loft, Ruby can see that he's got a queen-sized bed on a low frame up there, with enough room for a nightstand and a lamp.

"This place is incredible. Are any of your neighbors selling their places?" she asks, holding onto the rope railing as she steps back down into the living space.

"Didn't you just buy an enormous house on the beach on Shipwreck Key?" he asks, smiling at the way she's picking up his miniature tea kettle and touching the half-sized blender on the kitchen counter.

Ruby shrugs and walks back through the open front door, which Dexter closes behind them. He seems relieved to be outside again. Ruby stands on his front porch and looks at the wooden walkway that winds amongst the tiny houses and ends at a hard-packed sand parking lot, where posts with charging stations sit ready to charge up golf carts at night. The charging stations are painted with red and white stripes like candy canes, and in front of several of the tiny homes are pink plastic flamingos with Christmas wreathes around their necks or Santa hats resting jauntily on their pink heads.

"This place," Ruby says, shaking her head. "Although I guess Shipwreck Key does go a bit overboard on the pirate stuff."

"But it suits you?"

"Oh, yeah. I love charming places. As soon as I set foot on Shipwreck Key years ago, I knew I wanted to live there. It's not quite as small as this island, and it's only about ten miles south of Destin, so it's not difficult for me to be on an airplane within an hour or two, but it's removed enough from the real world that I can sometimes forget about everything else. It's ideal."

"You think you'll stay there?" Dexter leans on the railing next to her, looking out over the plot of mini houses.

Ruby tips her head to one side. "I think so. I love my bookstore, and my house is perfect. My girls seem to like it there, so I know they'll consider it a second home base as time goes on. And Sunday Bond is moving down soon—she bought a place of her own," she says, cutting a glance at him. She's giving him a scoop and she knows it, but it's not like Dexter is a tabloid journalist or anything. "This is completely off the record, of course, but she's leaving Peter and starting over on Shipwreck, so I'm going to be there for her as much as possible through all that."

Dexter has an extremely practiced poker face, which he employs now. "Hmmm," he says, nodding noncommittally. "Sounds like a good move for her. And you'll have one of your close friends there, which will be nice, right?"

"Of course. I'm finding that the older I get, the more I need strong, loyal, interesting women in my life." Ruby stares at the plastic flamingo in front of the house next door to Dexter's as she talks.

"Still completely off the record, naturally, and just out of pure human curiosity, but do you think there'll ever be another man in your life?"

A feeling washes over Ruby that she can't quite describe. It's one of awareness, mostly—awareness that she's taken her own life off its old course and sent it in a whole new direction. It would have been so easy to just stay in D.C., and to get a townhouse or a condo in Georgetown so that she could attend the functions that everyone still invited her to attend. She would have spent weekends sharing brunch with Sunday or Athena, and sprinkled in a trip to New York every few weeks to see people there and to visit Harlow. Of course she never needed to work or get a job again—everything Jack had became hers when he died—but falling asleep thinking of the bookstore and of how to make it profitable has her brain working in ways that feel invigorating. She's taking charge of everything in her life, including her role in Dexter North's book.

Ruby takes a deep breath. "Who knows? I'm not even fifty yet, and now that Jack's been gone for a year I can finally start to breathe again. I don't think I'm done with love. Jack didn't break me, and—with any luck at all—I still have half my life left to live."

"I love your optimism," Dexter says, watching her profile with open admiration on his face. "Sometimes other people do break us a little, and it's hard to imagine getting back out there again. I think it's great that you haven't closed that door."

Ruby nods and then turns her head to look at Dexter. "You know," she says. "In the end, this book might screw me over. I might be giving people far too much insight into my marriage or my life, but in a way, it feels good." A gust of wind from the ocean blows across the plot of tiny homes, sending sand across the wooden walkway and lifting Ruby's blonde hair from her shoulders. "You asked me before what I had to give up to be First Lady, and it's pretty much everything. You tuck away your own hopes and dreams, your thoughts, opinions, and plans. You are essentially at the whim of a machine that only wants you to be one thing: perfect. Or as close to perfect as possible. Hair done, clothes that always send the right message, a smile for the world no matter how much you don't feel like smiling. I've missed having a voice and I've missed being Ruby Dallarosa, which is who I'm starting to feel like again rather than just being Ruby Hudson, First Lady."

Dexter watches her intently. "I'm not recording this," he says, "but I kind of wish I was."

Ruby shakes her head. "I just said those things for you, not for everyone else. I want you to understand why I was so eager to come here and talk to you. I think I'm ready to be the real me again."

Dexter looks at her with a serious expression, like he's about to ask her for a deep, dark truth. "Does the real you feel like having a cheeseburger at Jack Frosty's?"

A slow smile creeps across Ruby's face as she nods. "Yeah, the real me does," she says. "And a beer."

* * *

The next twenty-four hours are over in a flash and Ruby is back on Shipwreck Key feeling windswept and happy. She loved Christmas Key, and the thought of partnering with Vance from A Sleighful of Books to come up with events and ideas excites her. Talking to Dexter felt liberating, and even watching Banks switch gears and relax as he talked to the locals had made her happy.

After having a cheeseburger on Main Street with Dexter at Jack

Frosty's, and then chatting with the islanders at the Ho Ho Hideaway that night as she sipped fresh coconut rum and danced to music that took her back to her college years, Ruby felt like she'd been on a true vacation. No one had asked her for an autograph or a photo, and no one treated her like an outsider. It was the most refreshing forty-eight hours she's spent in ages, and Ruby is ready to keep thinking about Dexter's book and her part in it.

But when she wakes up the next morning it's to middle of the night texts from both of her daughters, three messages from Sunday, and several emails and messages from Ursula with information about news outlets requesting a comment.

"What the..." Ruby sits up in bed, scrolling through everything she missed while sleeping. "No," she says, closing her eyes and falling back on the pillows. "No, no, no."

One of Athena's texts is a link to an online story, and her stomach flips just reading it, not to mention looking at the photograph that someone had obviously taken of her on Christmas Key, laughing and riding shotgun with Dexter in his golf cart on Main Street. The photo looks like it was taken from the sidewalk, and the graininess of the shot makes her think it's from the smart phone of a curious civilian, and not the work of a professional.

Former First Lady Ruby Hudson Canoodles on Christmas Key and Conspires to Write Tell-All Book.

Ruby sighs. It is what it is at this point, but she'd certainly hoped to keep the fact that she's talking to Dexter North to herself for as long as possible.

With a few muttered curse words, she tosses off her blanket and gets out of bed. She's annoyed. This is not a new sensation, having someone watching her every move, but she'd let her guard down on Christmas Key. And maybe she'd even overshared with Dexter. Should she have really spoken about her desire to love again and to be her old self? Suddenly everything she's doing feels questionable. The sensation of taking her life back and of making her own choices feels corrupted, and a small part of her even considers slinking back into the shell that she was *supposed* to stay in. There are plenty of people who won't like her talking to Dexter North, and she could easily hide out on Shipwreck Key forever and stay mum on everything.

Ruby shakes this thought off immediately, thinking of the book club and of her daughters. She thinks of how hard Marigold is working to make sure that women in the middle of their lives still have voices that are heard, and she knows there's no way that she'll actually just sink into silence and disappear. There's no way Ruby wants to live the next fifty years of her life in a color-coordinated pantsuit and pearls, smiling placidly. She's not taking Jack's secrets to her grave, and she's not going to live in shame because of his choices. It won't happen, but in some ways it is tempting.

Ruby pulls on a pair of sweatpants and slides on her glasses. She needs a cup of coffee before making any rash decisions.

After that, she'll be ready to face the world.

Ruby

Harlow jokingly refers to her mother's book club gatherings as "the meeting of the minds," which tickles Ruby. She knows that Harlow is only ribbing her anyway, but it's so much more than that. Already, Ruby looks forward to seeing Molly, Heather, and Marigold sitting around the back room of the bookstore, and to having Tilly and Vanessa there, Vanessa perched on the edge of her chair like a young woman who isn't quite sure that she's really been invited to join the grown ups, and Tilly slumped in hers with a brooding look like a kid being *forced* to sit at the grown up table against her will.

"Okay," Heather says, holding a cup of tea over her saucer at the start of their next book club meeting. They've decided that this meeting will be simply tea and cookies, and Ruby is using the box of blue and white chinoiserie-patterned china that she brought with her from the White House. "Let's debrief. We're all dying to get down to business."

Ruby allows a small smile, thinking of how the very word "debrief" feels presidential, but instead of discussing matters of national security, they're a group of wonderful women chatting about a two-day trip to a little island that's decorated for Christmas, and a meeting with a dashing man who wants to dissect every detail of Ruby's life.

"Well," Ruby says, dropping one cube of sugar into her hot tea with a pair of miniature silver tongs. "First of all, Christmas Key is amazing. I loved it there and I would go back in a heartbeat." There are murmurs of agreement from the other women. "But next we need to address the rumors, because I feel like my face is plastered everywhere, and I think it would be silly to not mention it."

"I saw it," Molly says, holding her teacup not daintily by the handle like the other women, but with one hand wrapped around the delicate bone china like she's holding a thick ceramic coffee mug. "What kind of people have nothing else to do with their lives but run around taking photos of other people who are just minding their own business? "

"Paparazzi," Marigold and Ruby say at the same time.

Athena, who is walking around with a teapot and refilling people's cups, stops to look at the women gathered in a circle. "They're relentless," she adds, turning back to Heather's cup and pouring more tea into it.

Marigold takes the lead here. "When I was married to Cobb, they were *everywhere*," she says, referring to her much photographed and written about marriage to (and ensuing divorce from) legendary rock singer Cobb Hartley. "Sometimes you would think you were completely alone, just walking on the beach or eating a sandwich on a park bench, then BAM, the next day there's an unflattering picture of you doing one of those things with a crazy headline like 'Is Cobb Leaving His Wife Because She Overeats?' It's outrageous."

Heather sips her tea and looks at both Ruby and Marigold guiltily. "I'm not going to lie to you all," she says. "I love a good celebrity tabloid. I can't help it. I'm sorry."

"That's human nature," Ruby says, letting her off the hook gently. "No need to apologize. And I'm used to it, I just let my guard down this time."

"Who took the photo?" Molly asks. "Someone who was being paid?"

"I'm actually not sure. I called the B&B and the owner very nicely told me that she couldn't say who her guests were while I was there—which I understand, and respect—but she did a little cough and said she thought that 'maybe' someone who was staying on the island with a relative innocently snapped a photo for posterity and then realized they could sell it and make a few bucks."

Heather shakes her head. "I never really thought about the fact that the stars I love to see eating street tacos or sitting at a red light in my *Us* magazine are just going about their business when someone swoops in and invades their privacy." She cringes at the thought.

"I'm a firm believer that if you're in the public eye, one of the trade-offs is that you don't always get to flip the switch and say when you are and aren't in the public eye." Ruby presses her lips together. "With some exceptions, of course," she says, holding up a hand. "When my husband first died and I was just trying to get out of bed everyday and be there for my girls, I wasn't having it with the paparazzi. Not at all. Seeing them camped out on the sidewalk outside our home or following me everywhere with their giant cameras really pissed me off."

"That's just unfair," Molly says, looking disgusted.

"It was," Harlow says from where she's standing by a bookshelf. Instead of sitting down with the group, this time she's busied herself with examining different books, and Ruby can't help but wonder if talking about the photo of her mother on Christmas Key laughing with another man hasn't upset her in some way. Harlow re-shelves the book in her hand and finally chooses a seat, sitting down heavily and crossing her legs. "And this is unfair, too. My mom deserves to go out and live her life, and she can do that with whoever she wants, whenever she wants. People don't get to scrutinize you forever, do they, Mom?"

Athena has stopped pouring tea and is staring at Ruby, waiting for an answer to her sister's question.

Ruby is caught off guard by the sting of potential tears behind her eyes; she had no idea that her daughters felt this strongly about her right to privacy, or that they'd moved past their father's death enough to support her moving on with her own life.

"I do think we need to have some basic understandings," Ruby agrees, blinking her tears back. "If someone shows up here and wants to take pictures of me carrying a cup of coffee from The Scuttlebutt into my bookstore in the morning, well, then so be it. This is a public island and Seadog Lane is a public street. I have no say in that. But if one of my daughters were to come to Shipwreck Key to get over a heartbreak and someone snapped a photo of me consoling my crying child on the beach, I would consider that an invasion of privacy," she says, looking between her two daughters meaningfully.

"But the paparazzi don't feel that way," Marigold says knowingly. "They don't have normal human boundaries."

"Okay," Molly says, standing up to pick out a shortbread cookie from the plate that Heather has brought. She takes a bite but starts talking anyway. "So what now? The world knows you were on an island with Dexter North, and apparently everyone knows that he's the king of the tell-all biography, so...is that really newsworthy?"

"He asked me about Jack's death," Ruby says, rushing ahead and ripping off the band-aid. Molly sits down heavily, the cookie in her hand forgotten as she swallows her first bite. "He wants to write about when I found out about Jack's affair, and he wants to talk about the way my husband died, but he wants to do the whole book from my point of view, which was not what I expected at all."

"Whoa," Heather says, her voice quiet and breathy. "He is not messing around."

Ruby shrugs. "I expected to be more put off by it, but there's a part of me that wants to talk." She looks down at her fingers, which are knotted together in her lap. "I want to heal. I don't forgive Jack entirely yet, but he's gone. Spending the rest of my life feeling angry is not the way I want to live."

"Amen," Marigold says. She reaches for a frosted cookie. Ruby already knows from watching her snack at the last book club meeting that she'll nibble on this one cookie endlessly, making it last for the next hour. It's easy for Ruby to imagine Marigold as a youthful model in her twenties, staying slim by counting calories and sipping black coffee, but now she's known more for the intense workout regimen that she posts about on Instagram, and on her firm belief in moderation in every-thing. Wine, cookies, pizza, and french fries are all allowed—in small amounts. Marigold is always aware of everything going on around her, of what people are doing, saying and thinking, and of how what she does is perceived by others, which Ruby greatly admires, but also finds exhausting. She's done that herself for enough years, and what Ruby wants more than anything at this point is to *not* scrutinize or be scrutinized.

"So let's talk about the book," Ruby says, picking up her copy of the Monica Lewinsky biography.

"Eh," Molly says, waving a hand and going back to her cookie. "The book was good—we all know that. I got up to bake my morning scones and muffins on two hours of sleep one time because I couldn't put the damn book down and get my shut-eye."

"It was pretty compelling," Athena agrees. She's sitting forward on her chair, legs crossed and fingers laced together around her knee; she looks so grown up, and Ruby desperately wants to hear what her daughter thinks. "I love the way he didn't villainize her or make her overly sympathetic. Clearly she knew she was The Other Woman in this scenario, but he cut her a lot of slack for her youthful naiveté, which I think made the book even more readable."

"I was once the other woman," Heather says, holding her teacup in one hand as she looks at the window just beyond the circle of women.

"Only once?" Marigold jokes.

"Yep, only once," Heather admits. She brings her gaze back to the other faces around her. "The wife was on life support—"

"Lord have mercy," Molly says. She takes a sip of her tea, but she is clearly listening.

"Yeah, it sounds like it would be a pretty yucky situation, right?" Heather nods at Molly. She could have easily been offended by Molly's tone, but she's obviously not. "This was my fourth husband. His wife had been suffering from dementia for more than ten years, and at the end of her life she was completely unable to communicate or care for herself. I think it was understandable that though he loved her and hired wonderful caregivers for her, he'd emotionally moved on. That's why I allowed it to happen."

"I think that's reasonable," Ruby agrees, offering her support. It's not a path she's ever walked in life, but she can at least imagine a scenario where the romantic part of a marriage is completely over due to illness, even if the love and loyalty lives on.

"Why the attraction to older men?" Molly asks plainly.

Heather thinks about it for a second before answering. "I think there's something safe about it," she finally admits. "Men my own age might find something lacking about me. It would be easy for them to reject me, to leave me, to find someone better. But to an older man— one who is more likely to be an old-school gentleman, which I love— I'm a catch. If a guy is over seventy, I mean, c'mon: a woman of forty-two is a vixen. But if a guy is in his forties he's going to look right by me and go after the woman in her twenties."

Marigold is nodding in understanding. "That's not wrong," she says, wagging a finger at Heather like she has a point. "Every guy who makes a negative comment on any of my social media posts appears to be in his thirties or forties, and he actually seems weirdly angry towards women our age. Why are they all so mad at us? They love to point out that we're 'tired, old, dried-up, done'...what's with that?"

The women all look at each other with no clear answer until Harlow speaks up.

"I think," she says, clearing her throat as she holds her teacup and saucer in both hands, "I think they're intimidated by you."

Heather and Marigold frown, but Ruby gets her daughter's meaning instantly. She nods at Harlow encouragingly.

"I mean, look at all of you," Harlow says, glancing at each woman in turn. "You're all smart, beautiful, accomplished, and you don't *need* a man. Most of you—sorry if I'm making an assumption here—are done having babies, so you don't need them for that, and you make your own money and take care of yourselves. They're angry at you in a vague way because you're happy and self-sufficient and deep down they know that they're just gravy in your lives at this point."

Ruby wants to applaud; Harlow has hit the nail completely on the head. As she looks at the other women in the group, she knows this is completely the truth. Heather and Marigold both own their own homes near the water, and Molly has been a solo business owner for forty years. She herself does not *need* a man, but has the luxury of deciding now, as she enters her fifties, whether or not she *wants* one. And while Vanessa is still at the starting gate to that part of her life, looking around desperately for someone to run the race with, and Tilly is quite probably going to end up living in her grandfather's house for the rest of her life with a bunch of cats and books about serial killers, the rest of them are precisely as Harlow just described: self-sufficient and confident enough in who they are to not dress, act, or openly desire male approval. It's a revelation to her.

"Honey," Ruby says to Harlow, "you are so right. Thank you for that."

"Correct, my girl," Molly says. "You've got a good head on your shoulders." She lifts her teacup in a toast to Harlow, then turns to the other younger women in the group, giving a nod to Athena, then Vanessa, and finally Tilly. "The future is bright for womanhood with smart, interesting, sharp young ladies who go against the grain." She casts a glance at Tilly as she says this last part. "It's a pleasure being in a book club with so many different women and their varied perspectives."

"You know," Ruby says, picking up the thread. "It really is. Getting to know all of you is making this transition to living on the island so much easier. Thank you for being willing to come here, read books with me, chat about life, and just be your authentic selves."

The women take a moment to smile at one another in acknowledgment, but then Marigold speaks up.

"Okay, we've patted ourselves on the back and we all agree that this is a special group," she says, measuring her words and looking serious. "But now we need to get down to the nitty gritty." Almost in unison, the other women lean forward in their seats as if Marigold is about to impart some top secret information. "We need to figure out how Ruby can use this situation to the best of her advantage. She has the opportunity here to use this book as a platform and to tell her story the way she wants to tell it, so let's choose our next book carefully."

"Right!" Heather says, leaping in to the discussion. "You are so right, Goldie. This is Ruby's moment to really shine."

"Then I have a book suggestion," Athena says. Everyone looks at her in anticipation. She bends over and pulls her oversized purse from beneath her chair and takes out a dogeared copy of a book that she's obviously already reading. "*Jacqueline Bouvier Kennedy Onassis: The Untold Story*," Athena says, holding up the book for them all to see.

"Ooooh," Marigold says, nodding in agreement.

"Good choice," Heather adds.

"Jackie O." Molly inhales and holds her breath before releasing it. "A First Lady with a successful second act. I like it. Very inspirational."

A slow smile spreads across Ruby's face. "Me too. Okay, just to be official here—quick show of hands: who's on board with the Jackie O. book?" Every hand shoots into the air. "Fabulous, ladies. Let's meet again in two weeks."

Athena

Diego texts on a Thursday in June. Athena is on a leave of absence from work, and for the first couple of weeks she was determined to get over her broken heart, bad feelings, and shame, then pack her bags and head back to her life in D.C. But as time has gone on, she's gotten increasingly comfortable on Shipwreck Key. She loves waking up to the sound of the ocean and the smell of coffee that her mom has already woken up to brew, and she adores walking through the front door of the bookstore and flipping on the lights to see shelves and shelves of beautiful books, just waiting to find good homes.

Is Shipwreck Key a den of romantic possibility? No, it is not. But right now that's part of what makes it so appealing. The absolute dearth of young men looking for love suits Athena just fine. But that doesn't mean she's not bitter on some levels, because she is. Who does Diego Santana think he is to rob her of her trust in men like that? How can he wake up and look himself in the eye everyday knowing that he made a mockery of love, intimacy, and trust—both for her, and for his new wife?

"Hey, Bean," Ruby says, walking into the kitchen where Athena is sitting at the table nursing a cup of coffee and holding her phone in one hand, the message from Diego still sitting there unanswered.

Ruby walks over to the refrigerator and pulls open the door. She's wearing a pair of bright red running shorts and a white tank top, and her hair is in a bouncy ponytail. Athena's life might be falling apart, but as she watches her mom, she realizes that the pace and lifestyle on the island are doing amazing things for her mom.

"Want an omelette, hon?" Ruby asks, setting a carton of eggs on the island and turning back to the refrigerator for the milk and a wedge of aged cheddar.

"Mom," Athena says, ignoring the offer of food for the time being. She screws up her face in a frown and holds her coffee mug tightly in both hands. There's no reason to feel as nervous as she does. "I think I want to quit my job."

The kitchen is spacious and full of sunshine. The light glints off the stainless steel appliances, and every surface is clean and shiny. Athena realizes in this moment that she loves this kitchen. She loves this house. Everything about this life here on Shipwreck Key suits her, and she wants to start feeling and looking as relaxed and at home as her mother does.

"Bean..." Ruby abandons the eggs, milk, and cheese and comes over to the table. She pulls out a chair and plops down across from her daughter, setting both elbows on the wooden tabletop and lacing her fingers together. "Let's talk. I want to hear what's going on in your head right now."

Athena blows out a breath, lifting a long, stray curl that hangs over her forehead with the force of her exhalation. The hair falls again, and Athena meets her mother's eye.

"I don't think I can go back. What do I have in Washington if you're not there?" Her look is lost, pleading. "I can't see myself wandering around a silent library for the rest of my life, feeling like everyone who works there knows my business and thinks I'm just a dumb girl who got screwed over by a guy."

Ruby unlaces her fingers and reaches across the table to take Athena's hand in hers. She holds it and stares at her oldest child with a long, loving look. "My sweet," Ruby says earnestly, squeezing Athena's fingers in hers. "The first thing you've got to do is learn to let go of what other people think about you. Your life is your life, and this was—of course—a horrible thing that happened to you. But if people look at you in judgment, then let them. I can promise you that not a one of them has lived a life free of mistakes or mishaps."

"But you care what people think of you," Athena counters carefully. "You're talking to Dexter North so that he writes a book that makes you look good."

"Fair. Not entirely true, but fair," Ruby says, letting her eyes drift to the window over her daughter's shoulder. The beach is gorgeous today, and there's not a soul in sight. "I want to tell my story, sure, but I like to think it's more of a search for catharsis than simply an attempt to cast myself in a flattering light. Of course, human nature is human nature, so sure, maybe I want to come out smelling like a rose, but I am willing to do the hard work, Bean. I am willing to ask myself the tough questions and to uncover truths that might not be totally flattering to me."

Athena nods and stares into her coffee mug. "I'm not even sure how to do that," she says softly. "But there must be some things that are my fault in this situation."

"No, no, no, honey." Ruby shakes her head firmly with each word. "None of this is your fault. I mean, what—you're guilty of liking a guy? Of accepting his invitation to dinner? Of wanting to be intimate with someone? You're twenty-three. None of that is wrong."

"I just didn't want my first time to be with someone who treated me like that," Athena says so quietly that her words barely carry. "Now I'm afraid to put myself out there again."

"Sweetheart..." Ruby's eyes well with tears as she watches her baby girl across the table. "I didn't know that this was your first time."

Athena shrugs, trying to look tougher than she feels. She swipes at the tears streaming down her cheeks. "It's whatever, really. I just didn't ever find anyone I liked enough until him."

"Well," Ruby says, looking unsure about what to say next. "All I can say without saying too much and making you squirm is that for most of us, our first time isn't anything like the movies. It's awkward and sometimes sad or funny when we think it's going to be romantic and perfect. Humans are always imperfect, but never more so than when we're in a vulnerable situation, which, frankly, sex is."

Athena nods and wipes her cheeks dry again. "That's true."

"So don't beat yourself up too much, okay? You were vulnerable and hopeful, and you went into the situation with good intentions. His bad actions are *not* on you, nor do you need to take them as your own, do you hear me?"

"I do."

"Okay." Ruby gives one firm nod and moves on. "Now, let's talk about this whole business of you wanting to quit your job." She stands up and walks to the island, where she starts cracking eggs into a bowl and then pours in a dab of milk. "And pardon me for cooking here while we chat, but I'm going to feed you. Tears and coffee alone are not enough to jumpstart the day."

Athena gives a wan smile. "Okay, Mom. And I just think I want to quit the library. I want to stay down here with you."

Ruby nods as she grates aged cheddar into the bowl of eggs that she's already whipped with milk. Behind her on the gas range is an omelette pan that she's dropped a pat of butter into so that it will be ready for her egg mixture.

"Obviously I love having you here, sweetheart—I love having both of you here," Ruby says, turning to the pan and carefully pouring her eggs into it so that it will firm up as she chops the large piece of ham that she's also pulled from the fridge. "But I don't want you to make any rash decisions. Have you thought of the pros and cons?"

The door that leads from the kitchen out to the wraparound deck opens and Harlow walks in. She's out of breath and bends forward at the waist, stretching as sweat drips down her temples. She's already kicked off her shoes outside on the wooden deck and she stands there in her white running socks, checking her mileage on her Apple watch.

"Morning," Harlow says, glancing at both her mom and her sister. "Oooh, breakfast? And why does everyone look so serious?"

"Omelettes," Ruby says, gesturing at the table with the spatula in her hand. "Sit down and I'll make you one too. And we're talking about Athena wanting to stay here on Shipwreck Key."

"Permanently?" Harlow pulls out a chair next to Athena and sits. Through the window they can see Eldrick standing on the deck, arms leaning on the railing as he faces the water. He followed Harlow on her run down the beach, and now he'll settle in outside and watch the waves until he and Banks coordinate who will trail the three women for the day.

"Yes," Athena says, sounding more certain than she has for most of the conversation so far. "I think this place suits me way better than Washington does."

"Of course it does," Harlow says, reaching into the bowl of fruit that's sitting at the center of the table. She chooses a banana and starts to peel it. "There are no men here to hurt you."

It's simple and it's true and it hits Athena right in the center of her heart. She averts her gaze.

"Sorry, Athena," Harlow says, breaking off the top third of the banana with her fingers and taking a bite of it. "But it's true. You got burned badly, and it's going to sting for a while. And the easiest way to protect yourself is to stay the hell away from men who can hurt you again. I've seen it happen many times," she says sagely. "And I get it, but don't stay off the horse for too long, so to speak. Or you'll be afraid to get back on."

Ruby turns her upper body as she stands at the stove and lifts one eyebrow at her younger daughter in warning. Harlow shrugs back at her helplessly.

"I get you—loud and clear," Athena says. "But I think I've made up my mind. Mom, if you'll have me, I want to stay. I can find my own place as soon as I figure out a job situation."

"If Athena is staying," Harlow says, though not with any sense of petulance or competition in her voice, "then I want to stay too." She leans her head onto her sister's shoulder and rests it there.

"Wait," Ruby says, lifting the pan from the stove and sliding the first omelette onto a white plate before she drops another pat of butter into the pan for the next round. "You want to stay here too, Lolo?"

Harlow is quiet for a minute before she lifts her head from Athena's shoulder. "Yeah. I think so." All of her normal bravado and bluster are gone. "I'm kind of freaked out by the big city. I always loved living there and I never felt afraid, but being in the bar that night just made everything feel so...violent. And random. I hate that," she adds, sounding like a little girl who is admitting that she hates the burned meatloaf on her plate or something equally innocuous.

"It's understandable that you'd feel that way," Ruby says, staying busy at the stove as she talks. "Do you think your therapist is helping at all? Not to be nosey at all—I'm just wondering."

"She is. And it was her idea that I stay down here for a bit."

"Oh?" Ruby reaches for the grater and the cheese again and shreds a bit more onto the flat egg mixture that's bubbling in the pan.

"Yeah, she suggested it," Harlow says, eating the rest of her banana. "Maybe Athena and I can find a place together on the island."

"Girls," Ruby says, turning off the heat and lifting the pan to slide the second omelette onto a plate of its own. "You're both welcome to stay here. I didn't buy a five-bedroom house planning to live here alone forever. Now, I know you won't *want* to live with your old mom forever, but for now, let's be each other's ports in the storm, okay?"

Ruby walks over to the table with the plates and sets them in front of her daughters. Harlow jumps up and grabs utensils and the salt and pepper shakers, then sits down next to her sister again.

"We can work out all the details," Ruby says, watching with a happy grin as her girls tuck into their omelettes with gusto. "But I think you've both been through some stuff, and being here is just a pitstop on the road to you feeling like you have some agency over your lives again."

Athena stops eating and looks up at Ruby. "You don't think we're losers, Mom?"

Ruby reaches out a hand toward each of her girls. "Not at all. I think you're humans—and relatively young ones at that. You've been through some tough stuff, and you need a re-set."

Just hearing her mother's words warms Athena from the inside. She's been feeling like a total loser just thinking of giving up her job and her apartment, but with her mother's approval, she knows that it's not the wrong thing to do.

As she demolishes her omelette, she feels a thousand times better about herself and her life choices, but then she feels a few hundred times worse again remembering that there's an unanswered message from Diego just sitting in her phone.

Harlow

"So you're not coming back?"

"I'm not coming back." Harlow is standing in the ocean up to her calves with her phone held out in front of her as she FaceTimes Dart, once her closest work friend and now someone she barely even thinks about.

"But what about your apartment?" Dart is standing on a subway platform, her short, black pixie haircut barely ruffled by the strong breeze of an oncoming train. They wait for the rumble of the train to pass through the station before carrying on with the conversation. "Are you going to sublet it?"

"I think so," Harlow says. "I don't want to give up a rent-controlled apartment in Manhattan entirely—that would be insane."

"So is moving to an island full of pirates in Florida, of all the God forsaken places," Dart says, making a face. "My grandparents live in Florida."

"Well, I'm happy here," Harlow says. "I'm going to keep working part-time from here for as long as it makes sense, and if it's not working out, then I'll quit and find something else."

"Huh," Dart says, looking unconvinced. Her full lips have been lined and filled in with a deep burgundy color today. She watches someone walk past her then returns her gaze to the screen and to Harlow's face. "Are you doing okay though? Like, in general. I think we're all a little messed up after what happened."

Harlow chews on her lower lip as a wave rolls in and washes over her bare feet, covering up her ankles before it slips back out and leaves her standing on wet sand.

"I'm okay sometimes," she says grudgingly. "I have nightmares. You?"

"Same," Dart admits. "I knew Ulysses for eight years. I miss him a lot. I think I'm going to talk to a therapist."

"Oh, you should. Definitely," Harlow says. "I have been, and it's helped a lot."

"I'm glad to hear it. But I'd be more glad to hear that you were coming back to the city."

"I can't," Harlow says, shaking her head. "Not now. But at some point. I'm just gonna ride it out here. You should come visit."

Dart gives a smug laugh and Harlow knows that there's a zero percent chance that her friend will make a trip south to the land of palm trees and Mickey Mouse.

"My train is coming," Dart says. Harlow can hear the screech of metal and the oncoming rumble of another train. "I'll call soon, okay? And don't forget that no one can actually make you wear sandals with velcro or force you to play pinochle, got it?"

Harlow laughs. "Got it, boss. Talk soon."

Dart ends the call first and the screen goes black. It takes Harlow a long minute of watching the surf to know what she wants to do next, but once she has it in her mind, it's a done deal.

She quickly Googles the Library of Congress and finds the number for the main switchboard there.

"Hello, can you please transfer me to Diego Santana?" she asks sweetly. She'd insisted that Athena show her the Instagram of the douchebag so that she could see for herself what had reeled her sister in, and yeah, she has to admit that he's pretty hot. But every one of his recent posts (following a long break of no posts at all) screams "gym bro" to her, with him showing off his gains in tank tops, or posing with one arm around another handsome guy wearing a nearly identical polo shirt as they both hold bottles of Heineken in a bar. There's also a new wedding photo posted, and this one fills her with the kind of rage that finally pushed her to make this call.

"This is Diego Santana," a deep voice says in her ear.

Harlow waits a beat. "You don't know me," she says, keeping her tone even. "But I know you, and I know your type. You might think you got away with what you did to my sister, but you've only gotten away with it *for now*. I've seen your Instagram, and I have your wife's info. So stop texting Athena—I don't want to hear that you've *ever* reached out to her again, am I making myself clear?"

"Wait...is this—"

"Yes. Do the math, jackass. You know who Athena is, so if I tell you she's my sister, you know who I am. You're a nobody, and I could crush you and your sham of a marriage if I wanted to. But as long as you forget Athena ever existed, I won't do that."

"Are you seriously calling to threaten me?"

"YOU. ARE. NOT. LISTENING," Harlow shouts, enunciating every word. "I do not want my sister coming to me ever again and saying that she got a message from Diego Santana asking when she was coming back to D.C. I do not want you reaching out to her and messing with her ever again. Athena might be sweet and innocent, but I'm not, and—
"

"Hey, whoa. Athena was all over me. She wasn't sweet and innocent at all, so I don't know what you're getting at."

Harlow narrows her eyes as she listens to this guy try to defend himself. He's worthless and spineless and if she were in D.C. at that exact moment, she'd wait outside the Library of Congress and confront him face to face. But she's not, so she has to settle for a phone call.

"Athena *was* sweet and innocent," Harlow confirms calmly. "But she's not anymore. You can thank yourself for that. And if you think someone high up has done a pretty decent job of covering up political scandals since the beginning of time, then you better believe that it would be a piece of cake to cover up any sort of mishap that might occur to a total nobody like Diego Santana." Harlow takes one deep breath and lets it out. "But hey, congrats on your recent wedding. Watch your back."

She hangs up and puts her phone into the pocket of her cut off denim shorts with a smile. *So long, Diego Santana.*

And so long to city life, five-star restaurants, the subway, art museums that stay open all night, concerts at Madison Square Garden, and her own freedom. Harlow knows she should feel sadder about giving up those things, but right now she just feels free.

She turns and walks back to the house, ready to put on a sundress and sandals and head over to Seadog Lane to have lunch with Athena.

Ruby

This time Jack is crying in the dream. He's sitting on one of the benches that runs the length of the boat, and they're not moving. The water is remarkably still, and the sky overhead is dark and foreboding.

"Jack," Ruby says to him in the dream, standing over him and looking down at his shoulders as they shake with his sobs. "Please, you have to tell me what's wrong."

But he doesn't. He either can't or he won't—which, she isn't sure—and when he looks up at her his face is tear-stained and he's distraught.

"Jack...you have to say something. You're scaring me," Ruby pleads. Still he says nothing. "Look," Ruby says. She's starting to feel angry in this version of the dream. "I can't help you if you won't tell me what's going on. I'm your wife—your partner—and I'm supposed to be able to help you. But I can't if you just sit here—"

"You can't help me anyway," Jack finally says. This is the first time Ruby has heard his voice in one of the dreams, and it sounds remarkably like him. "No one can help me, Ruby. You just need to keep your eyes open."

"Keep my eyes open for what?" Ruby nearly shouts, her frustration mounting. She reaches out to grab her husband by the shoulders. "Keep my eyes open for what?" she yells again.

She wakes up in her bed saying the words aloud: "Keep my eyes open for—"

Ruby sits up in bed, the sheets falling away from her satin nightgown. Outside her curtained windows, the sun is beginning to rise, though it's early—still only five-thirty, according to the clock by her bed. She pushes her sleep mask up onto her head and sits there, feeling defeated. No matter how the dream goes, she always wakes up too soon. There's never quite enough time to hear what Jack needs to tell her, or to make sense of what goes on in the dream.

Ruby gets up and walks straight to the shower. Even though it's early, she can still get dressed, make coffee, and go to the bookshop.

Today is the first day of an annual event called "Pirate Days," and Ruby's been warned over and over by the locals to expect what will feel like ten thousand visitors traipsing around the island. Of course this sent Eldrick, Banks, and Corbin into a tailspin, trying to figure out how to watch over the Hudson women and keep things under control, but Ruby has assured them that things will be fine. They've been living in the limelight for the majority of the girls' lives, and they're all used to being on high alert in larger than normal crowds. Of course, Marooned With a Book will be a point of interest to some of the visitors, but Ruby is prepared. Her dream about Jack has rattled her cage, which it always does, but she's got her game face on and she's ready to shake hands and do what she knows how to do best.

Seadog Lane at six-thirty in the morning is a peaceful place. Banks pulls over to the curb, parking directly in front of Marooned With a Book. He shuts off the golf cart and gives Ruby a thumbs-up.

"All systems go," Banks says, leaning back in the seat and waiting there for Ruby to make a move.

But rather than heading right into the bookstore, she climbs out of the cart and walks down the sidewalk, heading for the bench that overlooks the beach. It's the same one that Harlow and Athena had sat on together while Athena cried, and it has a view of the sunrise over the water that's unbeatable. Ruby sits, dropping her purse on the bench next to her as she looks out at the sea, which is bathed in the golden light of the sunrise.

Waking up early has always given her time to get her mind set for the day ahead, but waking up early after one of her Jack dreams just means she has more time in the day to obsess over what exactly he wanted to tell her, because she believes in dreams and premonitions. She knows in her heart that there's something she's missed, and that what she's been told about her husband is only the tip of the iceberg.

Ruby glances back at Seadog Lane, and sure enough, Banks is stationed there patiently, keeping his eyes on the street and on her. Ruby looks back at the ocean, turning slightly to the east so that she can watch as the sun begins its climb up over the water and into the sky as she thinks.

When Jack died a year ago, Ruby knew instinctively that there was far more to the story. It was a Wednesday, and she was sitting in a strategy meeting to discuss their upcoming reelection bid for the White House. Jack's first term was almost up, and he was abroad, supposedly meeting with England's Prime Minister in London. Some of their discussions while he'd been on that particular trip had been curt or done entirely by text, as Jack had claimed to be busy and on London time, but Ruby has never been one to sit and wait idly by for her man to return, so she kept herself moving, taking meetings, having lunches, and attending to the girls. Nothing seemed amiss to her, and so when Helen —then Jack's Chief of Staff—had walked into her private quarters and barged into her dining room where she was eating with two of Jack's advisors and her own personal secretary, Ruby had looked up in surprise.

"Helen," she said. "You're not with Jack?"

"Not this time," Helen had answered tersely. "Can we talk privately?"

Looks were exchanged all around the table as Ruby stood. She knew instantly that something was wrong.

Sitting on the couch in her private living area, with framed photos of her family on the polished credenza, Ruby had tucked her hands between her knees and felt her body turning in on itself protectively.

"Ruby," Helen said, sitting close enough to her to reach out and put a hand on Ruby's back, which she had. "You need to listen carefully, okay?"

Ruby had nodded; she knew instinctively what was coming.

"Jack has been in an accident on the Bay of Biscay. He was in Bordeaux, and something happened."

"Why was he in Bordeaux?" Ruby asked, frowning. The fact that her husband had been in an accident hadn't fully settled in yet. "He was supposed to be in London."

"Ruby, I'm not sure of all the details yet. I just know he was in a small airplane over the Bay of Biscay, and he had to make a water landing."

Jack had gotten his pilot's license at seventeen, and after a stint in the Air Force, Ruby considered him one of the best—if not *the* best—pilot she's ever known. His ability to just take a plane out had been entirely curtailed by his position as President, and how he'd managed to get airborne in a small plane on his own was as much of a mystery to Ruby at the moment as anything else that Helen was saying.

"Wait—a plane crash?" Ruby stood up and walked over to the credenza, pacing absentmindedly. Later, she would look back on this moment and not remember her reactions or responses. How does one appropriately process the news that their husband has crashed into a body of water in a country that he wasn't even supposed to be visiting? "Jack's plane crashed? I don't...I'm just..." Ruby put her head in her hands and stopped pacing. She closed her eyes. "What was Jack doing flying a small plane? He only ever flies Air Force One..." Nothing was gelling in Ruby's brain. *France?*"

Helen stood and walked over to her, taking Ruby by the shoulders. "You need to listen to me, Ruby. I'm serious. Jack died in this accident. He was alone. I don't have all the details yet, but you need to understand that this is going to move fast. The world will know in a matter of minutes that the President of the United States has died, but I wanted to be the one to tell you. Are you hearing me?"

It was a valid question, because Ruby found that both her hearing and vision were shutting down. The light was dimming and a loud buzzing was filling her ears and overpowering her brain. Helen continued to hold her by the shoulders, and at this point, she gave her kind of a hard shake.

"Ruby, do you need to sit?" Helen asked, her face and voice full of concern. "Here, sit on the couch." Helen led her back to where they'd been sitting just minutes before and Ruby sank onto the cushions grate-fully, letting her head fall to her knees.

After a few minutes of breathing as Helen rubbed her back, Ruby lifted her head, feeling a sense of calm wash over her. While this had always been an outcome that she *didn't* want to experience, it was one that she'd been prepared for many times and in many ways. Being married to the President meant that you were intimately familiar with all of the horrible things that could happen to him and to your entire family, but you lived each day by pushing it to the back of your mind and essentially suspending your disbelief.

"Okay," Ruby said, breathing in and out one more time and centering herself. "I'm ready. I'm here." There were tears inside of her, and there was panic waiting to bubble to the surface, but instead of giving in to that feeling, she stayed as quiet as possible. She needed to be present to find out what happened next. "I'm with you."

"I'm told that the airplane has been recovered, as has the body."

Ruby nodded slowly. Instinct kicked in then and she began to understand what was happening. "His body has been recovered," she repeated, nodding slowly. She needed her girls. No, she needed to under-stand everything before sitting down and talking to Harlow and Athena. She needed all the information first.

Helen looked at her knowingly. "There's more to this story, and I'm sure we'll hear it eventually, but for now, I need you to be briefed and ready for the onslaught. Because there *will* be an onslaught. Everyone will want a piece of you. Everyone will want a story, a tip, a comment, a photo, or something to report."

"There will be no comment—at least not for a while," Ruby said firmly. "I need to think. I'm going to need a lot of time to think before anything else happens."

"Of course."

"I need the girls," Ruby said, already in crisis mode. She stood up again, unable to stay seated.

"They're both en route. They've been told nothing but that there's a situation at the White House, and they're both being driven rather than flown so as to keep them safe from any news for as long as possible."

Ruby had been grateful for Helen's friendship and for her professionalism at that moment, and once she knew for sure that her daughters were on their way, she allowed herself one frustrated, sad, angry sob before pulling herself together again.

She sits on the bench now, remembering as much of it as she can: the meeting that had been interrupted by Helen; the walk to her private living space; the news delivered to her like a bomb that had exploded in the middle of their lives. Ruby has no idea how she sifted through it all, or how she survived the relentless speculation of a 24/7 news cycle that never dropped the topic—not even for one minute. But she has survived it, and she sits here on Shipwreck Key now, watching a sunrise as the street behind her comes to life in anticipation of Pirate Days.

Ruby stands and puts her purse over one shoulder as she walks back to the sidewalk, leaving the beach and the ocean behind.

"Morning, stranger," Bev Byer calls out. He's in front of The Frog's Grog with a hose, cleaning off the sidewalk. "You ready for the pirate invasion?"

Ruby laughs and walks over to him. He stops spraying the sidewalk. "Is it really an invasion?"

Bev considers this. "Of sorts. You'll see people dressed like runaway cast members from *Pirates of the Caribbean*, but most people will just buy a t-shirt and call it good. Every adult stops in for at least one grog."

"That's a lot of limes."

"Indeed it is," he says, nodding at the open door of his bar. Ruby can see straight through to the counter, where Tilly is stationed, squeezing limes with a sour look on her unmade-up face. She looks like a much younger girl without the red lips, dark eyebrows, and heavy foundation that she usually wears.

Ruby lifts a hand and waves at Tilly, who scowls back at her. "I see you've got my sunniest employee hard at work in there."

Bev laughs. "She'll learn how to do a day's work come hell or high water," he says with a shake of his head. "Kids these days, wanting to sit around on their phones or play their damn video games all day and night."

Ruby watches him as he talks, noticing that while he seems perturbed by his granddaughter's youthful penchant for electronics, he also has an unmistakable look of pride on his face. He knows that he's a salty old island-dweller, but that somehow he's taken an orphaned little girl and turned her into a young woman who is headstrong and unique.

Ruby reaches out and touches his arm. "She's one-of-a-kind, Bev. You've done good work."

A smile twitches at the corners of his mouth from under his gray mustache and his eyes take on a grandfatherly twinkle. "Thank you kindly, madam," Bev says, shaking out his hose. He's ready to get back to work. Ruby steps onto the empty street to cross over to the bookstore. "Keep your eyes open today, alright?" Bev says loudly over the spray from his hose. "There'll be pirates and unexpected things everywhere."

Ruby stops in her tracks. A chill runs up her spine. "Keep your eyes open" is exactly what Jack said to her in the dream. But keep her eyes open for what? Men with hooks instead of hands? Planks? Scurvy?

Ruby scans the street: A banner hangs from one side of Seadog Lane to the other that reads *Avast ye! Welcome to Shipwreck Key!* and on the front of most stores are welcoming signs that say things like *Ahoy!* or *Sink me! It's a pirate!* Over the front window of Marooned With a Book, Ruby has hung a smaller banner that reads *Yo ho ho, let's find you a book to go!*

But for as charming and festive as the street looks, with its anchors and ropes and nautical touches, there's a touch of something dark and unknown about the day ahead.

"It's just the dream," Ruby mutters to herself. "But I *will* keep my eyes open."

At some point during the day, Ruby is aware that her face hurts from smiling and her feet hurt from standing. People have come into the bookstore in droves, wanting to see the former First Lady, to get photographs with her, which Ruby always indulges, and to buy books that they can proudly display back home and say they bought at Marooned With a Book.

Even with the front door closed to keep the air conditioning inside,

Ruby can smell the sweet butter and cinnamon of the elephant ears being fried and sold out on Seadog Lane, and she can see people wandering up and down the street that's been closed to everything but foot traffic. There are tons of people in pirate outfits—eye patches pushed up onto foreheads so that people can pull them down as necessary over one eye for effect; pantaloons with long socks and loose, flowing shirts; dresses with plunging necklines and cinched bodices— and plenty dressed in shirts covered with images of Captain Hook, the Jolly Roger flag, and words that pertain to pirates or Shipwreck Key.

There's a brief lull in foot traffic around three o'clock while a theater group from Destin performs funny scenes from the musical comedy *The Pirates of Penzance*, and Ruby sits down with Harlow on the front step of the bookstore as they eat two hot dogs slathered in mustard that Harlow picked up at a booth next to Chips Ahoy, the island's fish and chips shop.

"Good day so far?" Harlow bites into her hot dog and gets a dab of mustard on the end of her nose.

Ruby reaches over with her napkin and swipes at the mustard playfully. "Great day," she says, smiling at her youngest. People are walking by and eyeing them with curiosity, but for the most part, they just smile or nod and keep walking. From the end of Seadog Lane, the actors can be heard performing a scene from the movie to applause and laughter.

"I hope you don't mind that we're not working in the store today, but Athena somehow got us roped into pitching in at the dock."

Ruby holds her hotdog in both hands as she watches Harlow's profile. It's a wonder to her how resilient Harlow has been in light of the terrifying nightmare of the bar shooting, and while Ruby knows that she sleeps with her nightstand pushed up against the door (she won't do this forever), and she sits on the floor of her closet with the door closed to have her Zoom calls with her therapist (a self-protective mechanism), she's definitely coming around. Ruby has caught her laughing with her sister, and looking and sounding more like the funny, lighthearted Harlow she's always been. And while neither of her girls seem ready to go back to their old lives anytime soon, Ruby has to admit that having them there is kind of like an opportunity to re-enjoy them. After all, so much of their lives were spent with Ruby elbow-deep in First Lady duties, and now that all of that is behind her, she's looking at her daughters with fresh eyes and an uncluttered life, both of which allow her much more freedom to enjoy her time with them.

"Honey, I don't mind at all." Ruby takes a bite of her own hotdog and chews it with a smile while Harlow takes a swig from her can of Diet Coke. "Being part of a small community like this means pitching in and being part of everything."

"Even something corny like Pirate Days," Harlow says with a lopsided grin. "Actually, it's pretty fun. Some of the boats that are coming in to the dock have Jolly Roger flags on them, and the people are all really excited to be here. It's charming."

Ruby pops the last bite of hotdog into her mouth and wads up her paper napkin in both hands. She's about to stand and brush off the back of her shorts when a shadow falls over her there on the front step of her store. She looks up to see a woman standing before her with a pre-teen boy at her side. Ruby squints against the afternoon sun.

"Good afternoon," the woman says, sliding her sunglasses off her face. She's lovely—approximately forty years old, dark wavy hair, and the kind of easy, quiet beauty that comes with a lot of money.

Ruby instantly feels off-balance; something is wrong here, though she doesn't know what. She looks back and forth between the woman and the boy expectantly, assuming that they want a photo or to tell her that they were huge Jack Hudson supporters.

Instead, the woman rubs her lips together nervously. "Mrs. Hudson," she says, glancing at Harlow. "Hello," she says, giving Harlow a slight nod.

Ruby's blood runs cold, though it takes her a moment to realize why: it's the French accent.

"Mrs. Hudson, I didn't want to come here like this, but I need to speak with you. It's urgent."

"Who are you?" Ruby asks, her voice no more than a rasp.

The woman looks at her—a long, burning look of understanding and uneasy familiarity. "I'm Etienne Boucher, and this is my son, Julien."

Ruby

Etienne Boucher is here. Etienne and Julien are here on my island, Ruby thinks. Instinctively, she reaches out a hand and sets it on Harlow's thigh protectively, as if this will do anything to shield her daughter from the woman who Ruby had hoped never to meet.

Ruby stands up slowly, her balled up napkin still in one hand. "What are you doing here?"

"As I said," Etienne explains carefully, "I need to speak with you, and I wasn't getting a response any other way."

Ruby looks up and down the street, but no one is watching them with much interest. "Come inside," she says, opening the door to the bookstore briskly and ushering Etienne and Julien inside.

Harlow stands. "I'm going to get Athena," she says flatly, turning and walking toward the dock without another word.

Inside the shop—which is empty at the moment—Ruby turns the sign from Open to Closed and twists the lock on the door.

"I can't believe you would come here," she says, trying to calm herself. She steps behind the counter to put something between herself and this woman, and to her credit, Etienne looks as uncomfortable as Ruby feels. "This is so inappropriate, and such bad timing," Ruby adds, nodding out the front window at the crowd of people on the street. "There are a million sets of eyes on this island right now."

"Listen, Ruby," Etienne says carefully, pointing her son wordlessly toward the center room. As if he understands implicitly what his mother wants, he wanders away, looking at the books on the shelves but not touching anything. "I came here because there's something important that you need to know, and frankly, I think it should stay between you and me. No one else needs to know this."

"What? That my husband had a mistress and a child outside of his marriage? Too late—everyone already knows." Her words are laced with hurt and anger; this is the culmination of her disappointment and rage, feelings that have built in her over this past year, ebbing and flowing as she's worked to come to terms with the real facts of her marriage.

Etienne sets her purse on the counter and unzips it loudly. "Here," she says, taking an envelope out and laying it on the counter. "I would have mailed it or sent it via our lawyers, but a part of me understood that it may never reach you that way. And it's important."

Ruby stares at the envelope—on the front is her name, scrawled in Jack's familiar handwriting. Time stands still as she stares at it, unwilling to reach out and touch the letter for fear of being burned.

"What the hell is this? Have you read it?" Ruby looks up at Etienne's beautiful face. "And does your child know what he's doing here? Does he understand what's going on?"

Etienne's mouth curls into a shadow of a smile, and it's clear that she has empathy for Ruby in this situation. "We're French, Ruby, we're not aliens from another planet. Of course he understands—at least to the capacity that a twelve-year-old boy needs to or can understand. For a long time, he was unaware that his father was the President. Jack would visit when he could, and all Julien knew was that his father traveled a lot and visited when he could. I knew I wouldn't be able to keep it from him forever, but then he and his school friend took that DNA test, and it led to all kinds of questions that I'd hoped to never answer."

Ruby remembers Harlow opening the results of the DNA test for her college course. "I can understand the surprise. When Harlow took the test, we were completely blindsided by the suggestion of a sibling."

Etienne looks down at her hands on the counter and is quiet for a moment. "Can I ask how Jack responded to that?"

It all feels surreal in that moment: the woman her husband had loved and impregnated is standing before Ruby, asking her for something that only she can give. There's a slight shift in the power dynamic as Ruby weighs whether or not she wants to divulge any information to this stranger.

She ultimately decides that she should, given that this may be the only time she ever meets Etienne Boucher in her life.

There's a knock on the front door and Ruby's head snaps around. She's ready to shout that they're closed for the afternoon and to point at the sign, but then she realizes that it's Harlow and Athena. Harlow looks determined, but Athena's eyes look wild and frightened. She lets her girls in and re-locks the door behind them.

Etienne takes a step away from the counter, suddenly outnumbered by the Hudson women. She looks appropriately intimidated, and for a second, Ruby pities her.

"Jack immediately lied," she says, returning to the question at hand without introducing her daughters. She knows that Etienne is well aware of who the girls are, and now that Harlow has retrieved Athena, she guesses that Athena's been brought up to speed as well. "We were in Palm Beach and he sat across from us at breakfast and said that it was impossible, and that DNA tests were an inexact science."

Etienne nods, still looking at her hands. "I see."

"Did you expect him to rejoice?" Ruby asks, though not meanly. "To claim this child as his own without any sort of preamble?"

In the next room, Julien is picking up books from the shelf, examining them, and sliding them back into their slots carefully. Ruby has to hand it to Etienne: he seems incredibly calm, polite, and well-adjusted.

"If I'm being honest, in a perfect world, he might have owned up to both lives he was living and tried to integrate them somehow."

Ruby snorts in disbelief. "In this case, being French is the same as being aliens from another planet, Etienne," Ruby says, using her name for the first time. "That's simply not how things are done here. Maybe in France, where having a mistress is as common as having a glass of wine with dinner—"

"No need to disparage the French," Etienne says, holding up a hand. "We're just slightly more evolved about some things."

Ruby can feel Athena piecing things together, and she knows Harlow well enough to know that her daughter is about to speak up, so she talks instead.

"You're here now," she says, feeling a frost to her words as she waves a hand in the direction of Julien, who is still wandering the store as he was told to do. "This is your one chance. My girls are plenty old enough to understand what's going on, and if you want to introduce them to your son, then you may."

"To their half-brother," Etienne says softly, but with the protectiveness of a mountain lion.

Deep inside herself, Ruby knows that Harlow and Athena have every right to develop a relationship with their half-brother—or to refuse to do so. The choice is not hers to make.

Etienne says her son's name and he turns to face her. In French, she explains something and he puts the book in his hand back down on the table before walking to the front of the store.

"Harlow and Athena," she says to the young women who are still standing side by side near the front door. "This is your brother, Julien. Julien, my love," she says, turning to him and speaking in English for everyone else's benefit. "These are your sisters, Harlow," she points at Harlow, "and Athena." With a nod, she gestures to Ruby's oldest daughter. "While the circumstances that bring us together are not good ones, the three of you have the right to determine what relationship—if any—you choose to have with one another in your lives. I wanted nothing more than for all of you to meet. It's the right thing to do."

"How did you know we'd be here?" Harlow asks stubbornly.

"I knew you would, because I called your office in New York and they explained to me that you were available remotely. It was a safe bet that I'd find you here. And you," she says, turning to Athena, "posted a photograph of Shipwreck Key on your public Instagram account three days ago, so I hoped to find you still here."

Julien clears his throat before speaking, and his accent is much thicker than his mother's, his English less fluent. "I am happy to meet you," he says to his half-sisters, looking at them shyly. "I'm sorry about your father."

There's a sweetness and an innocence to the way Julien says this, and it tugs at Ruby's heart in a way she hadn't expected. She finally comes out from behind the counter, compelled to be real—to be human—to this little boy. She can be as angry as she wants to be toward Jack (though it's far too late for that to do any good), and she can be as cold as she feels toward Etienne, who should have known better than to take up with another woman's husband, but Julien has done nothing but be born. He's just a child with a tender heart.

"And you," Ruby says to him, walking past Etienne, who bristles slightly, "we're sorry for your loss as well. You lost your father too, and that has to be hard."

Quickly and quietly, Etienne translates this into French for her child. Julien's eyes well with tears and he nods.

Everyone stands there in the bookstore without speaking for a long minute.

Finally, Athena speaks. "Do you want us to tell you more about him?" she offers to Julien. Athena is Ruby's deeply sensitive, caring child, and offering to share her father with a boy she's never met is right in line with how she operates.

Julien nods.

"Let's go sit down," Athena says to him, and then she reaches out, offering him a hand. Though Julien is nearly as tall as she is and not really much of a child at all, he takes her hand willingly, and the of them go to the back room of the store, where they sit down in the mismatched floral chairs together. Ruby has no idea what they'll talk about, or whether the language barrier will be a problem, but she knows her daughters will handle Julien with care, and Etienne is absolutely right: it's up to the three of them to decide how and if they want to continue to have any sort of relationship.

"You don't have to read the letter," Etienne says now, looking at the envelope on the counter.

"I can't even imagine what it contains," Ruby says. She's tired and overwhelmed. She runs her hands over her face and sighs deeply, feeling like she just aged thirty years since her first bite of the hotdog on the front step with Harlow. "What could Jack possibly have to say to me from beyond the grave, and why am I just reading this now, a year after his death?"

"It's what he wanted," Etienne says with hesitation. She's treading on thin ice here, presenting facts and information that proves her intimate knowledge of what Jack would or wouldn't have wanted. "He left me a letter that I read right away, and in it, he asked me to wait a year before presenting this to you."

"That's bullshit," Ruby says, swearing angrily, though she normally measures her words much more carefully. "Why do you get to read a letter immediately from *my* husband, and then why do I have to wait a full year to find out what the hell went wrong with our marriage? That pisses me off." Her voice has grown loud, and when she looks through the store she can see the three kids looking back at her from their huddle of chairs. Ruby drops her voice. "Once Jack was dead, why didn't you send me that letter immediately? Who cares what he wanted—he wasn't there to know whether or not you carried out his wishes."

Etienne keeps her mouth pressed in a straight line, but folds her arms over her chest protectively.

"And why are there even letters for us at all anyway? If Jack died in a small plane crash unexpectedly, then why the hell did he have letters for his wife and mistress in the event that he died?" She watches Etienne's immovable face. "Are there letters for the girls as well?"

Etienne shakes her head. "No. One letter for you, one letter for me. I think if you read it for yourself, you'll have more answers."

Ruby thinks of her recurring dream, and of how badly she's always wanted answers directly from Jack's mouth. Every single time she dreams about them on that damned boat together, she wakes up wanting more. She wants answers. And now here they are—maybe, possibly—in an envelope right here on her front counter, and she wants to run away from them.

Ruby seeks out her daughters with her eyes, suddenly desperate to be alone with them. She looks at Etienne and knows that this conversation is over. Pulling herself together, she stands up straighter and takes a deep breath.

"Thank you for the letter. I'll read it when I'm ready. I'm glad the kids had the opportunity to meet, and if they wish to have further contact, then of course they should." Fumblingly, Ruby reaches for a business card to the store and picks up a pen. She scribbles her personal email address on the back, because really, now that she's met Etienne, is there really a monster left to avoid? She's just a living, breathing woman like any other, and whether Ruby likes it or not (she does *not*), they shared a man, and their children share genes. "Here's my information if you need to reach me."

Etienne takes the card from Ruby's hand and gives her a tight nod of understanding. "Thank you," she says, and Ruby understands that it's a show of gratitude for everything from speaking to her in the first place when she showed up on the doorstep of Marooned With a Book, to encouraging their children to foster any sort of relationship at all. "Julien," she says, calling for her son. Julien stands and offers his hand to both of his half-sisters, which they shake in turn. It's a formal goodbye, but not an unfriendly one, and Ruby observes her daughters' faces as they watch Julien go. They look curious and guarded, but she knows they'll never shut him out if he wants to know them.

Ruby unlocks the door and lets Etienne and Julien out, then closes it behind them, locks it, and closes the curtains. As Harlow and Athena watch, she presses her back to the door, slides down it, and lands on the floor with her forehead pressed to her knees.

There on the floor, Ruby succumbs to the tears that have been building since the second Etienne introduced herself. They are the tears of a woman who had to pull herself together the moment she heard that her husband was dead. They are the tears of a woman who never got a straight answer from her husband about his other life—his other family. They are the tears of a woman who is angry, lonely, sad, confused, and, maybe most of all, they are the tears of a woman who is afraid of what she'll find inside that envelope on the counter.

Athena

Thank God Aunt Sunday is on Shipwreck Key now. This is the first thing Athena thinks when she wakes up a week later to hear voices on the deck below her bedroom window.

"But Rubes, you need to read it," Sunday is saying when Athena walks outside from the kitchen with a mug of coffee in her hands. "Morning, sweets," Sunday says when she looks at her. "You're looking lovely as a daisy bathed in the sunshine of a summer day."

Athena laughs out loud and plops down in an Adirondack chair. "Doubtful," she says, holding her coffee between both hands. "But thank you."

Sunday turns back to Ruby. "That letter could have the answers you need, Ruby," she argues, pacing back and forth on the deck wearing a pair of yoga pants and a tank top. Ruby is watching from a chair of her own. "That woman had the nerve to show up here after *carrying out* Jack's stupid wishes, but what if the letter tells you how sorry he is, and explains everything you ever wanted to know about why he did this in the first place?"

"It won't," Ruby says with a firm shake of her head.

Sunday sighs dramatically. "Okay. Well, I won't be able to convince you before my yoga class starts," she says, glancing at the watch on her wrist. "And I need to go and meditate on how I'm going to handle my own marriage, so call me later on, alright?"

Ruby gives her a small salute and she and Athena watch as Sunday bounces down the steps of the porch in a pair of flip-flops. She hops into her new golf cart and backs out of the driveway.

"The phrase 'firecracker' was invented solely to describe Sunday Bond," Ruby says, watching her friend with amusement as she drives away. "I'm thrilled that she's here, Bean, but sometimes your aunt Sunday acts like a kid who ate too much sugar, and you just need to let her burn it off."

Athena laughs because it's a completely apt description of Sunday. "Harlow was sometimes like that when we were kids," she says, sipping her coffee.

"Yeah?" Ruby turns to look at her daughter, then shifts her gaze to the beach in front of the house. "I never had a sister, so I guess I wouldn't actually know what it's like."

Athena shrugs. "It's mostly cool—at least it is once everyone is grown up. Being sisters when you're both kids is a whole other story."

Ruby takes a sip of her coffee. "I'm glad you and Harlow are such good friends now. That's important to me, and you two have lived a shared life experience that not many people get to have. When you say your dad was the President of the United States, that's something that most people can't fathom—even I can't. I went into the White House willingly and as an adult, but you two grew up in the spotlight without ever having anyone ask you whether you wanted to or not." Ruby's eyes fill with tears.

"Hey, Mom," Athena says, watching her with a worried look on her face. "It's okay. Really. Harlow and I are totally fine." She pauses and makes a face. "I mean, we *will* be fine, but our current circumstances have nothing to do with us being the daughters of Jack and Ruby Hudson. I promise you."

"That's not true," Ruby says, shaking her head emphatically. "I hate the thought that Harlow not only had to live through such a nightmarish experience, but that it was covered every second of the day on the news, with her face splashed all over the story like she was the only or the most important person there in the bar. And I absolutely hate the thought that some guy—some predator—broke your heart and potentially did it just so he could say he slept with Athena Hudson."

"Mom," Athena says, stopping her. "It's all okay. I've had lots of time to think since I've been here, and, yeah, Diego is an asshole. He used me, but I'm going to tell myself it was just because I was so obviously into him that I was an easy target. No one likes to think of themselves as a glamorous notch on some guy's belt."

"You're right, baby—I'm sorry. I shouldn't have said that."

Athena laughs softly. "Hey, that's okay too. Part of being an adult is learning to hear what people have to say, and then deciding what you're willing to take on and what you're not. I'm fine knowing that *maybe* that's the reason Diego targeted me for a one-night stand, but I'm not fine with labeling myself as some sort of prize. I'm just not. So it's all good, and I'll keep processing it and getting myself back to where I was."

Ruby watches her daughter with awe and pride. "You're such a remarkable young woman, Bean," she says, swiping away a tear. "And so is your sister. I'm really proud of both of you."

Ruby stands and walks over to Athena, bending at the waist so that she can plant a kiss on her daughter's head.

"We're proud of you too, Mom," Athena says, smiling softly as Ruby walks back into the house, leaving her there on the deck alone with her coffee.

This time on Shipwreck Key has done more to improve Athena's mental state post-Diego than any amount of therapy could ever do. Not to detract from Harlow's need to speak with a therapist—good God, Athena totally supports that and would for anyone who needs it—but being on the quiet island, breathing in the ocean air, and surrounding herself with books in a totally different way than she had at the Library of Congress has all done great things for her. She's even stopped looking up Diego's Instagram to see what he's posted, and she did herself a favor two days ago and blocked both him and his wife on all social media platforms so that she won't even be tempted to check up on their lives. Because really, who cares? It's not her life, and Diego's actions don't define her unless she lets them. And she won't.

In a final display of self-worth and strength, Athena picks up her phone from where she's set it on the arm of the deck chair and opens up her text chain with Diego. There's not much there beyond his message that she'd haltingly answered with a series of hurt questions and angry retorts, but she opens it anyway and reads everything one last time. Unfortunately, Diego will always be the first person she slept with, but he won't be the man who got under her skin and ruined things for the next guy she meets.

Athena's thumb hovers over the screen for a minute, but then she taps it a few times, effectively blocking Diego's number. After she does that, she gives their shared messages one determined swipe, deleting them from her phone forever.

Just like Sunday leaving Peter in D.C., or her mom letting Etienne and Julien into the bookstore so that she can start to say goodbye to the mystery and shame that surround her own marriage, Athena wants to embrace the power of womanhood and let go of the things that hurt her.

And Shipwreck Key is turning out to be the perfect place to do just that.

Ruby

"You haven't read this?"

"I have not read this," Ruby says, shaking her head and holding the envelope from Jack in her hand.

Nearly three weeks have passed since Etienne showed up during Pirate Days, and Ruby has kept herself as busy as possible, waiting for this moment right here.

"And you want to read it with me?" Dexter North asks, looking surprised. They're on a boat together, somewhere between Shipwreck Key and Destin, and Dexter has cut the motor so that they're drifting in the middle of nowhere, with no spectators, no paparazzi, and no ears to hear them. The boat bobs in the water as they stare at one another in anticipation.

"I think I do." As soon as she'd gone through all the emotions that Etienne's visit had stirred up, Ruby had a vision about how she wanted this to go down. After all the dreams she's had about being on a boat with Jack, it only seems appropriate to her that she hear his final words —even if they are written ones—here on a boat.

"Let's talk about the pros and cons of us reading this letter together," Dexter says. It's obvious to Ruby that he wants nothing more than to read the final words from the President to his wife right alongside her,

THE CASTAWAY

both as a curious human being and as the author of the biography he's working on, but Dexter North has proven himself to be a stand-up guy, along with being a stellar author, so he waits patiently to be convinced that this is truly what Ruby wants.

"Well," Ruby says, sitting back so that she's leaning against the side of the boat. Now that it's three o'clock, the sun has crested and is moving lower in the sky, but it's still summer in Florida, so even the breeze off the water doesn't entirely erase the humidity that hangs in the air around them. Ruby pulls her tank top away from her body and lets it snap back against her skin as she tries to get a little wind on her body. "The cons of reading this personal letter with anyone else are that I'm sharing something private and hurtful. I'm also opening myself up to the possibility that you won't honor your journalistic integrity and that you might share the information in an unauthorized way." Dexter looks back at her, his face blank; he is wise enough to listen to her concerns and not be offended.

"And the pros?" he prompts, leaning back on his side of the boat and folding his arms. A bigger wave sneaks up on them, lifting the boat and rocking it a few times as it rolls past.

Ruby considers this. She could have read the letter alone, which she's sure is what Jack would have wanted. She could have read it with her girls, hoping to give them some much-needed insight into their father's life and death. She could have refused to read it altogether (but she's not superhuman, and who could actually do that?) Instead, she wants to read it with the man who is going to document her husband through her eyes.

"The pros are that you get to be present—as a biographer—for a truly authentic moment. You're also relatively impartial to my marriage, and I think it's safer to read the letter with a man who might be able to offer a male perspective, should it be warranted, rather than with a female friend, who will jump to my defense regardless of what the letter says."

"You're thinking of Sunday Bond?" Dexter asks, lifting one eyebrow from behind his Ray-Bans.

"She'd be a natural choice," Ruby admits. "But this is what I want, and I'm sure of it." She holds up the sealed envelope just as the breeze picks up unexpectedly, blowing her hat off her head and into the water. Startled, Ruby jumps up and instinctively lets go of the letter, which is taken by the wind. "No!" she screams, leaning over the side of the boat as she reaches for the envelope.

She catches it between her first and middle finger, holding onto it with a prayer as she feels her feet coming out from underneath her; she'll be in the water—along with the letter—in just seconds.

But before she can feel the unmistakable sensation of going headfirst into the water, Dexter is up and his arms are around her waist. His body presses against the length of hers as he pins her to the side of the boat, reaches out with one hand, and plucks the letter from her hand.

"Got it!" he says, using the arm that's still around her body to pull her down to her feet again. They both stand upright, carefully brushing themselves off as Dexter holds the envelope out to her.

With a nervous, shaky laugh, Ruby takes the letter, presses it tightly to her chest, and casts one glance over her shoulder at her straw hat, which is bobbing away merrily on the water. "I never liked that hat anyway," she says.

"Okay, take two." Dexter runs a hand through his hair as he catches his breath. He sits down on the bench again on his side of the boat, watching her intently.

Ruby nods as she sits down, still clutching the letter tightly. "Maybe I should have given more thought to the practicality of this situation. But yes, take two. Here we go."

She opens the envelope with fumbling hands, putting it under her bare thigh on the bench to keep it from blowing away after she extracts the single page from within.

Dexter is watching her with his body leaned forward eagerly, arms resting on his knees. Ruby takes a deep, shaky breath and starts to read.

The minute she's done, she knows what she needs to do.

* * *

The next book club meeting is laced with an undercurrent of expectation. The women are all well aware that Ruby has met with Dexter North for a second time, and while they'd read the Jackie O.

biography and discussed it at length at their last meeting, this time they don't even have a book to hide behind as they sit in their circle, eyeing one another and waiting for Ruby to speak.

"You ladies have quickly become my favorite part of living on Shipwreck Key," Ruby starts, sitting in her chair and looking around. In addition to the original five—Heather, Marigold, Molly, Vanessa, and Tilly—she's got her girls in attendance once again, and as an added bonus, now Sunday is officially a member of the Marooned With a Book Club, though not without some disbelief, as the other members of the book club still occasionally seem stunned as they look around the circle and see both the former First Lady and the former Second Lady sitting amongst them.

"And I can't even imagine going forward without knowing that we're going to get together every two weeks to talk about books," Ruby goes on. As she says this, Heather's face falls.

"But you're dumping us," Heather says knowingly. "You're leaving the island."

Ruby is stunned. "No! God, no. Does this seem like an 'I'm leaving' speech?" The other women make fleeting eye contact with one another as they nod. "Not at *all*," Ruby says firmly, shaking her head. "Actually, quite the opposite. I want to thank you for your friendship so far, and to ask you all for a huge favor."

"As long as you aren't leaving," Molly says, her arms folded across her chest protectively, "then we'll do anything you ask us to."

"I'm not leaving!" Ruby assures them with a laugh. "But I am going to need your help. All of you."

Marigold is watching her intently, running her fingertips along her jawline as she watches Ruby to see where she's going with this.

"Spit it out, Mom," Harlow says. "You're making everyone nervous."

"Okay, okay. This is hard to talk about, but I need to get comfortable with it fast." Ruby wipes her damp palms over her jeans. "Like I told you at our last meeting, my late husband's mistress showed up on the island and we talked."

Molly shakes her head and makes a *tsk-tsk* sound. "Takes some nerve, doesn't it?" she mutters rhetorically.

"And she left me a letter from Jack that I waited for quite some time to read." Ruby pauses. "But when I did, I realized immediately that it wasn't just a letter for me, and it wasn't just a letter for my girls." She glances at Harlow and Athena, who are both studiously looking at the floor as they try not to cry. She'd read the letter to them both the minute she got back from the boat trip with Dexter North, and with their encouragement, she's decided to go forward with her plan. "It's a letter for everyone."

The small group of women shifts in their seats, looking at one another with confusion.

"Like, a letter for all of us?" Marigold asks with a frown.

"More than all of us here in this room," Ruby says. "When I say everyone, I mean *everyone*. And I want the world to hear it, which is where you all come in."

Ruby looks at each of them in turn, then shares her plan with the women, who silently take it all in, heads nodding in understanding.

"Sweet, fancy Moses..." Molly looks stunned. "Honey, are you absolutely sure about this?"

"I am absolutely sure," Ruby says.

"Then if this is what you want, this is what you'll have," Heather says, standing up. "Let's get to work making it happen, shall we?"

The sun hasn't even set outside on the late June evening, but the women get to work inside the bookstore, planning and scheming together until it gets so late that they all drive their golf carts home under a bright, full moon with the sound of the waves crashing in the near distance.

Harlow

Being away from New York has been amazing. For the first couple of weeks Harlow was so traumatized by the shooting that all she did was eat, sleep, and hide inside her mother's house. Talking to her therapist has given her strength to make all kinds of baby steps, and now being a part of her mother's book club (while at first a seemingly lame thing to do) is restructuring her life and giving her purpose.

As soon as Ruby told them all what she wants to do with Jack's letter, Harlow had jumped into action. She's been working remotely for the marketing firm in only the most bare bones way, answering emails, taking phone calls from existing clients, finishing projects, and kind of drifting away from her job as she sits on her mom's porch with whatever book they're currently reading for book club, or taking shifts at the bookstore and laughing at whatever dark or twisty thing Tilly is currently saying. There's only the tiniest sliver of the old Harlow still kicking around inside of her, feeling worried that she might be fired from her job, lose touch with pop culture, or become totally irrelevant and morph into a middle aged woman in a young woman's body. The rest of her is a new, more relaxed Harlow—one who is learning how to be her real, authentic self outside of the public eye—and she likes this new Harlow a heck of a lot more than she ever thought she would.

Sitting at a little table by the window inside The Scuttlebutt, Harlow sips her chai latte and skips the Taylor Swift song that's playing in her AirPods in favor of an upbeat 90s dance jam. Molly has kindly given her a spot to do her work and use the coffee shop's WiFi, and Harlow loves having a place to work that's not her mother's house or the bookstore. The added bonus is that she can hit pause on her music and keep her AirPods in, listening to people come and go and as she picks up on all their gossip while still pretending that she's not able to hear them.

So far, Harlow has discovered that: the original teacher for the entire island was a beautiful thirty-one-year-old Canadian woman who left with a boy named Jeff Absos the minute he had his diploma in and hand and had turned eighteen. The scandal rocked the island, but apparently Miss Breck and Jeff are happily married now, living in Saskatchewan and raising two kids on an alpaca farm. Harlow also overheard two women discussing the fact that the former owner of Chips Ahoy was arrested for money laundering and had some connection to the mob, and the very minor detail that Bev Byer has been in love with Molly for almost twenty years.

This last bit of gossip interests her the most, as she's grown to love and appreciate Molly's totally down to earth persona, and finding out that there's even a whiff of romance to the staunchly loyal widow's life is completely intriguing. Harlow tucks this information away to share with her mom and sister over dinner and refocuses on the task at hand.

Her immediate concerns are all about making the event her mother wants to hold a raging success. She chews on her pen and looks out the window at Seadog Lane as the dance song playing on her AirPods changes to a jazzy lounge cover of Radiohead's "Creep."

Hearing her dad's words read aloud by her mom had been eye opening for Harlow—and for Athena, based on the way her sister had cried wordlessly as they both listened—and now she is wholly committed to making sure that they do something big here. This event will be everything Ruby needs it to be on a personal level and on a public level, because if there's anything that Harlow can do well right now, it's coordinate and market the crap out of this shindig.

So far, Harlow has arranged for the weekend in question to be a full package deal: The Flora—Shipwreck Key's only inn—has agreed to only rent out all of their rooms as part of the package, which also includes coffee and pastries both mornings at The Scuttlebutt, lunch and dinner both days at the cafe and restaurant on the island, and entrance to the actual event, which is going to be held at Marooned With a Book.

As for the event itself, Ruby wants to make sure that it will be highly covered and reported on, but only by a select few news outlets, which is why she's asked Harlow to coordinate the weekend and present it as an opportunity for the ten highest bidding journalists or organizations to attend, film, and report on exclusively. And it's working: so far, the website that Athena built to host the auction for tickets to this exclusive weekend is showing high levels of traffic, and the bids are currently at fifty thousand dollars for each of the individual packages. With ten rooms up for grabs, Ruby is already banking on half a million dollars that she'll be able to turn around and donate once everything is said and done—and that's assuming that the bids aren't driven even higher than that, which Harlow predicts they will be.

The whole thing is fairly genius, in Harlow's opinion, pitting news organizations against one another to drive up the bids and benefit charity, and it will also give Ruby the opportunity to use this platform in the way that she wants to. Harlow and Athena know exactly what's going to happen, but no one else does, although the book club is aware of the event and each woman has offered to chip in and help to ensure that the weekend is successful. It will be, of course, because Ruby never does anything halfway, and Harlow has seen her when she sets her mind to something, pulling together functions, getting people to do things they wouldn't normally do, and turning anything she does into solid gold.

But this...this is personal. This has meaning. And if it goes the way Harlow thinks it's going to go, it could possibly bring closure not just to her and her mom and sister, but to anyone who felt touched in any way by Jack Hudson's death. A lot of people took the sudden death of a relatively young president quite personally, and Harlow hopes that they feel the same sense of peace and understanding that her family has felt since reading her dad's letter.

"Hey, kiddo," Molly says, walking over to where Harlow is sitting by the window. "How's tricks?"

Harlow takes a sip of her chai latte. "Everything is good. Thanks again for letting me set up shop here."

"Not a problem." Molly is holding a blue and white checkered rag in one hand and she slaps it into the palm of the other, tugging on both ends of it nervously. "Hey, Harlow...question for you."

"Shoot."

There's no one else in The Scuttlebutt at the moment, so Molly pulls out a chair and sits across from Harlow.

"Is your mom really okay with this whole book thing? I mean...she's a special lady, which I'm sure you know, but I worry about her having pressure from everywhere to share the kinds of things that most of us never have to share with the world. Do you think it bothers her?"

Harlow squints her eyes as she thinks about this. "Actually, I don't think it does," she decides. "My mom has always been a First Lady, even when she wasn't technically one. She understands that being a part of people's lives means that you're there through thick and thin. And she didn't just lose her husband when my dad died—the whole country lost a president, and all those people want answers just as much as we do."

Molly folds her arms and leans on the table, shoulders slightly hunched. "When my husband Rodney died, I didn't want to do anything for a year—even get out of bed. I didn't want to see anyone, talk to anyone, or explain how I felt to a therapist, to my mother, or to my friends. I just wanted to close my eyes and make it all go away, and some days I still feel that way, even though it's been forty years," Molly says with a sad smile. "So watching your mom get her life in order is inspirational. I consider myself a relatively tough old broad, but your mom's got real gumption, and I admire it."

Harlow feels a warm glow of pride spread through her. "She does have a lot of gumption," she agrees. "And so do you. You're a business-woman with a fierce love of the island, and everybody knows you. I've been sitting here long enough to realize that every single person who walks into this coffee shop feels like they're your friend, and that's a gift, Molly. Not everybody can put the people around them at ease, but you do. And I didn't know him, but I think Rodney would be proud."

Molly smiles at her indulgently. "He would," she agrees, nodding her salt and pepper head up and down slowly. "He definitely would.

That man was a lot of things that drove me insane—he was stubborn, a loud and off-key singer of love songs when he drank a couple of beers, and he never remembered to leave his sandy shoes on the porch—but he was the most supportive husband you could have imagined. I miss him everyday."

Harlow bites her lower lip before saying what's on her mind. "Have you ever thought about dating since he died?"

Molly gives an unexpected whoop of laughter as she leans back in her chair. Her eyes twinkle with mirth. "Dating? Honey, I've dated a plenty since then," she says, watching Harlow's surprised face. "I'm still a woman even though the love of my life is gone—I'm still breathing!"

Harlow laughs. "Wow...I guess I just assumed that you hadn't gone out with a man in all these years."

"Well, you know what they say about people who assume," Molly says, standing up and pushing in her chair. She whacks the table with her dish towel and gives Harlow a wink before walking behind the counter to greet the woman who has just walked in.

Harlow finishes sending an email to the boat services that she's hoping to hire to bring the highest bidders to the island, then closes her laptop and packs up her things.

Shipwreck Key is no New York City, but with every passing day it's getting more interesting and beginning to feel more like home. Harlow is almost happy to have traded the nights on the town, the fast subway rides, and the frenetic energy of the big city for nights at home playing Scrabble with her mom and sister, slow walks on the sand, and the peacefulness of life on a tropical island.

And with the event that she's currently planning, she knows in her heart that there's no better place to be once the contents of her dad's letter hit the world square in the face. She, her mom, and her sister are going to need to be someplace where they can huddle together, ride out the storm of publicity, and start the process of healing and letting go.

Ruby

"Tell me more about that time in your life."

Ruby is sitting cross-legged on her bed with just the lamps on in her room. She's got her hair pulled up into a bun, and her thick-framed glasses on instead of contacts. It's nearly eleven o'clock at night, and she and Dexter are having a Zoom call while she sips a cup of tea.

"You want to know more about my life in Santa Barbara when it was just me and my mom?" Ruby leans over and sets her mug on the bedside table, disappearing from the screen for a moment before sitting back against the pillows and showing up on her laptop again. On his end, Dexter is sitting at his kitchen table in Manhattan with the darkened window behind him. It's a long galley kitchen, and there are copper pots hanging from hooks on the wall above the stove. He's got about four days of stubble and is wearing his reading glasses as he glances back and forth between the screen and his notes on the table.

"Yeah, I do. I think hearing about how your early life shaped you will give me more insight into how you functioned as First Lady."

Ruby tries to smother a smile, because she's starting to wonder whether Dexter North is interested in her life on some personal level, or if it's truly "just for the book." There have been moments when they've talked in their nightly Zoom calls when she catches him gazing at her with a rapt look as she speaks, and it reminds her a lot of the way a smitten man might watch a woman from across the table on a date.

But no! Ruby thinks. *He's just an extraordinarily thorough researcher. There's no way a man in his mid-thirties could be romantically interested in a woman whose fiftieth birthday is right around the corner.* She tells herself that every night after they end their call, which sometimes goes on until after one a.m., and then she reminds herself of it each morning as she's putting on her makeup in the mirror and turning her head from side to side, examining her crow's feet, looking at the pull of the skin on her neck, and cataloging the way her frown lines linger between her brows even when she relaxes her forehead. *Dexter North could do better*, she tells herself over and over, but then mentally berates herself for even thinking that a man might be interested in her, because that's not how a woman in her shoes should be thinking or behaving.

"Okay," Ruby says now, uncrossing and recrossing her legs so that the opposite leg is tucked under the other. She gets comfortable by fluffing her feather pillows behind her back and then sinks into them. "Let's see. So my mother, Patty, was and is the most elegant woman on the face of the earth. I'm not kidding. When my father died, she pulled herself together and planned the funeral herself. I remember silver candlesticks, hot dishes that she prepared the night before the service, and the way she washed all the windows so that when people came to our house after being at the church, the sunlight flooded through the house and made it feel warm and quiet." Ruby closes her eyes for a moment, remembering. "Six months after my dad died, my mother decided that she was going to use her law degree and go back to work, so she did. My grandmother watched me after school and in the evenings, and my mother became an incredibly successful lawyer at one of the biggest firms in Southern California. She dated judges, young and hungry lawyers, actors, and musicians."

"Your mom did?" Dexter asks, laughing. "Wow. What a minx."

"She's a force, Dexter, you have no idea. She still loves younger men, and she's in her seventies now."

"Could I get an introduction?"

Ruby can't help but laugh at this. "Sure. I'd love for you to meet her. She was here when the bookstore opened, and she'll be here again for the event."

"Let's do a sidebar from our discussion and talk about the event."

"Let's not," Ruby counters. "You're invited, and you'll stay here at my house for one night so that you can attend with the other ten news outlets."

"But I'm not a news outlet," Dexter argues good-naturedly. "And I don't want to cramp your style or make you feel like you have to say 'off the record' every time you burp in your own home."

Ruby collapses in a fit of giggles, actually falling sideways onto her pillows as her glasses get knocked off-kilter. "You think I'm going to *burp* in front of you, Mr. North? First Ladies don't belch."

"I bet they do lots of things that regular people do," he says seriously, watching her face.

Ruby sobers instantly and sits upright. "You're right," she says, clearing her throat. "We're real people. And I would tell you to get a room at the inn, but I've booked it up entirely for the event, so your only other choice is to stay at Sunday's house. And while that girl has my heart, I can tell you honestly that she could talk a gate off its hinges. You will never be prepared to keep up with Sunday Bond."

"So then you would actually be saving me by putting me up in your guest room?" Dexter asks, amused.

"I mean...in a sense." Ruby shrugs. "But if you want to find out for yourself, Sunday is the nicest person you'll ever meet, and I'm sure she would put you up."

"Tempting. So tempting," he says, smiling at her. "But if you'll really have me for one night, then I accept the offer."

"Done." Ruby pushes her glasses up the bridge of her nose and then shoves her bun back to the center of her head, as she can feel it listing to one side. "Now, let's talk more about my mom, who is truly a wonder." Ruby pulls her knees to her chest and hugs them with both arms. "So, Patty Dallarosa was dating her way through the Golden State during my teen years, and at one point she brought home Harrison Ford, who was filming *Indiana Jones* at the time."

"You are absolutely kidding me."

"I would never," Ruby says, holding up one hand in Scout's

Honor style. "My mother has always had a way with men, and she's extremely classy. Outspoken, but classy. I think I learned the right ways to behave in every situation from watching her, to be perfectly honest. And yet, as a kid, she let me have a pretty normal California upbringing."

"So surfing, skateboarding, cut-off jeans, and joints in the back of some long-haired guy's van while the sun sets at the beach?"

Ruby intentionally makes a stunned face. "Wait, were you there?" They both laugh. "No, but honestly, it was a lot like that. I hung out at the mall, went to beach parties, Disneyland, and concerts at the Hollywood Bowl."

"Best concert you ever saw there?"

"I'm an 80s girl—I saw them all: Prince, Madonna, U2, Michael Jackson. And they were all amazing."

"I can't lie," Dexter says, "it does sound idyllic. The California part, I mean," he adds quickly, "not the part where your dad died and your mom had to work her butt off at a law firm while you were a teenager and probably needed her around."

He's prodding for more emotion, but Ruby respects this because it feels more like a conversation than like a reporter giving her the third degree.

"I probably did need her around a bit more. I had to turn to my friends for guidance on birth control when I was with my high school boyfriend, and there was a brief moment when I considered getting a chain of roses tattooed around my ankle, but I went with a tiny rosebud on my right hip where no one can see it. I've never mentioned it publicly."

"A First Lady with a visible tattoo would make a statement. Do you think any of the other First Ladies have been hiding ink from us?"

"Oh sure. I think Lady Bird Johnson had a giant eagle on her back. Maybe its talons were made to look like they were leaving trails of faux blood down her spine." Ruby curls her hands into talon-like claws as she says this.

Dexter chuckles at the image. "So is this off the record—about you having a tattoo that no one knows about?"

"On the record," Ruby says decisively. "I'm about to share a whole hell of a lot more with the world than a little story about a tattoo I got at Woodstock '94."

"You definitely did not mention that this happened at Woodstock '94," Dexter says, surprise written all over his face. "Did you camp out? Were you one of the mud people?"

"I camped, and I got muddy, though I didn't dive right into it like the people you're thinking of. True story: the porta potties overflowed and mixed with the mud, so that wasn't just mud."

Dexter gags. "No wonder it was mostly young dudes popping up in front of cameras looking like swamp creatures."

Ruby shakes her head, remembering. "It was a different time. I was twenty and in college. I took the trip with a couple of girls I knew from doing commercials in L.A. at that time, and we actually had a lot of fun until one of them took a massive hit of acid from a guy with waist-length dreadlocks and ended up on a bad trip." Ruby frowns as she recalls the girl, whose name was Summer, passed out in the grass while everyone around her body-slammed to the Red Hot Chili Peppers and raged to Nine Inch Nails. "She was fine though," Ruby adds breezily.

"So, in your misspent youth, you got a teeny tiny tame little tattoo at a giant music festival, smoked a wee bit of weed, and cruised the mall for hotties, but I want to know more about your internal life. Was the high school boyfriend your first heartbreak?"

Ruby gives a soft laugh. "Isn't the high school romance always your first heartbreak? I mean...yeah. His name was Paul. He was my first, as you've gathered, and he was a nice enough guy in general, but he went to a party with some friends during our first year of college, met a girl, and then bing, bang, boom."

"Bing, bang, boom?"

"Yeah," Ruby says with a shrug. "He fell in love with her, apparently, and decided he couldn't live without her."

"So now they're married, living in Van Nuys, and their oldest son is about to make them grandparents?"

"I wish things had turned out that way—I really do. But actually it's a much more tragic story than that, so I'm going to have to ask you to keep it off the record because it isn't my story to share with the world."

"Done."

"Okay." Ruby takes a deep breath. "Paul and I went down completely different paths. Things didn't work out with that girl from the party—I don't even remember her name—but he started dating anything in a skirt, and within two years he found out he was HIV positive."

Dexter blows out a loud breath. "Wow."

"Yeah. This was the early-90s, remember. AIDS was everywhere, both literally and figuratively. It felt like the whole world knew about the dangers, but a lot of people had the 'it will never happen to me' mentality of youth."

"And Paul...damn."

"Yeah, and Paul." Ruby sits quietly for a minute, her eyes glistening with tears. She hasn't thought about Paul in a long time, and when she does, it's always fondly. He'd treated her well, and when they broke up she'd been crushed, but with time those sharp edges have softened a bit and it's easier to remember the good things. Senior prom. Kissing on the beach. Laughing. She sniffles and swipes at both eyes. "He died in 2002," Ruby says, forging ahead. "I went to the funeral and hugged his mom, and she said she blamed me for his death because I let him go and he went crazy."

"No way," Dexter says loudly. "Are you serious? She said that?"

"She did, and it was a great lesson for me in the years ahead, because I really understood that people can project onto you basically anything they need to project in order to get by. The American public can see you and project their fantasy of a perfect, well-behaved woman standing next to the man who leads their country. A man can see you and project his dreams of ending up in the White House with a photogenic, smiling, Stepford wife sleeping prettily beside him in bed. A woman you don't even know can project her fantasy of having a relationship with the President of the United States behind your back because she thinks you're nothing more than a political partner, a wife on paper, and a woman with her own agenda."

"Is this still off the record?"

"This part is on. You want to know me and how I feel, so anything I tell you about me and my life is fair game unless I say otherwise."

"Got it."

195

Ruby sighs and leans her head back against the tufted, cornflower blue headboard. "I hate to cut us off for the night, but I really need to get some sleep."

"Same time tomorrow?" Dexter asks, resting his tired looking face on his hand, elbow propped on his kitchen table. He has a pencil tucked between his fingers and his glasses reflect the glow of his own laptop screen.

"Same time," Ruby confirms.

Dexter sits up straight and closes his notebook. "One more thing, Ruby."

"Yes?"

"I think you're really brave. Not just because I'm the one writing this book and I think it's going to be ground-breaking, but because it takes guts to share yourself. And this event is going to be unprecedented. You don't have to share any of this with the world—not your story, not your marriage, and not Jack's death—but you are, and I think that's extremely generous."

Ruby smiles at Dexter, thinking of the Jackie Kennedy biography that she and the book club read, discussed, and parsed for meaning as she sought counsel on how to proceed with telling her own story.

"I'm going to lean on the words of the immortal Jackie O. here when I say, 'You cannot separate the good from the bad. And perhaps there is no need to do so.'" Ruby pauses. "It's simply my story, Dexter. The good, the bad, and the ugly. And I think every person can relate, because no matter who we are, we've got our own good, bad, and ugly."

Ruby

Event weekend. It's hot, muggy, and the sky is threatening a storm the likes of which Ruby actually welcomes. She races around the island in her cart with Banks behind the wheel, checking items off her to-do list and mentally preparing herself for the shift in her life that's about to occur.

In the end, Athena's website logged over three point five million dollars in bids on the ten packages to attend Ruby's big event. It's a staggering figure, and Ruby already knows that the news organizations who won spots (all of the biggies: NBC, CBS, ABC, CNN, Fox, Harpo Studios—Oprah's people are already trying to finagle a private sit-down with Ruby during the course of the weekend—and a handful of others) will most likely make eye-popping donations afterwards in an effort to elbow one another out of the way and prove to the world that they care the most about the cause at hand.

But the real highlight of the event will be the chance for Ruby to put a period at the end of a chapter of her life. Obviously there's more to her marriage that will carry on and be with her until the end, and she's well aware that simply meeting Etienne and Julien doesn't mean that she can put them on a back shelf and pretend that they don't exist, but for now, this chance to speak and share will officially end her time as

Jack Hudson's smiling, loyal wife. His silent, dignified widow. The sole keeper of his memories. From this point forward, she will be a footnote in American history, but she will be the main story of her own life: a woman who was tattooed at a rock festival, someone who loves wine and music and laughter, a human who still wants to find love, be loved, and really *live* this second chapter of her life on her own terms, with no professional stylist, no stage makeup, no speech writers.

The bookstore is sparkling. The women have been true to their word, showing up in their free time to stand on ladders and clean each crystal, bead, and light bulb in every chandelier. They've waxed every wood surface and reorganized the bookshelves. The entire center of the store has been cleared out and set with rows of chairs for Ruby's expected guests, and Dexter has arrived and is documenting everything quietly, following Ruby around as she talks, asks questions, and makes requests of her daughters and friends.

At five minutes to six on the evening of what would have been Jack's sixty-second birthday, everything is in place. The journalists are there, looking serious and overheated from walking around on Seadog Lane in the thick evening air, and Ruby is in the tiny back office of the bookstore, getting a pep talk from Athena and Harlow as Dexter sits in the corner and listens in—a fly on the wall in the very best sense.

"Mom," Athena says, holding both her mom's and sister's hands as the three women stand together in a tight circle. This is all they have now: a circle of three forever, and no matter what happens or where they all end up living in the future, they need to stay as tightly knit as they've become this summer. "You're making us really proud, and I fully believe that Dad would be proud too. This might not be what he planned when he wrote the letter, but you're doing something that's honestly going to help a lot of people."

"You think?" Ruby asks, looking at her daughter nervously. "Because I just forged ahead on this without really and truly asking for permission from the two of you. I'm opening up your closets just as much as my own, and I'm letting all the skeletons fall out for the world to see."

Harlow shakes both of their hands abruptly, like they haven't got time to waste. "Mom, it's for the best," she says, sounding absolutely certain, and also as grown up as Ruby has ever heard her sound. "Just wait until this hits the news this evening—you'll see. Now get out there and kick some ass, okay?"

Ruby laughs, still feeling the tiniest bit shaky. "Yeah," she says, nodding her head to encourage herself. "Yeah, this is what I'm doing, and it's going to be great."

"Go get 'em," Athena says, kissing her mom on the cheek. Harlow leans in and does the same.

"Love you, girls," Ruby says, smoothing the front of a carefully chosen pale pink linen dress that highlights the healthy tan she's gotten while living on Shipwreck Key. She'd slipped it on in the back room of the book shop and then hasn't sat down since, hoping to keep it freshly ironed and wrinkle-free until the cameras are on her. Sunday came by the house that afternoon to help her with her hair and makeup, and then Ruby had added her wedding rings, a pair of gold hoop earrings, and a gold bangle bracelet from her mother, who is sitting in the front row of the gathered press corps out in the bookstore.

Ruby walks out of the back room and into the hotly lit shop. Cameras and lights are set up all around and aimed at the podium that's stationed at the back of the store, with the chairs positioned in rows to face it.

Ruby steps up to the podium with the letter held carefully in her hands. She sets it in front of her and smoothes out the folds so that she can read.

"Thank you for coming," Ruby says into the microphone. Though she wouldn't need one if it were just the twenty-five people gathered there in the bookshop, she wants to be heard and recorded clearly so that her message can be relayed to every news outlet in the world.

The folding seats in the shop are filled with every notable face from every huge news show in the country. Had Ruby not already encountered them all a number of times in her life, both in formal and in social settings, she would have needed to take a moment to really soak in the level of power in the room. But at that moment, she knows that she alone holds all the power in the bookstore.

Ruby clears her throat before continuing and slips her reading glasses on. "I understand that this is an unusual situation, with a highly unusual structure, and I hope that my motives become clearer as I share with you all." There are clicks from the cameras around the room photographing everything for posterity, and along one wall, Molly, Marigold, Heather, Tilly, and Vanessa stand, watching with silent support all over their awed faces.

"First of all, I want to acknowledge that you've all taken a bit of a journey to get here, which I appreciate. I've taken a bit of a journey myself. Just over a year ago, I was the First Lady, preparing to support my husband in a bid for a second term in the White House, when I learned that he'd been killed in a small plane crash." The room is silent except for the occasional camera click. "Shortly after, I learned that he'd died in France while visiting his mistress and their twelve-year-old son, something that has come to light and been a point of interest for many people—and understandably so. We trust our leaders to be fair and honest, and finding out that the President of the United States has been anything but honest in his personal life is unsettling. What I'm about to share with you today is not an apology, and not an excuse for anything that my late husband did or didn't do, but it is a piece of the puzzle that we've all been missing as we've tried to understand exactly what happened."

In the front row, the lead anchor of the NBC Nightly News shifts in his chair, eyes glued on Ruby like he's never heard a more interesting news story than this one.

"Not long ago, the woman my husband was visiting in France came to me with a letter from Jack. He'd left her one as well, and asked that she wait until a full year after his death to give me mine. Why, I don't know, but that was his wish, and she honored it. My daughters and I have read the letter, of course, and now I want to share it with you." Ruby looks directly into each of the cameras and gives a long, meaningful look at the people who will be watching and listening. "I think this letter actually belongs to all of us."

The room is absolutely silent as Ruby spreads the paper flat again on the podium. Then she begins to read.

My Ruby...if you're reading this, it's because a year has gone by and I'm not with you. By now, you will undoubtedly know everything—every one of my transgressions, misdeeds, and choices. You will not necessarily know why, because even I don't know why I've made all the choices that I have. But there will be no more secrets.

You know by now that I fell in love with the sister of one of my best friends. This was not to hurt you, Ruby, and it was not to in any way take away from the life we made with our girls. You were and are the best wife and First Lady that a man could ever hope for, but at some point, my heart went left and we went right, and life changed in an instant. I would apologize for what I've done and for hurting you, but to do so would be to say that I wished my son had never been born, and I don't wish that. So I want to take responsibility, to own my actions, and for everyone to know that I understand that there was wrong in my actions, but in a lot of ways, there was also right. There was love, there was happiness, and there was pride—in all three of my children. I hope you can forgive me for not wishing to undo anything. You know who I am, Ruby, and you know that I'm a man who forges ahead and never backs down. I have been that man till the very end.

But right now, I'd like to clear up one last thing: the final secret that I've been keeping from everyone. Three months ago, I was diagnosed with Creutzfeldt-Jakob disease (CJD), a rare and fatal brain disorder. About 70% of people with CJD die within a year, and the symptoms worsen rapidly—much more quickly than in Alzheimer's or other neurological diseases. Not to sound glib, but "I ain't goin' out like that."

Ruby looks around at the people in the room. Their soft laughter at this, their shocked tears, and the way they're listening so intently have reminded her that she's not alone in the bookstore as she reads her late husband's words yet again. There are people in front of her who feel just as stunned by this news as she was the first time she read it.

So, how am I going out? Ruby reads on, blinking a few times against her own tears. *You know how much I love to fly. You know the freedom it gives me, and the way I can forget who I am and where I am when I'm looking out at the horizon.*

Once I'm up there, I won't be the President anymore. I will be the President.

I won't be Jack Hudson. I will be every version of Jack Hudson I've ever been.

I won't be the man who let you down, or the man who feels torn between two women, two families, three children. I will be the man who has let you down, whose heart is in love with two women, who has three beloved children.

I won't be someone who everyone watches and speculates about. I will be the person no one can watch anymore, but who everyone will speculate about endlessly.

I won't be a man facing an uncontrollable disease that will take away everything he knows about himself. I will be the man facing the ultimate decision about what to do when it comes to an uncontrollable disease that will take away everything he knows about himself.

And I know what I will do. Nothing will matter but the horizon. I will fly into it, and I will not return.

I am saving all of us from pain and anguish of a different kind. I love you all terribly, completely, infinitely. I have been honored to be called to serve our country. I have been blessed to have met every single person I've met. This life was more than I could have ever dreamed, Ruby. I wish you nothing but happiness in every way: in whatever work you decide to do; in watching our girls continue to grow into wonderful women; in someday (hopefully) being a grandmother; in friendship, and finally, in love. Thank you for believing in me when no one else did. Thank you for being by my side through every damn thing. Thank you for our daughters. Thank you for being my wife. Thank you.

Fly high, Rubes—your future is yours, and your power is boundless.

Yours,

Jack

Ruby stops and looks up, tears streaming down her face. She takes off her reading glasses and sets them on the podium as she watches the faces of everyone in the crowd. Surely the news has knocked them all sideways, but even still, these are professionals and Ruby can feel the curiosity brewing.

Helen had been kind of enough to fly down again and sit with Ruby on her deck, going over every potential question that a journalist might ask: *How did the President get diagnosed with a fatal disease and not a single other soul in his life knew about it for three months? How long had President Hudson been living this double life with a second family? Had you noticed any neurological changes—was he different? How in the world does a sitting President end up high over the Bay of Biscay in a single-engine plane, all alone? Where was the Secret Service? Do you wish he would have seen it through to the end? How does it feel finding out the truth more than a year after your husband's death?*

Ruby knows the questions are coming—from the people in this room and from the people of the world—but she's not ready to answer them just yet. The reporters will be here for the rest of the weekend and she'll encounter them all, granting some of them their requests for a one-on-one, if she feels up to it, but right now she feels like she's gotten to the end of a long book and needs to stand up and stretch.

"Again, thank you all from the bottom of my heart for being here. As you may have logically guessed at this point, the auction for spots at this event has been to raise money for further research into Creutzfeldt-Jakob disease, and I'm pleased to announce that, so far, we've raised three point five million dollars." Ruby's eyes scan the crowd, letting them know that she more than expects the various news organizations to up their donations to help fund research for a disease that would have ultimately taken the life of a sitting President if he hadn't taken matters into his own hands. "There will be plenty of time for questions this weekend, and for you to drink your weight in grog." She pauses here and listens to the appreciative laughter. "But if you'll excuse me, I need just a moment to catch my breath. Thank you."

The cameras keep recording under the hot studio lights, and the photographers start snapping their shutters like mad as Ruby steps out from behind the podium, making eye contact with her daughters and her mother. The three women stand and join her, walking straight through the shop as a unit and out onto Seadog Lane.

Ruby straightens her shoulders and holds her head high; the truth truly has set her free.

"Should we walk the beach, ladies?" she asks, taking her mother's arm as her daughters clasp one another's hands and walk behind them. The dark, stormy sky has morphed and given way to a fiery sunset over the water as Ruby guides them across the street and down to the sand.

"I raised one hell of a woman," Patty Dallarosa says, holding onto Ruby's arm tightly as they step onto the sand. "I'm proud of you."

"Thanks, Mom," Ruby says softly, watching the pinks and yellows of the storm-bruised sky as it bleeds into the water. "I've had some great examples of womanhood. All three of you inspire me."

They stop and naturally come to rest with their hips nearly touching as they stand in a straight line, watching the ocean. Each winds an arm around the waist of the woman next to her and they stand there like that, ignoring everything else in the world for a long moment as they turn into four silhouettes against the tropical evening sky.

Come back to Shipwreck Key...

Sunday Bond leaves her husband, the former Vice President, to join her best friend on Shipwreck Key. There's romance, betrayal, political scandal, and tons of female friendship to be found in Book Two—available on Amazon and in Kindle Unlimited!

Also by Stephanie Taylor

Stephanie also writes a long-running romantic comedy series set on a fictional key off the coast of Florida. Christmas Key is a magical place that's decorated for the holidays all year round, and you'll instantly fall in love with the island and its locals.

To see a complete list of the Christmas Key series along with all of Stephanie's other books, please visit:

Stephanie Taylor's Books

To hear about any new releases, sign up here and you'll be the first to know!

About the Author

Stephanie Taylor is a high-school teacher who loves sushi, "The Golden Girls," Depeche Mode, orchids, and coffee. She is the author of the Christmas Key books, a romantic comedy series about a fictional island off the coast of Florida, as well as The Holiday Adventure Club series, and the Shipwreck Key series.

https://redbirdsandrabbits.com
redbirdsandrabbits@gmail.com

Made in United States
North Haven, CT
13 July 2024

54757239R00117